DREAMS *of* ARCADIA

by

Brian Porter

Legacy Book Press LLC
Camanche, Iowa

To my wife Karen, with love

I come down to the water to cool my eyes. But everywhere I look I
see fire; that which isn't flint is tinder, and the whole world sparks
and flames.

—Annie Dillard, *Pilgrim at Tinker Creek*

One

The hills emerged after Nate left the interstate. He drove south, hugging the dips and curves, remembering the farm's green pastures dotted with cattle, long summer days and clear starlit nights, the wonder and agony of childhood.

At Hadlow, he turned east on Highway 17. Everett's clinic was two miles from town, a sandy brick house nestled among twisted live oaks. Toys and bicycles cluttered a long open porch, and an Open sign hung on a door at the far end.

Nate parked next to a truck, then stepped out and approached the door slowly. On entering, he saw a woman sitting behind a desk with a tall counter, hidden by an enormous orange cat. She stood when he walked over and introduced himself.

"Hey there, Dr. Holub. I'm Jennie, and this is Chewy. He's in charge here." The cat purred loudly as she scratched his arched back. "Doc should be free in a minute. Can I get you some coffee?"

Nate reached down and rubbed Chewy under his chin. "No thanks. I had a cup on the drive out."

To the right of the entrance, an open door led into a large room, the back wall lined by a sink, shelves filled with drug bottles, and a countertop with a centrifuge and microscope. As he walked over to the seating area, Nate saw Everett talking to a man in a red cap and green coveralls. He gave Nate a wave, then returned his attention to his client.

"It's that same bunch, Doc. These calves are coughing bad. I tried that stuff you gave me, but it ain't doing no good. I need something stronger."

"Are they still eating, Turk?"

"A little…but they're going downhill fast. One probably ain't gonna make it."

"Let me get you a different antibiotic. How many calves we talking about?"

"Well, let's see…there's four altogether, and another one that's just starting. You might wanna just give me a whole bottle. Maybe two."

Nate heard Everett opening drawers and rattling bottles as he prepared the medication. The waiting room was simple but tastefully decorated with bright walls, a potted schefflera plant by a single broad window, and a Rockwell print of a boy and his bandaged dog waiting for the vet. A shelf with flea collars, shampoos, brushes, and other pet supplies stood in the far corner.

Nate had met Everett at his uncle's funeral, a month earlier. During the reception, while Nate was talking to one of his cousins, a stocky balding man approached and extended his hand. "Dr. Holub, I presume?"

He looked a few years older than Nate and at least thirty pounds heavier. A bushy graying mustache hid his upper lip, and a pair of round glasses sagged halfway down his nose. His hand felt as leathery as his Tony Lama boots.

"Everett Templeton, the village cow doctor. I hear you practice in Houston."

"That's right. The west side, just outside the Beltway."

"I'm from the area…Tomball, back before the city swallowed it. My sympathies on Jerome."

"Thank you."

"I did a lot of work for him. I work for your Aunt Ruthie too. Good folks, your family…even old Viola." He winked. "She'll call me if the situation's dire, if she's exhausted every possible home remedy."

"That sounds like her all right. Are you the only vet in town?"

Everett nodded. "Old Doc Sullivan might pull a calf for a friend, if his arthritis isn't flaring up. Then there's Jill Anderson and Mike Hruska over in Warrenville, but that's it for vets in this county. I had a guy working for me recently, but he decided mixed practice wasn't his cup of tea and moved to Austin. You know anybody wanting to work long hours for low pay?"

Nate smiled. "Not offhand, but I'll give it some thought."

"It *is* hard work, but being inside all day would have me climbing the walls. There's never a dull moment in a practice like mine. Case in point—Wanda Kostelnik, just last week. Wanda lives down in the river bottom. Runs an animal sanctuary of sorts. I've had every kind of crazy call you can imagine out there, so when she called and told me her goat Merlin was on the roof, I didn't bat an eye.

"So I get out to Wanda's, and sure enough, there's Merlin, prancing around like a mountain goat in the Rockies. How he got up there, I haven't a clue. Wanda was in a tizzy, about to hyperventilate, so I put a ladder against the house and climbed up. When I reached the top, Wanda said, 'I should probably mention…he's got a bit of a temper.' I looked down at her, not sure I'd heard her right. When I turned back around, I was looking right into Merlin's yellow eyes. He lifted his front feet and turned his head, rearing back to ram me, but he slipped on a loose shingle and came sliding down. I grabbed him, lost my balance, and we came tumbling down together. After we rolled to a stop, I lay there on my back, in pain, wondering why I didn't go to dental school like Mother wanted. Then I sat up and rubbed my head, trying to clear the cobwebs. Behind me, I heard Wanda say, 'Are you okay? Are you okay?' She sounded pretty emotional, so I told her not to worry. I was a little bruised up, but nothing was broken."

Everett shook his head sadly. "You know what? I don't think she heard a word I said. When I turned around, she had her arms wrapped around Merlin and was giving him a big kiss. She said, 'It's all right, baby. Mama's here. He almost dropped you, didn't he?'"

Everett rocked back on his boot heels and laughed. Then his phone rang. He pulled it out and checked the display. "Ah hell, it's Gilbert Falke. He called earlier about a cow trying to calve." Everett put the phone to his ear. "Gilbert, hold on a minute." He pulled a business card out of his wallet and handed it to Nate. "Well, I've gotta run. If you get a wild hair and want to get out of the city, give me a call. Come by and visit my clinic sometime. It's not much to look at, but it's functional."

Nate hadn't taken the offer seriously, yet here he was.

Everett suddenly entered the waiting room, followed by his client. He greeted Nate and then introduced Turk Wehmeyer, who had a thin hawkish face covered with gray stubble, a lazy eye, and a habit of licking his lips. Everett later confided that Turk was the local "witch doctor," and a few people relied on him to treat their animals for a small fee—probably only beer—using a combination of over-the-counter feed store medications and home remedies. He came to Everett only when his usual bag of tricks didn't work.

"I give him only enough medication to treat animals that need it, and animals I've examined. If I gave him a whole bottle, he'd be treating half the animals in DeLeon County, proper indications be damned. I should probably run him off, but I try to keep the peace."

Everett took Nate on a tour of the clinic, which didn't take long. To Nate's surprise, the large room served as exam room, surgery room, pharmacy, radiology room, and laboratory. A door led from there into a narrow office with two desks along opposite walls, a row of filing cabinets, and a large bookshelf extending from floor to ceiling. An alcove with a washer and dryer and small half bath was tucked into the far end. The office had two other doors, one leading into the kitchen and the other outside to the porch. The kennel was at the other end of the waiting room, connected by a long hallway. Separated from the house by a broad circle drive was the large animal facility—an open metal-roofed barn with a loading chute, pens, and a hydraulic squeeze chute. A horse stock with a concrete slab stood near the barn in the shade of a post oak tree.

Overall, it was an odd setup, but Everett apparently made it work.

"Working out of my home is not my first choice," Everett said as they walked back to the house. "I tried to buy Doc Sullivan's old clinic years ago, but it needed a lot of work, and by the time he was ready to sell, I'd put far too much money into this place. I plan to build a new clinic someday. We've got no privacy here. We close the gate after hours, but believe it or not, people climb over it."

They went into the office through the side door. Everett told Nate to have a seat while he went to the kitchen and got himself a drink. Nate heard another voice in the kitchen, and when Everett returned with a glass of ice water, he was accompanied by a sturdy woman with a mop of bleach blond hair and red hoop earrings.

"Nate, this is my wife, Audrey."

Nate stood. "Nice to meet you."

"Sit down, sit down. The pleasure's mine." Audrey had a dimpled chin and a sunny smile. "So I hear you're coming to the rescue. Everett needs help in the worst way."

Everett sighed as he collapsed into his chair. "That's my girl. Gets straight to the point, no fooling around. But in her defense, she deals with teenagers all day, so being direct is essential."

Audrey smiled. "I teach at the high school here…Algebra I and Geometry. Plus I coach softball."

"I admire you," Nate said. "Teaching is tough work."

"And done with minimal compensation, thanks to the erudite members of our state legislature." Everett took a big swallow of water, then wiped his mouth with the back of his hand. "You know, a few years ago, we were on a plane coming back from Colorado, and I started talking to this guy next to me. I mentioned I was a vet, and he said, 'No kidding? I work with animals too. I'm a middle school teacher in Atlanta.'"

Audrey laughed. "Between this place and school, I *do* feel like a zookeeper sometimes."

Everett set his glass down. "Well, I better see what Jennie's got on tap for me this afternoon. We close at noon on Saturdays, but that doesn't mean much."

Nate followed him into the waiting room and up to the reception desk. Everett leaned on the counter. "Jennie, how're we looking? Time to close her down?"

Jennie looked down at her appointment book. "Dr. Strickland has a colicky mare and wants you to come out. And Vernon Smolik has a cow with a prolapse. Sounds like it's uterine. He said she's in the pen. Not at his house, but at the river. Said you'd know where to go."

"The river?" Everett furrowed his brow. "Oh yeah, now I remember. It's a lease pasture. Why that's just down the road from the Holub farm." He grinned at Nate. "Jennie, tell Vernon I'll be out there in a half hour or so. I'll stop by Janet's first and take a look at her horse. Dr. Holub, you got time to stick around and experience a little ambulatory practice?"

Nate hesitated. He started to answer, but Everett had turned and was halfway across the room. Over his shoulder, he said, "Jennie, order us some burgers. We'll pick them up on the way. Nate, let me get a few things together, and we'll hit the road!"

A few minutes later, Everett and Nate were speeding toward town in Everett's truck, which smelled of rubbing alcohol and betadine and was littered with coffee cups, soda cans, and syringe cases. A stethoscope, a receipt book, and a yellowing dog-eared copy of *The Merck Veterinary Manual* sat on the seat between them. After picking up the burgers at the Dairy Queen drive-thru, they headed south through town, crossed a high bridge over the Soledad River, and then snaked up the steep bluff on the other side.

Hadlow's bluff was a geologic oddity, a heavily wooded vein of limestone jutting above the south bank of the river for half a mile. It would have looked more at home on the Edward's Plateau a hundred miles to the west. The earliest inhabitants of DeLeon County camped for centuries at its base, eating venison and pecans from the river bottom. Nate remembered his father showing him an arrowhead he found along that stretch of the river as a boy.

Everett slowed the truck to a crawl as they made the sharp switchbacks. About halfway up, Nate suddenly felt an odd sensation—a slight tingling that started in his legs and radiated up his spine. His hands felt clammy, and his stomach started churning. He closed his eyes and gripped the armrest with one hand, his knee with the other, and tried to take deep breaths. Once they reached the top of the bluff and left its shady canopy behind, the feeling passed as quickly as it started. He wondered if he was coming down with something.

They turned onto a winding county road, passing through open pastureland broken by wooded tracts of post oak, pecan, and live oak with a dense understory of yaupon and cedar. It was unusually hot and dry for June, the green pastures of spring baked to a russet hue.

Everett drove through a stone and wrought iron gate with the sign Lazy S Ranch. "Janet Strickland is one of the town's physicians. You can tell when a local owns a place or somebody that's moved in. It's generally new folks that build the fancy entrances and give their place a cutesy name. And most of them have horses. You won't see your average rancher putting money into a horse. Places around here are small enough that you don't need horses to work cattle. The few that do just like to play cowboy."

A paved lane led to an impressive home with a nice view. They pulled up near a barn where a young man with a short black beard was walking a horse. Nate had taken only a few bites of his burger, while Everett had finished not only his burger but also his fries, and he had somehow managed to do so while talking nonstop.

Everett got out of the truck, opened up one of the compartments in the back, and started getting out what he needed. "*Hola, Roberto! Es malo!?*"

The man stopped walking the horse. "No, Doc. But she wants to lie down."

Everett nodded as he continued getting his supplies, then he walked over to the mare. She was a sorrel quarter horse, her neck and flanks glistening with sweat. He checked her eyes and gums, took her temperature and heart rate, and listened carefully to her abdomen with his stethoscope as she pawed at the ground with a front hoof.

He wrapped the stethoscope around his neck. "Probably just a touch of sand colic. Has she colicked before?"

"No, but this one's been here only a few months."

The treatment consisted of an intravenous injection of an analgesic and a gallon of mineral oil administered by nasogastric tube. Everett had Roberto twitch the mare, and then he deftly ran a thick plastic tube down her nostril and into the stomach. He first made sure no fluid refluxed up the tube, then he kneeled, connected the tube to a stomach pump, and pumped in the oil. By the time he finished cleaning off his equipment and putting it back in the truck, the mare looked more comfortable and was no longer trying to lie down.

"Roberto, we've got a cow to look at. I'd keep walking her. And give me a call if she's not doing better, okay?"

As they drove back down the lane, Nate said, "Do you do a lot of horse work?"

Everett shook his head. "Mostly just colics and wire cuts, and both of those tend to occur after hours. That treatment I gave will cure most colics. The rest need IV fluids and maybe surgery, and I'll refer those if the owner's willing to go that far. I don't court the equine crowd. I'll do the basics, but the serious horse people use Jill Anderson, and that's the way I like it. Cattle folks are more my kind of people."

They took a right turn onto the county road and started climbing a broad hill.

"I do about sixty percent cattle, thirty percent dogs and cats, and the rest is horses, goats, pigs…you name it. I'll look at anything."

After a few miles, they passed through the community of New Bremen, and Nate realized they were getting close to the Holub farm. New Bremen consisted of a small general store, a Lutheran church, a couple of houses, and an old school building that was rented out for family reunions and other gatherings.

The history of South Central Texas is written in its place names. The Spanish came first in their search for gold and converts, naming the rivers but establishing only a few widely scattered settlements. Then came Anglos from the Old South, who founded most of the major towns, organized counties, named the smaller streams, and brought their slaves and cotton culture to the area. Wave after wave of central Europeans, including Nate's ancestors from Moravia, arrived in the mid to late nineteenth century, and they soon outnumbered the old Anglo families. Most of the county roads and small farming communities bear the names of the immigrants.

They took a left onto Holzmann Road just past the church. A couple of miles later, they entered dense woods and approached an old wooden bridge. Nate caught a glimpse of an unpainted farmhouse on the right, almost completely hidden by vegetation. It looked strangely familiar.

"That's the Alois Holub place," Everett said, as if reading his mind. "Now there's a different kind of cat. How's he related? Great-uncle, maybe?"

"I believe so." Nate turned his head, but he couldn't see anything. "I've forgotten about him. He's still alive?"

"Last I heard. Doesn't get out much. Rumor has it he's got a daughter living with him, but if it's true, I've never seen her."

Nate gave Everett a curious look as they crossed the bridge, the boards clattering loudly beneath their feet.

Not far from the bridge, they passed Viola's entrance, consisting of only a rusty cattle guard. A mailbox leaned precariously nearby, Edwin Holub painted on it, faded and almost illegible. Nate's grandfather died of a heart attack shortly after Nate was born. He went by the nickname Cap most of his life. A dirt lane leading from the cattle guard disappeared into a thick tangle of yaupons.

Nate felt a tugging inside as they passed the farm, equal parts yearning and dread. He told Everett about his frequent childhood visits with his father. After his dad died, his mother didn't encourage any contact with his Holub kin. His first trip back wasn't until he was in college. He made only a handful of visits after that, each more wistful than the last.

"We've been real happy since moving here," Everett said. "Folks around here are good people. They're tighter than bark on a tree, but they work hard and pay their bills…well, most of them anyway."

A half-mile from the farm, the road forked. They took a right and made a descent into the Soledad River bottom. Before the construction of dams upstream, floods were a frequent occurrence along these lower stretches of the river. Heavy rains could still send the river raging, albeit rarely.

They pulled off the road and up to a gate. Nate got out and opened it, and after Everett had driven through, he closed it and got back in the truck.

Everett said, "Back when I was in high school, I spent a summer living with my grandparents in East Texas. I worked for this old vet, Dr. Percival Milner. What a character. Wore an old Panama hat and quoted Shakespeare. I rode with him and opened gates, fetched supplies, that kind of thing—my first experience with veterinary medicine. Every once in a while, when I got back in the truck after opening a gate, the cab just reeked of bourbon."

Everett turned and looked at Nate over his glasses. "I guess some jobs called for a little something extra."

An overgrown lane led to a cattle pen sitting under a towering bur oak tree. The sultry air buzzed with the sound of cicadas as they got out of the truck and approached the pen. Vernon Smolik wasn't around, but they were clearly in the right place. A cow paced the pen with a dark red mass extending from her vulva, already attracting a cloud of flies. Something moved in the grass near her feet, and Nate made out a newborn calf, still wet and blinking at its strange new world.

Everett took his shirt off and pulled on a pair of coveralls. He explained how he preferred casting cows when a reliable squeeze chute wasn't available. "Some vets will work with the cow just tied to a post, and I used to be one of them. But shit, I've been kicked one too many times."

Wearing work gloves, he leaned over the side of the pen and tossed a rope around the base of the cow's horns, wrapped the rope around the bottom of a post, and tied it off. Then he got into the pen and put another rope on the cow's horns, letting the end hang over her back. Using a shepherd's staff to retrieve the rope from between her legs, he made a couple of half hitches—one behind the forelimbs and another in front of the rear limbs—and then when he pulled hard on the end of the second rope, the cow lay down gently. Nate held the rope while Everett pulled both rear limbs straight back.

"If you get them in a frog-legged position, the uterus goes back in a lot easier."

After putting on obstetrical sleeves, Everett gave the cow an epidural and then scrubbed the uterus with betadine and rinsed it off. Using both hands, he slowly pushed the large unwieldy organ back through the seemingly too small space of the vulva. He then used a long Buhner needle to close the vulvar opening with a single stitch, leaving a knot at the bottom. After giving tetanus antitoxin and oxytocin shots, he untied the cow and let her back up. The whole procedure, start to finish, had taken only twenty minutes. Nate was dripping with sweat and hadn't done anything but hold the rope.

As Everett washed up, Nate tried to imagine himself doing horse and cattle work. Everett made it look easy, but he had years of experience.

They were soon on the road again, enjoying the cool blast of the truck's air conditioner.

Audrey called in on the radio. "Sorry to be the bearer of bad news, honey, but your day isn't over. A man has a sick puppy. Sounds like parvo. And Grace Lesky is bringing in a calf with a broken leg."

"Okay, we're on our way. Get a deposit on the puppy if it's someone we don't know." He looked at Nate. "I could use an extra hand. You have time to stick around a little longer?"

"Sure, why not?"

Nate braced himself as they drove back down the bluff, but fortunately, the feeling he had earlier didn't return. Back at the clinic, he helped Everett get an IV catheter inserted in the puppy's leg and fluids flowing. A fecal snap test confirmed parvovirus infection.

As they were coming out of the kennel, a green truck pulled up, and a woman in dusty jeans and a white t-shirt got out. Nate followed Everett out the door.

"Grace, I've been seeing more of you than Audrey lately. She might start getting jealous."

Grace took her cap off and wiped her forehead with a handkerchief. She had smoke blue eyes and tawny hair streaked with gray. "Third sick calf this year. I need to find a cheaper hobby."

Everett introduced Nate. Then he retrieved the calf from the truck's cab, carried her into the clinic, and placed her on the surgery table. A quick exam revealed a fractured left metacarpal bone.

"It's not bad. A splint should do the trick."

Everett rummaged around the room for materials. Then he had Nate extend the leg, maintaining gentle traction as he applied a layer of cast padding. He glanced at Grace.

"Nate here has ties to the area. He's Viola Holub's grandson."

Grace looked at Nate. "Well, I'll be damned. You'd be one of Ruthie's?" She frowned. "No, that couldn't be."

"Not Ruthie…Dennis." Nate said.

Grace stared at him, lips parted, then swallowed hard and looked back down at the calf. Everett was lining up a splint made of PVC pipe. Nate held the splint in place as Everett started applying strips of tape.

The room felt warm and stuffy.

Nate said, "Did you know him?"

Grace nodded, not taking her eyes off the calf. "Of course. Everybody knew Dennis." Her voice trailed off. Nate thought she might continue, but she just leaned against the table and traced its beveled rim with a crooked finger, following the curve at its corner, and then back again.

Everett finished taping the splint and covered it all with a roll of red bandage wrap. Then he picked up the calf, carried her out to Grace's truck, and put her on the seat as she held the door open. Everett tied the calf's three good limbs together to keep her immobilized.

"We'll need to keep this splint on for four to six weeks, Grace. Bring her back for a checkup in a week, or maybe I'll stop by if I'm out your way."

"Okay, Dr. Templeton. Thanks."

As Nate started following Everett back toward the house, Grace grabbed his arm.

He turned and looked down at her.

Grace held his arm, seeming to pull herself up to get closer. Her eyes were narrow, her features taut. In a hushed tone, she said, "Your father was a good man. Don't let anybody ever tell you different." She squeezed his arm with a strength that surprised him, then turned and walked back to her truck.

Nate stood there watching as she drove down the lane, and he kept watching until the truck disappeared from view.

A few minutes later, they left for another farm call, a calf delivery far west of town. By the time they arrived, the cow had given birth unassisted. On the drive back, Everett persuaded Nate to stay for dinner.

He grilled shrimp kebabs with vegetables from their garden. They ate outdoors on the back patio in the shade of a big oak, enjoying a late afternoon breeze.

When they had finished eating, Everett said, "So what's it gonna take to get you out of Houston?"

Nate was expecting the question, but he wasn't prepared to answer it. He listened carefully as Everett described the job, and before leaving, he promised to give it some thought.

His head was spinning on the drive back. It had been a better day than expected. Leaving his life in the city had gone from a half-baked daydream to something closer to reality, but he still couldn't come to grips with it. DeLeon County held so many memories and stirred up his emotions in unexpected ways. Moving there might open him up to heartbreak.

When he reached the edge of the Houston suburbs, Nate looked in the rearview mirror. The sun had almost completely dipped below the horizon, and a bank of low clouds glowed like a bed of hot embers. The sky was a canvas of the deepest blue swept with crimson and gold brush strokes. Fragments of rich luxuriant light hovered and danced on the surface of small velvety clouds, producing an ethereal effect.

It was breathtaking, and Nate turned to get a better look. He wanted to pull over and get out, lest the spell be broken upon entering the city, but traffic was heavy, a line of vehicles stretching far behind. He tightened his grip on the wheel and drove on, pulled along by the current, not looking back, not until all trace of the sun had faded into the city's murky glow.

Two

Nate got up early the next morning after a long harrowing night. Sleep had been elusive since the divorce. He staggered into the kitchen, started a pot of coffee, and popped a bagel in the toaster. The kitchen table was littered with newspapers, junk mail, and unemptied bags of groceries. He cleared off a spot and collapsed into a chair.

Almost a year had passed since Caroline and the girls moved out. She worked in hospital administration, and Vicente Esteves, a cardiovascular surgeon with hypnotic eyes and gleaming white teeth, found her a willing target. She moved with the girls to his place in the Museum District. The girls were fourteen and reluctant to change schools, but Vicente's posh townhouse helped make up for it. Nate chose not to fight for custody—teenage girls need their mother more than their wretched, burned-out father.

Nate was taking the girls to his mother's house for lunch. She had been inviting him over a lot lately, believing he needed her counsel to get his life back together. She would ask where he had been all day Saturday, so he wasn't eager to see her.

He picked up Marianne and Emma at eleven thirty. On the drive to The Heights, he tried to make conversation, but both girls seemed more interested in their phones. They pulled into his mother's driveway a few minutes before noon. Her house was a one-story Victorian, painted yellow, with graceful gingerbread under the front eaves, gray shutters, and a broad wraparound porch, complete with porch swing. Her second husband Rudy had made a living buying, renovating, and selling old houses before his death from prostate cancer. This house was a wreck when he bought it, and Nate's mother loved to show before and after pictures of his handiwork. She helped with the renovation herself, doing most of the interior painting.

She greeted them at the door over the barks of Gyro, her miniature schnauzer. "Make yourselves at home. I've almost got lunch ready."

The girls collapsed on the living room sofa. Marianne picked up the remote and started flipping channels, while Emma played with Gyro. Nate followed his mother down the hallway to the kitchen.

She stopped, turned, and put her hand on his cheek, pulling his face toward the light. "Nate, you look terrible. Are you getting enough sleep?"

He pulled her hand away. "I'm fine, Mom."

She squinted at him, shaking her head. Webs of fine wrinkles radiated from the corners of her eyes. She still wore her hair long, pulled into a grizzled ponytail. Nate sat down at the table and started thumbing through the Sunday *Chronicle,* and she returned to the salad she was preparing.

"So where were you yesterday?" she said. "I tried calling several times, both your home phone and cell."

"Yesterday? Well…I had to work past noon, and then I had some errands to run. I must've had my phone off." This explanation was entirely plausible. She knew he hadn't fully embraced the mobile phone as a means of communication.

"Didn't you work last weekend?"

"Yeah, but Joe and I swapped weekends. He's off on a fishing trip." He noisily flipped the page, pretending to read the sports section. "So what did *you* do yesterday?"

She studied him, then turned her attention back to the carrot she was cutting. "Oh, nothing much. Piddled around here. Worked in the yard some." She put her hands on the counter and looked at him again, frowning. "You know you work too much. You'll give yourself an ulcer."

Nate leaned back in his chair and sighed. Then he walked over and put his arm around her shoulder, giving her the biggest smile he could muster. "Don't worry about me, Mom, okay?"

She gave him a sideways glance, still frowning. "Have you seen any more of Phyllis?"

Phyllis Newberry was the niece of one of his mother's friends. She was a part-time court reporter and full-time crazy cat lady. She had seven cats, all named after Tolkien characters. After weeks of his mother's persistence, Nate had taken her out for dinner. He endured an hour of Phyllis detailing all of her cats' medical issues, highlighted by Frodo's gluten insensitivity and Arwen's obsessive-compulsive disorder. When Nate suggested that Gandalf's halitosis might benefit from a professional teeth cleaning, Phyllis was insulted. "His teeth are spotless. I brush them every day."

Nate shuffled his feet. "No, Mom, I haven't."

"You should call her. She's really sweet."

Nate nodded as he slid open a drawer and pulled out placemats. He set the table, and then, fearing more questions, he went to sit with the girls until it was time to eat.

During the meal, his mother asked the girls what they were doing for the summer. Marianne talked about her job as a swimming instructor, while Emma mumbled something about taking a summer school class. Nate tried to stay focused on the conversation, but his mind kept drifting back to his day in DeLeon County.

In describing the job to him, Everett said they would alternate weeks on after-hours duty, and both would work Saturday mornings, but Nate would have one afternoon off every week. The salary he offered was low, but the cost of living in DeLeon County was a lot less than in Houston. And as Everett put it, "The clean air alone should be worth what, $10,000 a year? Not to mention the lower crime. And you know we have only one traffic light here, right?"

He scored points with that last one, no doubt. When Nate expressed concern about his lack of large animal experience, Everett was ready. "You can ride with me for the first few weeks. I'll teach you everything I know, which isn't a lot, to be honest. Hell, this isn't neurosurgery." Nate had learned a lot in just one afternoon, so a few weeks seemed like a reasonable amount of time to get up to speed.

Nate returned to Houston thinking a new life might just be possible, but DeLeon County now seemed like a thousand miles and two time zones away. Mixed practice? Who was he kidding? The locals would see right through him in a heartbeat. He had city boy written all over him. He would inevitably do something stupid, like pumping mineral oil into a horse's lungs, and then his misdeed would be broadcast in every feed store and watering hole in the county. Or if he somehow managed to master the technical aspects of the work, he would get permanently disabled by some crazy-ass cow.

His mother said, "You're quieter than usual, Nate. Something on your mind?"

"I'm just in awe of this incredible salad dressing. Homemade?"

"No, it's a mix." She smiled, but he knew she wasn't buying it. "Emma, you haven't eaten any chicken."

Emma stared gloomily at the platter of chicken parmesan.

"She's a vegetarian now," Marianne said, as she speared a second piece of chicken and plopped it on her plate with a flourish. "I thought you knew that Grandma."

"Vegetarian? Since when?"

"Since we moved. She thinks eating meat is uncivilized."

Emma glared at her. "I've never said that."

"Yes you did. When Vicente told us about those pig farms in Argentina, you told him eating animals is cruel and barbaric. Don't deny it."

"I did not! Don't put words in my mouth. I just said that keeping animals in crates is cruel. I didn't say anything about eating them."

"All right girls, let's not argue," his mother said. "We'll have some brownies for dessert. I think that's something we can all agree on."

The girls were fraternal twins. Both had their mother's blond hair and blue eyes, but Marianne was nearly a head taller, confident and carefree, while Emma was more reserved and moodier. Caroline had once called Emma "daddy's girl"—not meant as a compliment, as it turned out.

Nate couldn't believe how his little girls had changed. Sometimes when he looked at them, he wondered how these were the same human beings who had once piled onto his lap for bedtime stories. He could once help them with their problems—console Emma when she lost a spelling bee, doctor Marianne's scraped knee when she fell off her bicycle—but now their lives were more complicated, and he wasn't equipped to handle it. Living apart made it a lot worse. He worried about them, especially Emma, who was less adaptable and had a harder time making friends and negotiating the minefield of adolescence.

After eating, they played a couple of games of Scrabble. The game was his mother's favorite, and she trounced them as usual. Nate could give her competition on a good day, but that afternoon he could barely put together three-letter words.

It was almost four o'clock when he took the girls back. He wanted to take them to a movie, but they had already seen the one he had in mind. Not wanting to see Caroline, he stayed in the car as the girls walked down the sidewalk and entered the townhouse. He sat there for a minute, staring at the door, his arms heavy on the steering wheel, unable to will his foot up to the gas pedal.

On the way back home, Nate felt a sudden urge to drive through his old neighborhood. He grew up on Grand Lake Street in Bellaire and hadn't seen the old house in years. Bellaire had been all shady rows of modest bungalows back then, but the area was undergoing a transformation, the places being bought up by Medical Center doctors, torn down, and replaced by massive two-story custom homes.

Nate pulled up to the curb in front of his old house, which looked abandoned and had a For Sale sign in the yard. The light blue siding had faded to a moldy gray, and the attached one-car garage had broken windows and peeling paint. New brick homes towered on either side. Its days were clearly numbered, so he turned off the engine and got out to pay his final respects.

He walked across the front yard in the shade of a sprawling magnolia tree. His father once attached a tire swing to that tree, despite his mother's objections, and it became a hit with the neighborhood kids. Nate spent many long summer evenings in that front yard, swinging or playing catch with his friends, chasing fireflies when it got too dark to see the ball. He looked down the street, remembering how heavy rains would flood it as high as the curb—a Grand Lake indeed—and he, his sister Sarah, and all of their friends would run around barefoot in their swimming suits.

Nate walked around the side of the house and entered the backyard through a gate in the chain-link fence. He recognized a cluster of tall pines in the far corner, but everything else looked different. The screened porch where his mother spent so many hours with her pottery had been walled in to make another room, and a wooden deck had replaced their small concrete patio. A pair of crepe myrtles hugged the side fence where their clothesline had been, and a storage shed stood over their old garden.

Nate's parents had been ill-matched in more ways than one, but the garden was one thing they shared. His mother, like many urbanites of her generation, saw gardening as a way to get back to nature, to grow non-processed, pesticide-free food for her family. For his father, who had grown up with dirt under his fingernails, growing food wasn't a novelty—it was all he had ever known.

A large cloud hid the sun, but the late afternoon heat was still intense. As he walked across the yard, Nate remembered an old photo his mother had of him and Sarah splashing around in a blue plastic wading pool, he spraying her with a water hose while she tried to pull it away. The pool must have been sitting between the patio and the garden, but he wasn't sure.

Nate could picture his father sitting on the patio on summer evenings. He worked as a mechanic at an oil drilling equipment factory, and his gray work shirt—his name monogrammed above the pocket in dark blue letters—would be soaked with sweat from working in the garden. He would sit with a beer and a small radio, listening to Gene Elston call the Astros game. He would stay out there past dark, having a second beer, sometimes a third or fourth, slapping at mosquitoes as he cheered the hits and cussed the outs.

The memories hounded Nate, trailing him back out to the street. Before getting into the car, he looked back at the house one last time. He saw the garage door open, the family station wagon parked snugly inside. The tire swing hung from the magnolia, rocking gently in the wind. His mother's azaleas bloomed in the flowerbed as she stood framed in the window above, looking out anxiously, waiting for her husband to return from yet another weekend trip to the farm. Nate closed his eyes and heard their voices, the walls reverberating with anger, echoes spilling out into the yard and down the street.

What did his mother feel on those Sunday evenings? Was it worry? Resentment? Bitterness? She must have realized that a part of Dennis Holub had never belonged to her, and that it never would. When he returned to the city, part of him stayed behind in the green grassy hills of DeLeon County.

Their marriage had reached a delicate equilibrium by that point, an unsteady truce, and it lasted until a sad Sunday one spring... the day he didn't return at all.

Three

Two months later, Nate found himself sitting on the front porch of his farmhouse, wondering if the cows were hungry. Three mistletoe-choked hackberry trees stood just outside his yard fence, while a few Herefords milled about in the shade, lazily chewing their cuds. Bruno Gaskamp, his new landlord, had been short on details. "Just give 'em a couple of square bales and a few cubes if they start looking peaked."

The farm was four miles northeast of Hadlow. Bruno, a used car dealer in San Antonio, had grown up on the place and couldn't bear to part with it. He kept the cattle around for tax purposes and offered Nate a ridiculously low rent in exchange for keeping an eye on them.

Nate had agonized over Everett's job offer for weeks. While wrestling with the decision, he took the girls to their favorite restaurant one night—Sal's, a small family-run pizzeria on Rice Boulevard. As they sat in a booth awaiting their pizza, he explained what he was considering. Marianne nodded along, while Emma just stared.

When he finished, he said, "So…what do you think?"

They exchanged looks. Then Marianne said, "That sounds awesome, Dad. You can wear a cowboy hat and boots and drive a truck. That would be so *you*." She glanced back at Emma. "What do you say, Em? Wouldn't Dad rock as a cowboy?"

Emma smiled dimly.

The waiter arrived with their pizza, and as Marianne reached for a slice, Nate looked at Emma. "Tell me what you're thinking, sweetie."

She shrugged. "You've been really sad lately. If you think this will cheer you up, you should go for it."

Nate didn't realize he had been wearing his emotions on his sleeve. He stared at his glass of iced tea, stirring it slowly with a straw. "This is the kind of job I had in mind when I decided to become a vet. I wanted to be outdoors, drive around the countryside…that kind of thing."

"So how'd you end up in Houston?" Marianne said.

Emma picked up a slice of pizza. "Think about it. Can you imagine Mom in the sticks? A hundred miles from the nearest Macy's?"

"Good point. She wouldn't last a week."

Nate continued stirring his tea. "That was a big factor, for sure. But remember I'm from the city too. I couldn't see myself fitting in."

"And now you can?" Marianne said.

"I don't know. This feels different. It's not…just any job. I've got roots there."

Nate wondered what the girls were thinking. Could they possibly understand? He finally leaned forward, his arms on the table. "It's you two I'm worried about. With the distance and all."

"How far is it?" Marianne said.

"About a two-hour drive from your place."

"That's nothing. We can teach you how to text. You finally have email down, so you can probably handle it. We can even video chat, but that might be pushing it."

Nate chewed on his lip. He looked at Marianne. "Are you sure?"

"Absolutely. I can tell you really want this, Dad." Marianne raised her glass of diet soda. "Let's make it official. A toast…to Dad's new job as a cowboy vet."

Nate slowly reached for his glass. Before raising it, he looked at Emma.

She held her glass up and smiled.

This was it then—no turning back now. He was relieved, but also alarmed. He had imagined a little sorrow at the idea of him moving away. Maybe even a token sniffle or two.

"We'll have to come visit," Marianne said. "You'll have a ranch with horses, right? We haven't ridden horses since summer camp, when we were what, eight or nine?"

"I'm not sure about the ranch, or the horses, but you'll definitely visit." They had been too young to remember their only visit to the farm. Their conceptions of rural life were based on country music videos and the Houston Livestock Show and Rodeo.

While driving the girls home, Nate mentioned he still had to tell his mother.

"Be prepared, Dad," Marianne said. "Grandma will call this a mid-life crisis and want you to see a therapist, but I wouldn't worry about it if I were you."

"A therapist sounds like really good advice," he said, hoping that was as bad as her criticism would get.

Nate went by his mother's house the next evening. He found her in the backyard, weeding one of her flowerbeds.

"Whew, it's too hot out here," she said as they walked over to a bench on her small shady patio, "but this darn nut grass is taking over the place." She took off her straw hat and wiped the sweat from her forehead with the back of her hand. "This is a nice surprise. What brings you by?"

"I just love visiting my favorite mother."

She smiled, then reached over and patted his hand. "I know you well enough to know when something's on your mind. Go ahead…out with it."

Nate started to speak, but he stopped. After taking a deep breath, he tried again. "I came by to give you some news." He looked down at the cracks in the patio concrete, rubbing his palms on his jeans. "This will come as a big surprise. I uh…quit my job this morning."

She leaned back and stared at him. "Quit your job? Well, it's about time. That man takes advantage of you." She had prodded him to be more assertive about the direction of his career for years. "So what are you going to do?"

"Here's the surprise part." He looked at the mound of nut grass she had piled up near the flowerbed. "You remember when I went to Jerome's funeral? I met a vet there, and he's been looking for help for years. I thought the idea was crazy at first, but I visited his clinic, and I liked it. He offered me a job, and after giving it a lot of thought, I decided to accept. It's definitely out of my comfort zone, but I need a change."

He turned to face her. Speckles of early evening sunlight danced across her face, filtered through the live oak leaves above. Seeing her confusion, he looked away. "The girls are supportive. I'll be coming back on weekends. I'm going to hold on to the house, at least for a while. It's only a two—"

She grabbed his arm. "Nate…are you…are you out of your mind?"

"I feel strongly about this, Mom, stronger than I've felt about anything in a long time. I'm not going to—hey, don't cry."

She had her elbows on her knees, her face buried in her hands. He moved closer and wrapped his arm around her. "Mom, don't cry. Please." She pulled away from him, sobbing uncontrollably.

He sat in silence, not knowing what to say.

When she finally caught her breath, she said, "You can't do this to me. You can't."

Nate went inside and brought back a glass of ice water, thinking maybe she had overdone it in the heat. She took the glass with a shaky hand, needing her other hand to steady it.

He lingered, trying to talk to her, wanting to get some resolution before leaving, but she said little. She clearly wanted to be left alone.

He drove away wondering what had triggered such a response. Emotional displays were rare for her. He had probably stirred up bad memories. Or was it the past at all? Maybe she was just lonely, much lonelier than he had imagined since Rudy died.

In the end, he couldn't escape the feeling that she was holding something back, something she couldn't quite face up to. He knew then that moving to DeLeon County was about more than dissatisfaction with his life in Houston or fulfilling his old dream of being a country vet.

It went a lot deeper.

The night before his first day on the job, Nate found sleep impossible. The warm night air felt suffocating, like all hope had been drained from it. He stared at the walls, paced the floor, and finally grew so restless he took a long walk down the county road.

It was almost midnight. A sliver of moon hung low in the sky, mostly hidden by a patch of dark ragged clouds. The soggy air resonated with cricket song.

What the hell was he doing in this place? He'd call Everett in the morning and admit it was all a huge mistake.

When he got back to the house, he was drenched in sweat. He took a quick shower and lay down on the couch. He watched the flickering shadows made by the ceiling fan on the scuffed hardwood floor, feeling lonelier than he had ever felt. As the hours stretched on, his doubts and fears swirled about him in an ever-narrowing vortex, threatening to pull him under.

He finally went to sleep, and when his alarm went off, sunlight streamed through the slats of the Venetian blinds. He sat up, realizing the panic had passed. Daylight always seemed to lift his spirits after long desperate nights. Fortified by breakfast and a cup of strong coffee, he drove to the clinic, determined to give it a chance.

When he pulled into the clinic driveway, Audrey was driving out in her minivan, heading to school with the kids. The Templetons had two adopted daughters: Olivia, a third grader from China, and Anastasia—or Ana—a kindergartner from Russia. Audrey waved and Nate waved back. He parked between Everett's old truck and his shiny new one.

As he walked toward the house, Nate saw two horses tied to the horse stock by the barn, nibbling on a few tufts of drought-burned grass. He entered the waiting room, stopped, and looked at the clock. Seven thirty and the place was deserted. How weird. His old clinic was hopping by then—clients dropping off their pets, kennels being cleaned, treatments being given, the phone ringing…bedlam from the get-go.

He walked into the office. A pile of the kids' stuffed animals sat on his desk, and when he reached down to pick them up, he stepped on a roller skate and lurched forward, banging his shin sharply on an open drawer. He grunted and dropped into his chair, grimacing and rubbing his leg.

Everett entered from the kitchen, carrying a cup of coffee. "Dr. Holub, you look chipper this morning." He walked past Nate and over to his desk. One of the family dogs, a pug named Oscar, trailed closely behind.

"Good morning," Nate said, holding his shin. He picked up the roller skate and tossed it onto a pile of shoes in the corner. He peered under his desk, looking for the other one.

Everett took a sip of coffee and put his cup down. "Your first day. Well, you picked a good one. Shouldn't be too busy. We've got a dog to spay, some heifers to work, and a couple of horses to geld." He reached down and patted Oscar. "I guess you haven't cut a horse since vet school, eh?"

Nate nodded, trying to remember if he had ever, in fact, castrated a horse. Surely he had, but if so, he had no memory of it.

"It's easy enough," Everett said. "I'll do the first one and you can do the other." He turned his attention to his computer screen.

Nate did the same, quickly doing a search for "horse castration."

Oscar walked over and looked up at him, his curled little tail wiggling, and Nate reached down and scratched him behind the ears. The Templetons had numerous pets and most had free roam—three dogs, four cats, an iguana, a goat, a gerbil, two hedgehogs, and an aquarium full of tropical fish. They also had two horses and a handful of cattle on the small acreage surrounding the house. The iguana, a male named Daisy, was kept in a large cage on the patio out back. Olivia named him when he was young and still of uncertain sex.

A few minutes later, the outside door opened. A burly youth with short blond hair walked in, wearing a green scrub top, jeans, and a baseball cap. "Morning, Doc. Welcome aboard."

"Hey Russell," Nate said.

Russell Prihoda was Everett's right-hand man. Nate met him the previous week, the day he moved his books into the office.

Russell turned to Everett. "Who left the horses?"

"Jimmy Kovar. He wants them gelded and vaccinated. Let's try to do them this morning, before it gets too damned hot."

"Sure thing."

Russell turned and walked into the exam room, and Nate followed. Russell had a business degree from Texas State and could make more money elsewhere, but he wanted to stay close to home and jobs were scarce. His father was a cattle trader and part owner of the local auction barn, so working with cattle came naturally to him.

As Russell started gathering supplies for the horses, Nate walked on into the waiting room, almost tripping over a flash of orange—Chewy, in a hurry to get somewhere. Nate didn't know the big cat could move so fast.

Jennie was turning on her computer. "Hi, Dr. Holub." She stood and looked over his shoulder, frowning. "Oh God…it's Floyd Riniker. What a way to start the day."

Nate turned and saw an old rundown white pickup parked outside. A round little man rolled out of the cab and approached the clinic. He stopped and talked to Everett, who had left the office through the side door. Everett said something and they both laughed, then Everett continued walking toward the barn. A truck was backing a trailer full of calves up to the loading chute.

The clinic door swung open, and the man leaned into the room. "Who wants a piece of Wild Bill!?" He grinned, hopped through the doorway, and shuffled up to the counter.

"Hi, Floyd," Jennie said.

Floyd Riniker had a double chin that bulged over his shirt collar, and his bald head glowed in the room's fluorescent lighting. "Hello, Miss Jennie. Wild Bill's not himself this morning. Didn't drink his milk. I know it's time for medical attention when that happens." He pivoted toward Nate. "Who's this?"

"This is our new vet… Dr. Holub."

Nate stepped forward and offered his hand.

Floyd cocked his head. "New vet, huh? Bill won't like that." He shook Nate's hand, then strolled over to the coffee pot in the corner. "Of course, he ain't real fond of Dr. Templeton neither." He chuckled as he poured himself a cup of coffee. Then he eased into a chair and picked up a magazine.

Jennie came out from behind the desk and motioned for Nate to follow. As they walked out and approached Floyd's truck, Nate saw a shadowy head at the driver's window, but it quickly disappeared. Jennie opened the truck door slowly. Nate looked over her shoulder and heard a low menacing growl. Then he caught a whiff of cat urine.

"Wild Bill's probably more bluff than bite." She moved out of the way to let him see. "But Doc doesn't take any chances. He always sedates him."

The cat was on the floorboard, crouched between the seat and the opposite door, only his kinked stubby tail visible. When Nate leaned in to get a better look, the growl intensified.

"Sounds like a wise policy," he said, backing out.

Nate had dealt with his share of fractious cats, but he couldn't remember anything quite like this. He went back into the clinic and returned with a syringe of sedative and a long Kevlar glove. Putting the glove on his left hand and holding the syringe with his right, he leaned over the seat, grabbed Wild Bill by the tail with his gloved hand, and tried to pull him back and quickly give the shot in his leg. The cat yowled—a loud unearthly scream—and Nate slipped and went down hard on the truck's floorboard, losing his grip on the tail. Wild Bill appeared suddenly from behind the seat, a gray blur, and ran up Nate's gloved hand to his shoulder, clawing wildly, and then leapt onto the dashboard. Jennie swung the truck door closed to prevent escape, catching the toe of Nate's right boot.

He winced in pain. "Shit!"

On his knees, Nate reached up with his gloved hand, but Wild Bill jumped off the dashboard onto the seat behind him, and then to the top of the seat, trying to crawl between the seat and the rear window. Nate managed to grab a leg before he got over the seat, pinned him against the glass, and gave the injection. He climbed out of the cab and slammed the door.

"I'm sorry about your foot," Jennie said.

Nate took off the glove, out of breath, Wild Bill's growls still coming through the closed door. "You kept him in the truck. That's the main thing."

He surveyed the damage—only one scratch on his biceps and another on his neck, just below the ear. Not much blood. He hobbled into the clinic and washed them off.

After the sedative took effect, Nate retrieved Wild Bill from behind the truck seat and took him into the exam room, still growling. The cat was a scruffy, flea-bitten old tom, his face scarred and disfigured by countless battles. He had a fever and a fluctuant swelling along the right side of his tailhead. Nate clipped the hair around the swelling, scrubbed it, and then aspirated thick yellow pus with a syringe. He lanced and flushed the abscess, gave an antibiotic injection, and prepared an oral antibiotic to send home with Floyd.

With Wild Bill taken care of, Nate walked out to the barn, where Everett and Russell were working on the calves. Nate watched Everett operate the levers of the hydraulic chute as Russell and another man pushed the next calf forward. Once the calf was in the head gate, Everett gave a brucellosis vaccination, and then he put the brucellosis tattoo and tag in the calf's ear while Russell gave a blackleg vaccination and poured dewormer on her back. They worked quietly and purposefully, with little wasted motion. Everett seemed a bit agitated, on edge. The other man wore dusty jeans, a sweaty t-shirt, and a dark blue cap. He leaned against the alley, waiting to push the next calf forward.

"How's Wild Bill this morning?" Everett said, finally seeming to notice him.

"A little cranky," Nate said.

"Too much partying over the weekend, I imagine. I've explained the benefits of alteration to Floyd more than once, but he'll hear nothing of it. I suspect little Wild Bills are running all over the county."

"That's a scary thought," Russell said.

Everett caught Nate's eye and nodded toward a man Nate hadn't noticed. He was sitting on a metal folding chair off to the side, surveying the scene.

"Nate, meet Mr. Woller," Everett said. "Mr. Woller, this is my new associate…Nate Holub."

The man rose as Nate approached. He looked to be around seventy, tall and lean, tanned, wearing a spotless Oxford shirt and starched jeans. He had close-cropped white hair under a gray Stetson. His manner was confident, his eyes a piercing blue. He extended his hand, a gold watch peeking out from his shirtsleeve. "Hello, Nate. Where you from?"

"Houston."

"Welcome to Hadlow. What brings you out to the country?" Woller was smiling, a faint frozen smile.

Nate looked back toward the chute. "I, uh…I guess I just needed to get away from the rat race."

Woller nodded. "Can't say I blame you. I avoid the place as much as possible."

Nate glanced at him, then looked back at the chute. "These are some good-looking heifers." He held his breath. What did he know about cattle?

"They're a bit lean. Not easy putting weight on them these days."

Nate nodded, exhaling slowly.

Woller pulled up the brim of his hat. "This drought's a bad one. Everybody's selling. Prices have bottomed out. It's a great time to buy though…if you've got the feed."

They watched as Everett and Russell worked on the last calf. Everett was rubbing tattoo ink on the inside of the calf's ear, and Russell was opening a new bottle of dewormer. Nate wanted to help, but he didn't want to get in the way.

Woller turned to Nate. "I didn't quite catch your last name. Hollis, was it?" The smile was still there, barren of any warmth or humor.

"No, Holub."

Woller scratched behind his ear and leaned in. "Did you say Holub?"

Nate nodded.

"You kin to the Holubs around here?"

"I am."

"How so?"

"I'm Viola's grandson."

Woller's hand froze, just below his ear. "So you're Dennis's son?"

"That's right."

Woller's smile vanished, his eyes hardening. He reached up slowly to his hat brim and pulled it down. He turned back to the chute just as Everett released the head gate and the last calf came barreling out. She pivoted left instead of right and came straight at them. Nate took two steps back, but Woller didn't flinch. He raised his hands and yelled, with sudden ferocity, and the calf veered off to join the others.

Russell and Woller's helper loaded the calves while Everett cleaned up. Woller walked back to his truck without a word to Nate, pausing only long enough to thank Everett.

After Woller drove off, Everett walked back to the clinic. Nate helped Russell as he finished cleaning up.

"What's that guy's story?" Nate said.

"Woller? You *are* new to Hadlow. The Wollers own half this town, and they're not exactly shy about letting people know about it. Did you like that comment about it being a good time to buy? Shit yeah, if you own a feed mill it is. Drought? What drought?" He laughed. "Doc gets uptight whenever Duke comes in. He hates kissing ass, but I guess you have to do it."

"Duke?"

"That's what people call him. Never to his face though. He's always *Mr. Woller.*"

"Why Duke?"

"I don't know. Because he acts like royalty, I guess."

Everett returned with a tray of surgical instruments soaking in disinfectant. It was time for the horses. "I'll do the bigger one. The other one's just a yearling."

Russell led the larger horse, a red roan, to an open area away from the barn, and Everett gave him an intravenous sedative. After a few minutes, the horse lowered its head almost to the ground and was having trouble keeping his balance. Everett then gave an intravenous anesthetic, and the horse lay down. Russell tied back the upper rear limb, and Everett scrubbed and rinsed the scrotum. He then injected the testicles and spermatic cords with lidocaine and placed the tray of surgical instruments at his side.

After putting on surgical gloves, he picked up his scalpel and made an incision through the scrotal skin to expose the glistening white parietal tunic. He cut through the tunic and applied gentle pressure to pop the testicle through the opening. He isolated and stripped the spermatic cord and then crimped it with an emasculator, crushing and cutting the cord simultaneously.

"Make sure you don't leave the tail of the epididymis here," he said, pointing the structure out. After leaving the emasculator in place for a couple of minutes, he released it and repeated the procedure on the other side. Then he stood and peeled off his gloves. "Nothing to it."

Everett gave the other horse its sedative. Three vehicles were parked at the clinic, and a truck and trailer had just pulled into the drive. He put a hand on Nate's shoulder and handed him the syringe of anesthetic. "You got it?"

Nate nodded.

"Keep an eye on this one," Everett said to Russell, motioning at the sleeping horse. "I'll see what these folks need." He turned and walked toward the clinic, whistling.

Nate tried to swallow, but it got caught in his throat.

"I'll get you a pair of gloves," Russell said. He walked over to the barn.

Nate eyed the horse warily. He was a bay not much smaller than the one Everett had done. After Russell returned with the gloves, they walked over to the horse. Russell untied him and led him to an open spot not far from the roan. Nate gave the anesthetic and stepped back. Russell held the halter firmly, protecting the horse's head as he tottered and went to the ground.

Nate tried to stay calm as he scrubbed the scrotum. *It's just another castration, only bigger—nothing to get excited about.* He glanced out of the corner of his eye toward the clinic. No sign of Everett. A drop of sweat ran across his temple and down his cheek. He held the base of the scrotum firmly to make the skin taut, took a deep breath, and then made a long incision, just as Everett had done.

Once he breached the skin and blood started flowing, he relaxed. Just simple surgery, after all. Opening the tunic and isolating the spermatic cord was easy, and although the emasculator was large and unwieldy, getting the cord crimped and cut wasn't so bad. He dropped the bloody testicle into the surgical tray, breathing easier. The other side went smoothly.

The roan was now sternal, and while Nate cleaned up, Russell went over and urged him to his feet. Then he walked him slowly back to the stock and tied him.

As they waited for the bay to wake up, Nate said, "You do many horse castrations here?"

"Not many. Maybe one every couple of months."

The horse moved his back legs and then raised his head slightly before lowering it back down. Blood dribbled out of the scrotal incision.

"So is it just you and Jennie?" Nate said, as he watched the incision.

"There's also Irene."

"Irene?"

"Irene Winfield. She fills in for Jennie most Saturdays and some weekdays. She goes to school part-time."

How did Everett manage it? Nate's Houston clinic had a staff of nine—three vets, two receptionists, an office manager, and three technicians. They also had a rotating cast of high school students who cleaned the kennels on afternoons and weekends.

The horse whinnied and sat up suddenly, bobbing his head back and forth. After a few more minutes, he was back on his feet. A stream of blood poured out of the incision and then slowed to a trickle. Nate leaned over and examined the incision site.

Had the first horse bled like this?

He walked over to the roan and looked—only a drop every few seconds. Russell took the bay over to the stock and tied him next to the roan. Nate watched the incision while Russell helped a man unload a bull for fertility testing. When he was convinced the bleeding had slowed, he went back to the clinic.

In the waiting room, Everett was chatting with a woman about her sick ferret, and a man was sitting with a dog needing its annual vaccinations. Nate led the man back to the exam room. The dog was an overweight cocker spaniel named Lacey. Eddie Hlavac, the owner, admitted he hadn't been giving Lacey her heartworm preventative, so Nate drew blood and did a heartworm test. Then he discovered an ear infection, which required flushing and instillation of an antibiotic ointment.

After sending Lacey home, Nate went back outside. Everett and Russell were standing by the horses, and Everett was leaning down and looking at the bay's incision site. Nate walked in that direction, his throat getting drier with each step.

Everett turned as he approached. "Everything go all right? Looks like you got a bleeder."

Nate looked between the horse's legs. The trickle of blood had not slowed. It now streaked the inside of the right leg, all the way to the hoof. Nate felt a band wrapped around his chest, slowly tightening.

Everett stroked his mustache with thumb and forefinger. "We could try packing it with gauze."

Nate wanted to say he had been careful, that he had done everything exactly like Everett, but he couldn't speak.

Everett frowned. "Jimmy will be back to pick them up right after lunch. We better put him back down and see if we can tie it off." He turned and walked back to the clinic, mumbling under his breath.

Nate stared at the ground, his face hot, blood pounding in his ears.

Over the next half hour, while Everett reanesthetized the horse, located the bleeding stump with a pair of long Carmalt forceps, and sutured it with catgut, Nate watched silently, chewing on the inside of his cheek until it was raw, sweat beading on his brow and dripping on the dusty ground. The man who brought the bull stood alongside him while they watched Everett work. Everett chatted with the man casually, as though this was all in a day's work, nothing out of the ordinary.

Nate looked toward the clinic. Several vehicles had pulled up. People were waiting. He wanted to go back inside, to get away, but his feet wouldn't move.

What went wrong? Did he catch a piece of scrotal skin when he closed the emasculator? Did he close it too slowly?

He went through the rest of the day in a cloud. He spayed a dog in the afternoon, finding some solace in the familiar, but then he had to go back out to the barn. It was blistering hot by then… August in Texas. Everett and Russell had the squeeze chute turned on its side and were working on a cow's foot. Nate didn't know the chute could be turned on its side, or how that was accomplished, or what conditions of the bovine foot he needed to be familiar with. Everett said it was a hoof abscess. How had he determined that?

Nate felt tired, light-headed, disoriented. It was so miserably hot—an absolute goddamned inferno. He just wanted to find a cool dark place and lie down, to pretend this day never happened.

After closing time, Nate sat at his desk in the dimly lit office, physically and emotionally drained, trying to collect his thoughts. Everett walked in with a glass of iced tea and sat down. He took a long drink, draining half the glass, then pivoted toward Nate.

"Not a bad day, actually pretty good for this time of year."

Nate stared at him. Not a bad day? Seriously? Was he just going to ignore his bungling and hope it corrected itself?

The day had been too much. He needed to be alone. He stood up slowly and plodded over to the door. With his hand on the knob, he stopped and turned to Everett. "Hey, I'm sorry about the screw-up today."

Everett set his glass down and leaned back in his chair. "Oh, you mean Jimmy's horse?" He dismissed it with a quick wave of his hand. "It could've been worse. Get yourself some rest. Tomorrow morning we've got cattle to work down on the river."

Tomorrow? With today's wounds raw and bleeding, Nate didn't want to think about it. He looked down at the floor and then back up at Everett wearily, not willing to bring him into focus. He gave a nod, turned, and walked out the door, back into the harsh relentless glare of an endless summer day.

Four

Nate's return to DeLeon County made him think a lot about his father. It had been thirty years since his death, and while Nate had long considered the wound completely healed, his recent emotions suggested otherwise.

He remembered the Saturday morning drives to the farm in his father's truck, just the two of them—the stories his father told, the sparkle in his eye, the way he sang along with the polka songs coming through on the radio as they got closer, tapping his hands on the steering wheel. Dennis Holub was a different person once out of the city, irritability and grudging acceptance replaced by something else, some vestige of a younger self that Nate could only imagine.

During Nate's childhood, his father still played baseball for the New Bremen Roadrunners, a member of the South Central Texas Amateur League. He played second base, while Jerome played first. Back in the team's glory days, the youngest Holub brother Sammy played shortstop, and the Holubs had the best double play combo anyone could remember. They were first, second, and third in the batting order, with Sammy leading off, followed by Dennis, and then Jerome with his power. Their legend had faded by the time Nate started attending games, but his father and Jerome were still a potent one-two punch in the lineup.

Nate recalled one game vividly. It was a warm pleasant afternoon, sometime in late spring or early summer. New Bremen's ballpark was half a mile from the community store, down a wooded dead-end road. It was the most basic of facilities, having only a backstop, benches for the players, a table for the announcer, and a tiny concession stand. Spectators sat in lawn chairs or on the tailgates of pickups or hoods of cars. Kids played pickup baseball games of their own with a stick and wadded up paper cup or chased after foul balls and home runs. Balls were easily lost in the surrounding woods, and returning one to the concession stand was good for a snow cone. Each home run ball sent a whole pack on a wild scramble, yelling and tripping over each other in hot pursuit.

Brilliant sunshine flooded the field that day. The dazzling green of the grass contrasted with the garish advertising signs lining the outfield fence and the deep green of the cedars beyond. Nate didn't remember the name of the opponent, but they wore red caps and jerseys with dark blue lettering and white pants. The Roadrunners sported their usual gray pants, blue caps, and white jerseys with New Bremen across the front in blue block letters. Probably no more than forty spectators were scattered behind the backstop and along the fences on both sides, keeping mostly to the cool shade.

Nate's Aunt Clarissa sat near the announcer's table with some other women. She wore a New Bremen cap and sunglasses and propped her long bare legs on a crossbar of the backstop, basking them in a shaft of sunlight that peeked through the trees, her thick brown hair hanging down to her shoulders. She was an attractive woman—a fact not lost on Nate, even at that tender young age. Although he didn't think about it at the time, he wondered how distracting those legs had been to the batters.

The game was tied heading into the bottom of the ninth. With the sun lower, long tree shadows danced across the left field line. His father came to the plate. He was a switch hitter and batting left-handed against a right-handed pitcher—a tall, lanky, pimple-faced kid who looked like he was still in high school. By that time, Nate's father and Jerome were in their late thirties, probably the oldest players on the field.

The New Bremen batters had been stymied all game. Nate stood behind the backstop next to Clarissa, watching anxiously. After a couple of pitches, his father stepped back, put his bat between his knees, and wiped his hands on his pants, studying the pitcher. Then he put his right foot back into the batter's box, looked back at Nate, and gave him a wink. On the next pitch, he dragged a bunt down the first base line. The ball rolled slowly to a stop, only inches from the line. The first baseman was playing back, and the pitcher didn't even attempt a throw. Jerome came up to bat next, and his father stole second on the first pitch. A few pitches later, Jerome hit a searing line drive to the gap in right-center, and his father raced around third to score the winning run.

Clarissa jumped to her feet, yelling and pumping her fists in the air. She turned and hugged Nate, holding on for what seemed like an eternity. He could still remember the soft fragrant crush of her embrace. She released him and hugged the woman to her left as Nate staggered backward, trying to catch his breath.

He followed the women over to the bench, where the players milled about, congratulating each other and passing around cans of beer. When his father saw him, he grabbed him around the shoulders with a sweaty arm and tousled his hair. Jerome and Clarissa stood nearby, and she had her arm wrapped around his waist. His father popped the top on a can of beer and tapped Jerome in the belly with it, the foam spilling across his hand and onto the grass.

"I didn't know you still had it in you, old man," he said, grinning. "I was about to steal third. I was hoping you might hit a slow roller somewhere to get me in."

Jerome laughed. "Good thing that catcher can't throw worth a shit, otherwise you'd been out at second. I figured I better get it to the fence to give your slow ass enough time to score."

The brothers bore a noticeable resemblance. Jerome was taller and a bit bulkier, but they both had square solid features with chestnut skin and gray dishwater eyes. Their sandy hair was thick and defied the comb. Nate's father always seemed to have a day's growth of whiskers, giving him a dusky look, and dimples appeared on his cheeks when he smiled.

Looking back on the scene, Nate considered the bond the brothers shared. They had grown up side by side, sleeping in the same bed, toiling under the scorching sun together for so many years, their bodies becoming lean and hardened. Not having a brother himself, and not having lived that kind of life, he knew he could never fully appreciate their relationship.

His father was drafted during the Korean War and trained as a truck mechanic. After returning home, he spent a few years living on the farm. He and Jerome worked with Cap and hired themselves out to other farmers when work was available. They hauled hay, picked cotton, chopped wood—any work they could find to earn a few dollars. To blow off steam, the brothers made the rounds at the area's dance halls on Friday and Saturday nights. Cotton farming was dying a slow death in the region, and economic necessity eventually forced the move to Houston.

His father had often talked about the old days fondly, a touch of sadness in his voice. When he was with Jerome, he would bring up things that happened when they were kids or during those later years at home, while Jerome nodded along, impatiently, clearly not enamored with the past. He would remind his brother that life wasn't so wonderful back then—there was the endless backbreaking work, the sweltering summer afternoons and icy winter mornings, droughts and floods, boll weevils and cockleburs—but his father wasn't listening. For him, the past was where Cap still plowed the fields and Sammy still played shortstop, where the cotton was always tall and the cattle fat, where the rains always came to breathe life back into the soil, a place far from the strife and chaos of his life in Houston.

He came back to the farm again and again, seeking something lost, needing to be reminded of the bonds of family, the mingling of sweat and soil, the ancient rhythms of crop and season. But in the end, he must have realized he was chasing an illusion, that the farm was only a shadow of what it once had been, and that the farming life, like his youth, was gone forever.

Five

Summer stretched on—implacable, pitiless, unrelenting. Nate went to work each morning hoping he would start feeling more comfortable, only to come home disappointed. He rode with Everett and Russell on most farm calls, which was awkward but a good introduction to the work and clientele. The pace was thankfully slow, but Everett assured him they would be a lot busier during the fall and spring calving seasons. He needed to learn quickly.

On a quiet Friday afternoon during his third week, Nate was relaxing at his desk after finishing the day's surgeries. He had spayed two dogs and neutered a cat, less than half of his typical surgery load in Houston. Everett and Russell were out on the road, and Irene was filling in for Jennie.

As Nate checked his email, Irene walked into the office and stood quietly by his desk. He was absorbed in his computer screen and didn't notice her until she cleared her throat.

"Hey, Irene, what's up?"

Irene was gangly—big-footed and small-breasted—and she wore her long auburn hair in a clumsy ponytail. Her husband Clint died in Iraq from a roadside bomb two years earlier, and she still bore the scar plainly.

"I just got a call from Tiny Sebesta. He's got a cow calving and needs help."

"Does he have her in the pen?" Nate had learned by now that this was always the critical question.

"No, but he said he would by the time we got there."

Irene wore a long-sleeved flannel shirt, despite the heat outside, and a pair of ill-fitting glasses sat precariously on her button nose. "I called Dr. Templeton, but he said he won't be back any time soon." She gave him a look he couldn't quite decipher, turned, and walked out.

Nate leaned forward, arms on his desk. He was on call that weekend, his first time on after-hours duty. The weekend felt like an approaching storm, dark and sinister. Should he take this one himself or wait for help? Tagging along with Everett was getting more and more uncomfortable.

With sudden resolve, he stood and walked into the exam room. He put a few bottles of medication and a couple of ice packs in a cooler, got the directions from Irene, and walked out to the truck. If he was going to see this thing through, it might as well start now.

Audrey had just pulled up to the house in her minivan, and she and the girls were getting out. "Hey, where you off to so fast?"

"Calving call."

"Where are Everett and Russell? Don't you want to wait for some help?"

Nate opened the truck door. "They're out on another call. I've got it." He hopped in and slammed the door, hoping he sounded more confident than he felt.

As he drove into town, he remembered a conversation with Everett one morning in the office. "Most calvings are easy," Everett had said, "and a good number of those didn't need any help in the first place." Then he leaned back and scratched his chin, his expression hovering somewhere between a smile and a grimace. "It's the bad ones that keep life interesting."

Nate had waited for him to continue, but Everett just stared at the wall, the specter of things unsaid, of grisly stories untold hanging in the air between them. Nate knew the complications well enough—malpresentations, fetal deformities, uterine prolapses, vaginal tears, ruptured uterine arteries—but to him they were little more than words on paper. To Everett they were battles won and lost, rope burns and aching joints, long nights and red-eyed mornings.

The Sebesta place was three miles south of New Bremen. The directions led Nate to an old farmhouse sitting glumly in a grove of pecans. As he pulled into the lane, a hulking man rose slowly from the front porch steps.

Nate got out of the truck and introduced himself. Tiny Sebesta stood at least six foot four and weighed nearly three hundred pounds. He had broad shoulders, a furrowed brow, and a graying unkempt beard. Nate's hand disappeared into his when they shook.

"Nate, I remember when you were no bigger than this here," Tiny said, bringing his hand level with his massive gut.

"I knew your daddy real good. We played ball together…for the Roadrunners."

The name sounded vaguely familiar, and now Nate knew why. "I remember you. Weren't you a pitcher?"

"Damn right. Pitched and played outfield. I was a bit lighter back in those days."

Tiny chuckled, then he looked off to his right, toward the pasture nearest the house. It was dotted with thick mottes of huisache, casting long dark shadows in the afternoon sun.

"Well, I couldn't get the old girl in the pen. She's normally gentle as a puppy dog—eats cubes right out of my hand—but she's a little spooked right now. If you follow me, we can drive right up, and you can probably get a rope on her real easy."

Nate nodded and walked back to his truck. What was he thinking, coming alone? He started the engine, waited for Tiny, and then followed him as he drove across a cattle guard and took a winding path through the brush.

The protocol in these situations, Nate had learned, was to make at least a token effort to rope the cow on foot. If that failed, Everett would drive alongside the cow and Russell would rope her off the back of the truck. Once the cow was dragging the rope, he would drive on top of it. The third option was to dart the cow with a tranquilizer gun. Everett said that some vets, the "smart ones," wouldn't come out to the farm unless the cow was penned. "But I'm the accommodating type, or maybe I just watched too many episodes of *Wild Kingdom* when I was a kid."

The cow, a tiger-striped Hereford-Brahman cross, lay near the fence in the far corner of the pasture.

"Ha, we got her cornered," Tiny said, after they got out of their trucks. "You can just drop a rope on her and tie off to a fence post."

Nate looked at Tiny, then at the cow, and took a deep breath. He put on work gloves, grabbed a couple of ropes and a shepherd's staff, and then approached the cow cautiously from her blind side, hoping he could get close enough for a throw before she spotted him. He saw two feet protruding from her vulva. Should be an easy delivery…if he could just catch her.

He walked toward her, his footsteps slow and measured. When he was thirty feet away, the cow turned her head and looked at him. He froze, then continued forward, creeping step by step. He dropped the shepherd's staff and one of the ropes. The other rope felt slick in his hands as he slowly uncoiled it.

The cow suddenly rose and wheeled to face him. Breathless, Nate took several steps back, gripping the rope tightly. He looked behind him. He was standing in the open without so much as a clump of brush to hide behind, and this cow was not the gentle beast Tiny had described. With eyes wide and nostrils flaring, she charged him.

Nate dropped the rope and ran. Realizing the truck was too far to reach, he ran toward a small post oak off to his left, his heart hammering. The cow's hoof beats got louder. He was pivoting to duck behind the tree when the world suddenly turned sideways, became a blur, and he hit the ground hard, his face driven into the dirt. A searing pain shot through his chest. He thought about his daughters…broken bones…a wheelchair.

The cow disappeared into the brush as Tiny lumbered up. "That fucking bitch!" He helped Nate roll onto his back. "You all right?"

Nate gasped for breath. *This is it. This is how it ends, only three weeks in.*

"I better get you to the hospital," Tiny said.

Nate shook his head, his face contorted. With Tiny's help, he struggled to a sitting position and began to take shallow breaths, then deeper ones, and the pain slowly eased. He swept dirt from his mouth and saw blood on his finger. With his tongue, he felt a raw place on the inside of his lower lip where a tooth had punctured it.

"I'm okay," he said finally. "Just had the wind knocked out of me."

"Shit, she tossed you like a sack of feed. I didn't think the old bitch had it in her. Good thing she ain't got no horns."

"It's my fault." Nate slowly struggled to his feet. "I'll have to dart her." He took a few deep breaths with his hands on his knees. He felt dizzy, but as soon as his head cleared, he stumbled to the truck, spitting out more dirt and blood on the way.

Not knowing how to prepare the tranquilizer dart or load the gun, he called Everett to get instructions. As he readied the gun, Tiny left in his truck to find the cow. Once the gun was loaded, Nate put it on the seat beside him and drove off to look for Tiny.

Tiny was parked near a stock tank, and as Nate pulled up alongside him, he pointed out the window. The cow stood below the tank's dam, partially hidden by trees. Nate drove closer and was able to get a shot off through the window, placing the dart squarely in her right hindquarter.

He drove back over to Tiny, and they waited for the sedative to take effect. Fifteen minutes later, the cow started stumbling. When she went down, Nate walked up cautiously, put a rope around her neck, and tied it to a nearby tree. He retrieved the calf puller, consisting of a long metal rod with an attached ratchet mechanism and a breach that rests against the cow's haunches. He looped obstetrical chains around the calf's feet, attached the chains to the ratchet, and then cranked on it to tighten the chains. When the head and shoulders emerged, he pulled the rod down toward the cow's feet and used leverage to tug the calf out.

He gave the calf an injection to reverse the sedative, as Everett had instructed, then pulled him away from the cow so she wouldn't step on him. When all of his equipment was back in the truck, he removed the rope and gave the cow the reversal drug. They drove off a short distance and waited. After a few minutes, the cow struggled to her feet, and it didn't take her long to locate the calf. She sniffed him, then began licking him tentatively.

"Looks like they're gonna be all right." Tiny reached into the bed of his truck, opened a cooler, and pulled out two cans of beer. He offered one to Nate. "*Pivo?*"

Everett had told him to expect offers of beer on evening or weekend calls, and it might be considered impolite to refuse. Nate glanced at his watch and saw it was past five. "Thanks. I need one."

Tiny chuckled and handed Nate the beer. He pulled the tailgate down, and they had a seat. "You sure you're all right?"

Nate still felt a dull pain in his chest when he inhaled. "I'm fine. I probably won't be able to get up in the morning, but I'll live." He knew he should get chest x-rays, just to be sure, but he wanted to put the whole incident behind him as quickly as possible.

A light breeze blew out of the south. A few slate gray clouds hung in the western sky, rimmed by an iridescent glow. The beer burned the inside of Nate's mouth where he bit his lip, but it felt good going down his parched throat.

"I don't get out here much anymore," Tiny said. "This pasture's gone to seed. Needs to be bulldozed."

"This where you grew up?"

"Sure did. Seven of us kids in that little house, if you can believe it. Me and my three brothers were in one room, and the girls had another. It didn't seem crowded to us—that's all we knew. That house didn't even have indoor plumbing or electricity until the '50s."

"Kids these days have it easy."

"Ain't that the truth. We didn't run off to the store for everything like nowadays. We had a garden, butchered hogs in the winter, had chickens, milk cows. And shit, we had to work. We were in the fields as soon as we were big enough to tote a cotton sack. Man, I spent many a long day in this field right here." He pointed at the ground below their dangling feet. "My daddy kept farming cotton longer than most, and this was all planted in cotton back then."

"That must have been hard work."

Tiny nodded. "Picking was the worst. All day long in the hottest part of summer. You'd pick bending over until your back hurt, and then kneeling until your knees hurt, so then you'd stand up again. Back and forth, all day long, something always hurting. And that old cotton sack just kept getting heavier and heavier. Your fingers would get raw and start to bleed, and you had to watch out for them stinging caterpillars that liked to hide under the leaves. I remember some nights I was so tired I'd fall asleep at the supper table, and Daddy would carry me to bed."

Tiny drained the rest of his beer in one big gulp, tossed the can in the bed of the truck, and took another one out of the cooler. He grew pensive, staring off into the pasture.

"You know, Nate, I liked your daddy a whole lot. Dennis was a good friend. All of them were—Dennis, Jerome, Sammy. Man, we used to raise some hell. Those were good times." He shook his head wistfully. "Damn, it's hard to believe they're all gone now."

Nate watched the calf try to stand, raising his back limbs slowly before collapsing under the cow's vigorous licking. "What was Sammy like? I never knew him."

"No, I guess you wouldn't have. He died in what…'66 or '67? Fucking 'Nahm. He was the apple of Viola's eye, I know that. Salutatorian of his class. Went off to UT. Was studying to be an engineer, I believe it was. He was on the baseball team too."

"I never knew he played college ball."

"Let me tell you, he was good...*damn* good. New Bremen was tough to beat when we had all three Holub boys. I don't know what the hell he was thinking when he quit school and enlisted. He wasn't drafted like me."

Tiny took a swallow of beer, then looked off toward the west. The sun had emerged from behind a cloud, and the cow and calf were now in the deep shade of a huisache. "I feel sorry for your grandma, Nate...with everything that's happened to the family. Losing Sammy like she did. And then what happened to Dennis and Clarissa. And now Jerome. Old Viola has weathered it all, but I know it's been hard on her. It's a good thing she still has Ruthie."

Nate hadn't seen Aunt Ruthie since the funeral. He needed to go by and see her. Lost in thought, it took a moment before Tiny's words sunk in. He turned suddenly, fixing him with a hard stare. "Wait...did you...did you say something happened to my dad *and* Clarissa?"

The furrow in Tiny's brow deepened. "It was her car that wrecked that night."

Seeing the confusion on Nate's face, Tiny set his beer down on the tailgate and grasped Nate's shoulder firmly with his oversized hand. "You mean you didn't know?"

Six

Nate decided to visit Viola the next day after work. He had been putting off his first visit to the farm, but he knew it would only get harder the longer he waited.

A thick cloud of dust trailed his car as he drove down Holzmann Road. Rain had remained scarce, and the landscape begged for moisture. Cottony puffs of cloud hung motionless in the sky, too scattered to provide any relief from the sun.

He gripped the wheel tighter as he thought about his conversation with Tiny. Afterward, he had returned to the clinic feeling a pain sharper than anything inflicted by Tiny's cow. He entered the charge in the computer, then sat at his desk staring at the monitor, not even noticing Everett walk into the room. When Everett asked how it went, Nate said little, only that it had been an easy delivery…routine. He barely slept that night.

Nate slowed down as he passed Alois's house. The fence line ran along a slight rise, and the fence was obscured by hackberry and prickly ash blanketed by grapevines and greenbrier. He tried to get a look at the house through gaps in the foliage, but he couldn't see much—half of the porch, a window, a pillar wrapped in vines, stone steps surrounded by tall weeds. The place looked lonely and forbidding, yet somehow compelling.

Who was this man, Alois Holub? Nate knew the name as soon as Everett said it—dust blown off the spine of a book long forgotten. But a daughter? He didn't remember a daughter.

He drove on, rattled across the Pettus Creek Bridge, and turned into Viola's lane, passing through a dense thicket of yaupon and cedar before entering a wide rolling pasture. Cattle clustered under live oaks, rhythmically chewing their cuds and keeping time with their swishing tails. The lane ascended gradually as the terrain on the right sloped down to the thickly wooded creek. The house soon came into view, looming ahead on the summit of a hill. Nate pulled to a stop and looked up at it, drops of sweat beading on his forehead.

Viola had always been an enigma. During Nate's childhood, she was never the warm cuddly grandma other kids had, the kind who bakes you cookies or sends birthday cards with a five-dollar bill. He thought he might relate to her better as an adult, but he still couldn't understand her. Life for her seemed to be one long, very desperate struggle.

Nate remembered his first trip back to the farm after his father died. It happened during the summer before starting vet school. He had driven down on a Saturday afternoon in June, finally acting on a long-suppressed need to reconnect with the family. He had been dating Caroline for several months and talked her into coming along.

They spent an uncomfortable few minutes trying to make conversation with Viola in her dark stifling living room. Then Jerome drove up, and after a brief and awkward reunion, Jerome asked if they wanted to help dig potatoes. Viola's garden was the largest Nate had ever seen, mostly long rows of potatoes, the leaves browning in the summer heat. Jerome drove a tractor down the rows, turning up the dark soil, and Caroline gave Nate a "you can't be serious" look when he grabbed a bucket and started down a row. An hour later, they were dripping with sweat, their clothes filthy, their arms covered with fire ant stings. That was Caroline's only visit to DeLeon County.

Nate continued driving up the lane. The house faced west, toward the creek, one and a half stories and rectangular with a broad open porch across the front and the kitchen jutting off the back. He parked in the shade of a crepe myrtle, just outside a crumbling picket fence that surrounded one side and the back of the house. He stepped out of the car slowly and looked around in sad disbelief.

The house's white paint was peeling badly, weeds choked the flowerbeds, and rust coated the steep tin roof. One of the porch pillars had rotted through at its base, and the swing at the far end of the porch rested against the house, just below a window with a broken pane. Most disturbing was the large live oak near the southwest corner that had always been anchored to the house in Nate's memory. A few branches had clusters of green leaves, but the tree was otherwise a skeleton, its naked lifeless limbs reaching hopelessly skyward.

The floorboards creaked loudly as Nate walked across the porch. His knocks on the screen door went unanswered, so he called out, and Viola eventually appeared at the screen. She had always been small and wiry, but age had shrunk her even further. Her back was bent and her shoulders gaunt. If she was glad to see him, it didn't show.

Nate opened the door and followed her into the dimly lit hallway. On the wall opposite the staircase were two photographs in antique oval frames of dark lusterless wood—two of his Holub ancestors, husband and wife, the weight of hard living etched on their dour faces.

The inside of the house had changed little. The furnishings were spartan, and nothing looked less than forty years old. The ceilings were tall, and faded wood paneling covered the walls. They walked back to the kitchen and sat down at the table.

An oscillating fan on the counter whirred softly, periodically stirring the spread-out pages of the *Hadlow Herald.* On the paper sat a zip-lock bag and a bowl of cracked and half-shelled pecans. The house lacked air-conditioning, but it felt surprisingly comfortable with the fan blowing and the windows and doors open to catch the hilltop breeze.

Viola leaned on the table and picked up a pecan. Her hair was white and disheveled, her skin sunspotted, her eyes the frosty gray of the sky on a winter morning.

"How is everything, Grandma?"

She frowned and shook her head. "It's too dry. This weather's gone to hell. Ain't like it used to be, that's for sure."

Nate nodded. Her voice hadn't changed. It was strong and thickly accented, with a vinegary edge.

He looked around the room. A wood stove of ancient vintage took up one corner. On the wall opposite the sink and cupboards hung a faded religious print in a gilded frame. It showed a grief-stricken Mary seated on the ground beside the cross, cradling the body of the crucified Jesus. The anguish on her face was palpable.

"Catching up on the local news?" he said.

"Just reading the obituaries. You're too damned old when you know more dead people in the paper than live ones."

She peeled the shell off the pecan slowly. "Hilmer Novotny died. That deadbeat owed Jerome money for years. Probably never did pay him. And Elsie Rudloff finally passed on. She was being treated for cancer, but it went to her bones and there wasn't nothing they could do for her."

The vigor in her voice and the glint in her eye belied her physical frailty. Nate recalled the way she once was, before his father died. Her rule of the farm was complete and exacting back in those days, and he feared her quick temper. He once cowered at that same kitchen table with his cousin Darrell while Viola scolded them for picking pears and throwing them on the barn roof. She usually didn't curse around the grandkids, but she made an exception that day. The response seemed greater than the offense, but his father later explained that wasting food was intolerable to someone like her who had grown up poor, not knowing if she would eat from one day to the next. Nate remembered that conversation like it happened yesterday.

"How've you been feeling?" Nate said.

"I've been better, and I guess I've been worse. I'm taking so many pills I can't keep up with 'em. I got pills for my joints…my bones…my blood pressure…my diabetes."

Nate rested his arm on the table and traced the lines on the red and white checkered tablecloth. He regretted not keeping up with her better. He would have to ask Ruthie about the diabetes.

She continued shelling the pecans and dropping them in the bag. "So how you getting on?"

"Just trying to get used to my new job. It's a big change for me."

"Templeton seems like a pretty good vet, but he charges too damned much. We had him out here to pull a calf last spring. Jerome was too sick to mess with it, and Raymond wasn't around. That reminds me, he's supposed to be coming by today. Should've been here by now."

Jerome's son Raymond was a lineman for the Soledad Valley Electric Coop, just as Jerome had been. He started working there during summers in high school. The coop covered a wide area, so his job had irregular hours and required a lot of driving. Viola was the only one in the family who called him by his given name. He was Wink to everyone else.

"What happened to the big live oak?" Nate said.

The pace of Viola's work quickened, her knobby fingers fumbling with the stubborn shells. The only other sounds were the pulsatile buzz of cicadas, the whir of the fan, and the ticking of an electric fence charger just outside the back door. Nate knew her mood could shift more quickly than the weather.

"How's your garden?" he said, trying to find a topic she might be willing to talk about, but then he regretted asking. Maintaining her garden had probably become too difficult.

"Got the fall plants in…beans, cabbage, squash…and put tomatoes in last week, but I don't know if they're gonna make with this heat."

Nate breathed easier. "No potatoes?"

Viola shook her head.

He reminded her about the potato-digging episode from years past, and she nodded. She remembered. He doubted there was much she didn't remember.

"We just plant 'em in the spring. Only a couple of rows. Nothing like back then. I don't hardly plant nothing no more. Ruthie tries to help, Raymond too, but they got their own problems."

What was it about that soil? His father. Viola. It was part of them somehow, inherent and vital.

Nate turned in his chair. "I'd like to go see the garden. Do you mind?"

Viola shrugged.

He smiled at her as he got to his feet. "I'll be right back."

He walked out the back door and through a gate in the yard fence, passing a corroded propane tank and the remains of an old windmill. He paused to admire the view, which stretched for miles in three directions. To the east, the densely wooded Soledad River bottom extended to the horizon, and to the west and south, he could follow the course of Pettus Creek almost to the river.

Live oaks kept much of the hilltop in shade. Decaying barns and sheds stood among the trees, their walls weathered and unpainted, their tin roofs red with rust. A cattle pen extended from the south side of an open-faced barn, shielded from the winter wind. Pieces of old farm equipment—plows, disks, a manure spreader, a hay baler—sat dejectedly in the weeds, their useful lives long since spent.

Nate's father took every opportunity to tell him about the farm's history. This had been virgin land when his great-great-grandfather purchased it, cheap because little of it was suitable for immediate farming. They cleared the fields along the creek one tree at a time, pulling the stumps out with teams of oxen. Hogs and turkeys grew fat on acorns and pecans in the creek bottom and were kept partially tame with handouts of corn. Cattle roamed free as well, and split rail fences were built to keep them out of the crops. The outbuilding closest to the house, part of its log walls still visible, had been the original home on the place, later converted into a smokehouse and tool shed.

The present-day garden was encircled by a barbed wire fence, mostly hidden by a thick layer of vines. Nate opened the sagging wooden gate and stepped in. The plot was overgrown, and even the small planting area needed a good weeding. A breeze stirred the long stalks of a clump of poppies, and he wondered if Viola still made the poppy seed kolaches he enjoyed so much as a kid.

Nate remembered picking green beans in the garden one summer evening. His father had spent the afternoon baling hay and still smelled of the hayfield. Nate watched him as he bent over the rows, his dusty brown arms disappearing into the thick green foliage, sweat dripping off his face and onto the leaves. He told Nate to use both hands, to grab the stalk with one hand and pull gently with the other. He must have picked ten beans for every one Nate picked, gathering a large bunch before walking over and dropping them in the bucket. He always seemed to work circles around him that way.

That was the Dennis Holub he wanted to remember at that moment—fatherly, responsible, sober. He tried to push out the other thoughts floating through his mind, darker ones wanting to swoop down and rip at that memory with sharp gleaming talons.

"A hoe's in the corner there if you want to get after them weeds."

The voice startled him. Nate jerked his head around and saw Wink leaning on the garden gate, eyeing him warily. He wore a blue SVEC work shirt with "Ray" monogrammed above the left pocket. It was the first time Nate had seen him since the funeral.

"Hey, Wink. I didn't hear you drive up." Nate walked forward and offered his hand.

Wink squeezed his hand tightly, not letting go. "I hear you're the new vet in town."

"That's right. I started a few weeks ago." With a jerk, Nate withdrew his hand.

"You sure there's enough kitty cats around here to keep you busy?"

Nate smiled. "Well…Everett lets me take a crack at the occasional puppy dog too."

Wink turned his head and spat. "You'll find folks around here ain't gonna pay for no high dollar doggy doctor."

Nate's jaw quivered, and he bit his lip to hold it still. He tried to keep his voice steady. "Actually, I'm not doing dogs and cats only. I'm doing large animal work too."

Wink's left eye twitched. "Large animals, huh? You mean cattle?"

Nate nodded.

"Shit, now *that* I'd like to see." He laughed.

Nate felt flushed, his throat tight.

"What made you want to come out here anyhow? You can make a lot more money in the city, can't you?"

Nate shifted his feet. "I just needed a change, I guess."

"A change, huh?" Wink searched Nate's face, as if looking for some hidden meaning. "I guess we could all use a change. I'm thinking about hauling my ass off to Houston and getting a house in River Oaks. Be living large then."

Wink laughed bitterly, then reached up and rubbed the back of his neck, looking down at his worn cracked boots. "Well cousin, I've enjoyed catching up, but I got work to do. You be careful around them *large animals*, okay?" He walked toward the tool shed, shaking his head and chuckling.

Nate wanted to say something, but he was too rattled. He paced around the garden, trying to calm his nerves. Then he went back inside and apologized to Viola for leaving so soon. He returned to his car, but instead of starting the engine, he leaned back in his seat, staring at the house.

What had he hoped to achieve by coming back to this place? It was no longer clear, if it ever had been. Instead of striding into the light, he was stumbling headlong into the dark, into a snarled tangle of lies and secrets. His mother had tried to warn him.

He started the car, backed up, and drove away, but the sudden buzz of a motor made him pull to a stop. He turned and looked back.

Wink had set up a ladder by the house, and he started climbing it, chain saw in hand. Viola stood on the porch watching him, holding a pillar for support. The saw's motor went from a coughing sputter to an angry high-pitched whine as Wink started sawing a limb of the dying live oak that sagged on the roof.

The limb slid off and crashed to the ground, causing Viola to wince. She shuffled slowly back to the screen door and opened it as Wink descended and started cutting up the limb. Pausing in the doorway, she looked back…just briefly…then disappeared into the darkness.

Seven

Nate woke Sunday morning to the brazen singing of a mocking-bird. He sat up and looked out drowsily at the eastern sky. Thin wisps of satiny cloud hovered parallel to the horizon, layered one on top of the other, shimmering in the morning light.

His sleep had been tortured and dream-filled. In one dream, he was visiting his old home in Bellaire with Caroline and the girls. When he knocked on the front door, his father opened it, looking like he was expecting them. He turned silently and walked to the back door. They followed him out into the backyard, but it wasn't the one in Houston—it was Viola's yard of Nate's childhood. They sat down in lawn chairs in the shade of the big live oak, its limbs dense with dark green foliage, extending out and down in graceful arcs. His father looked calm and satisfied as he gazed out over the lush green pasture. Calves loped through the tall grass and wildflowers, tails swinging, legs kicking wildly in the sunshine.

Nate saw a truck, and he watched while it slowly made its way up the hill. When it stopped, Jerome stepped out, wearing his baseball uniform and carrying a bat and glove. Nate turned to his father. He sat on the edge of his chair, his back straight, his eyes fixed on Jerome. Nate touched his arm, but he didn't seem to notice. They watched Jerome walk toward the house, his face expressionless, his bat balanced on his shoulder. When he stopped in front of them, the sun suddenly went behind a dark cloud, and a breeze shuffled the oak leaves above. Nate turned back to his father, but the chair was empty. He looked around frantically, but he was gone.

Nate got up and let the dog out. Shortly after starting work, Audrey had offered him a Pekinese cross named Roscoe. The dog had belonged to Virgie Johnson, a client who recently moved into an assisted living facility that didn't allow pets. Roscoe had the flat face and bushy tail of a Pekinese but with shorter hair, darker on the ears and muzzle. He had led a pampered, mostly indoor life with Virgie, but he took to the country as if he were born to it.

While eating breakfast, Nate considered going to Mass. He once went regularly with Caroline and the girls but stopped after the breakup. Being in St. Anthony's Church for Jerome's funeral had brought back memories of his father's. He had felt like a child again, huddled in a pew with his mother, almost feeling her grip on his hand, hearing the whispers in his ear. He had found himself fighting off tears, and he walked out before the service ended.

He couldn't go back to that place, at least not right now.

Ruthie had invited him over for lunch, and he was eager to talk to her. He checked his phone to see if he had missed any calls. Then he called the clinic to make sure the answering machine was working correctly. Saturday afternoon and evening had been eerily quiet, making him all the more nervous about getting a Sunday call.

He spent the morning catching up around the house—washing clothes, ironing some shirts, checking email. Marianne had sent him a message, asking if he had a cowboy hat yet. Nate cringed, realizing he hadn't called the girls all week. He wrote himself a note to call them that evening.

The old farmhouse was livable, but just barely. It lacked air-conditioning, so he slept on the couch under a ceiling fan. The linoleum in the kitchen and bathroom was cracked and coming up in spots, and paint was peeling on the cabinets and walls. A windmill and elevated storage tank supplied the water, and he had to wash dishes by hand. He spotted a mouse one night that week and needed to buy some traps.

Later on, he went outside and checked the cattle with Roscoe leading the way. Bruno's Herefords were a docile bunch—nine cows, a bull, and four calves. A couple of the cows looked geriatric, past reproductive age, but Bruno was apparently too softhearted to sell them. The pasture looked terrible from the drought, so Nate tossed out some hay and put half a bag of cubes in the feed trough.

When he came back into the yard, he walked over to the back corner, to a small shed sitting beneath a mulberry tree. He undid the latch and opened the door. Along the walls hung coils of wire, rusted tools, fan belts, chains, and other odds and ends. Two hoes, a shovel, and a posthole digger were propped in the corner, covered in cobwebs. A push lawn mower sat in the middle of the shed's dirt floor. Bruno expected him to keep the yard mowed, but the drought had taken care of the grass for now. Bruno hadn't said anything about watering, and there wasn't a hose or sprinkler anywhere to be found.

That corner of the yard looked like a good place for a garden. Nate once considered planting a garden in Houston, but Caroline insisted on building a swimming pool in the only suitable spot. The girls enjoyed the pool for a while, but then the novelty wore off, and Nate grew to despise it for all the maintenance it required. After the divorce, the pool became algae-covered and mosquito-infested, and he eventually had it drained and covered.

He stared at the shovel standing forlornly in the corner of the shed, and then he closed the door and latched it firmly. Maybe some other time.

Nate drove his work truck to Ruthie and Leroy's house, having left his car at the clinic when he returned from visiting Viola. The Kollatschny dairy was eight miles east of town. It was a small affair—forty acres of flat prairie divided neatly into fields radiating around the house and barns.

DeLeon County was beef cattle country, but it once had a smattering of small dairies. Leroy's father Walter started selling milk directly to the local populace in the 1940s, and Leroy spent much of his early adulthood delivering milk to homes and grocery stores around the area. Nate remembered drinking Kollatschny milk from glass bottles when he was a kid. The milk delivery business became unprofitable in the late 1970s. The dairy now sold milk to a regional cooperative, holding on by a thread. It was one of only two surviving dairies in the county.

Their house was a brick ranch-style with a shiny metal roof built in the 1960s to replace the original wooden farmhouse. The yard and porch were cluttered and homey with lawn chairs, toys, and potted plants. Cats lay on every exposed surface.

Ruthie greeted Nate at the door, and they walked back and sat down at the kitchen table. The kitchen was a bright sunny room with a large bay window overlooking an equally cluttered backyard.

"How many cats do you have, Ruthie?"

"Too many to count."

"They come for the milk or what?"

Ruthie laughed. She had plump rosy cheeks and eyes that disappeared when she smiled. "Now that I've got my own personal vet, I'm hoping to get some fixed on a discount."

"I'll see what we can work out. What does Leroy think about them?"

"He likes to fuss, but sometimes I catch him playing with one." She laughed again. "So how you been doing?"

"Okay, I guess."

"I took Mama to church last night. She told me you'd come by."

Nate nodded. "The farm looks really bad."

"Yeah, this drought is killing us. Luckily, we got some hay saved back from last year. Mama's got plenty of hay too, but if we don't get some rain soon, there ain't gonna be any winter grass. And our corn didn't hardly make this year."

"It's not just the drought. The place looks like it's falling apart."

Ruthie shook her head. "I know. It's been going down for a long time."

Nate looked around the kitchen, down at the faded parquet floor, and then at Ruthie. "Grandma mentioned she had diabetes. How long has that been going on?"

"For a couple of years. Things were a little rough there for a while, but she seems to be straightened out. I believe this new doctor she's got is doing her some good."

"She's been through a lot."

Ruthie nodded, running her stubby fingers along the edge of the table. "You know, Nathan, she'd never admit it, but losing Jerome has been tough on her. Almost too much to bear." She stared out the window, over his shoulder.

Nate waited, then he turned to see what she was looking at. When he turned back around, Ruthie was still staring, her eyes watery. She finally patted him on the shoulder and got to her feet. She wiped away a tear as she walked over to the stove, picked up a spoon, and started stirring a pot.

Leroy came in through the back door. "Hey Nate, good to see you." He hung his cap on a hat rack, walked over and shook hands, and then sat down heavily. His hunched shoulders and tired eyes made him look much older than he had at the funeral.

He turned to Ruthie. "We got another cow off feed."

Ruthie turned off the heat, removed the pot from the burner, then walked over and stood by Leroy, wiping her hands on her apron. "Nathan, we're having a stretch of bad luck with our cattle."

Leroy sighed. "Yeah, I don't know what the hell's going on. Some of our cows just don't eat like they should. They lose weight and don't produce enough milk. And then we've been having more mastitis than usual…more calves with pneumonia…more with diarrhea too. I've been in this business all my life, and I've never seen nothing like it."

"Have you had a vet take a look?" Nate said.

"Everett's been working on it. He's run a lot of tests, but nothing adds up."

"I think the place is cursed," Ruthie said. "Maybe it's our whole family that's cursed."

Leroy frowned. "Don't start that bullshit again, Ruthie. Something is causing it. We just need to get a handle on it. Nate, do you mind having a look while you're here? Ruthie didn't want me to ask, but since you're in your work truck and all, I thought maybe—"

"Sure. I can't promise any miracles, but I'm happy to take a look."

"I'm afraid this thing and the drought are gonna do us in," Leroy said. "I'm not worried for us so much as Darrell. This place is his, and we gotta keep it going."

Ruthie had prepared a chicken and rice casserole, green beans, rolls, and salad. Once they started eating, Nate said, "I'm surprised Grandma is still able to keep her garden going."

"Don't get me started," Ruthie said. "I tell her to let it go, but she's out there every day, rain or shine."

"She's pretty tough," Nate said.

Leroy stifled a chuckle. He glanced sideways at Ruthie, then down at his plate.

"Nathan, you probably don't know the half of it," Ruthie said. She leaned forward, her forearms on the table. "You know Mama's had a hard life. Her daddy was a drunk and mean as a snake. He was gone most of the time when she was growing up. My poor grandma had to raise six kids and keep a farm going pretty much by herself."

Nate knew little of Viola's early life. He had only a few vague ideas, things his father once told him. "Wasn't she the oldest?"

"Second oldest. She had to help raise them kids. There were only two boys, and they were the youngest, so Mama had to work like a man. She did some of the plowing and planting, as little as she is. And it was all mules back then. No tractors. Can you believe it?"

Ruthie leaned forward a little more. "I've never been able to get Mama to talk about it, but Aunt Cora once told me what it was like. She said the worst part was when their daddy was home. He'd get drunk and beat on Grandma and the kids both." Ruthie shook her head. "It must've been terrible."

Nate put his fork down and reached for his glass of iced tea. "Whatever happened to him?"

"I never knew him. He died not long before Mama got married, I think. I hate to say it, but that was a blessing for everyone. A year or so before he died, Grandma finally left him and moved the family to town. She got a job working in the courthouse. Worked there for twenty years or more."

"Didn't Grandma get married young? Before finishing school?"

"That's right. She met Daddy at the St. Anthony's Picnic. She went up to him and asked him to dance, figuring he was too shy to ask her." Ruthie smiled. "They got married not long after. That was 1932. Mama had just turned seventeen."

"And they moved right out to the farm?"

"Yeah. My granddaddy was still living on the farm then, but he was having trouble. That was Emil Holub. I never knew him, but Daddy used to say he wasn't much of a farmer. Had all kinds of harebrained ideas. About ran the place into the ground. He tried to raise Angora goats one time, but they all got sick and died. Another time he spent a lot of money on a used tractor, but it broke down. One year, during a bad drought, the cattle got out and ate some Johnson grass on the side of the road. Killed most of 'em."

"Prussic acid," Nate said, and Leroy nodded.

"Mama helped Daddy get the place back on its feet," Ruthie said. "I think she was out in the fields about as much as he was."

"My dad was born in 1934, I believe."

"That's right. And Jerome in '33. I came along in '38, and Sammy not until '46. Those must have been some lean years, but you know, Daddy used to say the Depression didn't change nothing. Life had always been hard."

For dessert, Ruthie served dewberry cobbler with vanilla ice cream, always Nate's favorite as a kid. Between mouthfuls, he mentioned his encounter with Wink at the farm.

"Oh boy, that one's got a temper," Ruthie said. "He's been like that ever since that rooster got him."

"Rooster?"

"His eye. I thought maybe you knew the story. When he was just a little fella, he was sitting by Mama while she was milking her old Jersey. Wink reached out to pet a rooster that was walking by, and it spurred him in the face. The wound got infected, and old Doc Purcell thought he was gonna lose his eye. It healed, but he ain't ever seen out of it quite right."

"I knew he had an eye accident of some kind," Nate said, "but I never knew what happened."

"Clarissa gave Mama all kinds of hell about it. You know she and Mama never did get along, and that made it even worse."

The sky was starting to cloud up by the time Nate went outside to look at the cows with Leroy. He checked his phone again—still strangely quiet. He walked over to the truck and returned with his stethoscope and thermometer. The milking parlor was a long cinder block building with a green metal roof. Nearby stood a holding pen, several side pens, and a dark blue elevated grain silo. Barns and sheds were scattered about, one flanked by a lot filled with calf hutches. Most of the cattle were out in the pasture, but a few milled about in the pens.

Leroy motioned toward a Holstein in the nearest pen. "This cow here has been sick for a couple of weeks. She still eats, but not like she should. She had a touch of mastitis, but we got that cleared up."

They walked the cow into the chute, and Nate checked her temperature, listened to her lungs and abdomen, and examined the milk in each quarter. Nate had Leroy restrain her head with a halter and lead rope while he examined her mouth. Everything looked normal.

"Leroy, do you know if she's bred?"

"Darrell palpated her last week and didn't think so, but he's not so good at picking up the early ones."

Nate went back to the truck and returned with a palpation sleeve and a bottle of lubricant. Holding the cow's tail with his right hand, he carefully slid his left hand, and then his arm into her rectum. At just past elbow's length, he located the two uterine horns along the pelvic brim. He gently felt the length of both horns, locating a golf ball-sized, fluctuant swelling in the right horn.

"She's early bred, Leroy. I'd say one to two months." He removed his arm and then everted the palpation sleeve and balled it up. "Well, I can't find anything obviously wrong. Let me talk it over with Everett and see what tests he's already done. Do you know if he's done any feed and water analysis?"

"Hell, he's done every test you can think of."

Leroy took Nate through the milking parlor, and Nate had him explain their operation in as much detail as possible—what they fed, when they fed it, what they vaccinated for, when they vaccinated—while he took down notes in a pocket notepad. Nothing seemed unusual, but considering that this was his first dairy investigation, he wasn't sure he would recognize a problem, even if it was something obvious.

As they walked back to the house, Nate's phone rang, almost making him jump. The display showed *Wilhemina Petru 261-484-4701*. Between bad reception and the woman's thick Czech accent, Nate had a difficult time understanding, but it sounded like she had a cow calving. He managed to get the directions and told her he would be right out.

He returned to his truck and washed up, and then he went inside to thank Ruthie for the meal.

"Thanks for looking at the cow," Leroy said, as he followed Nate back out. "Just have Jennie send us a bill."

"No way, Leroy. Ruthie's cobbler was payment enough."

As he drove off, Nate wondered what he had gotten himself into. Diagnosing an individual animal was one thing, but complex herd problems were quite another. What did he know about dairy medicine?

He felt like he was rappelling down into a deep cave without a headlamp, suspended in inky darkness, unsure if and when his feet would touch bottom. Maybe his confidence would grow with more experience, but then again, maybe not. Before things got any better, they might just get a whole lot worse.

Eight

The Petru farm was three miles northwest of town. The directions took Nate around the courthouse square, through a residential area, and then down a lonely county road. He descended into a shady creek bottom and crossed a low wooden bridge. A hundred yards later, he pulled up to a weathered farmhouse and parked under a tall sycamore.

As he got out of the truck, a spotted one-eared dog was urinating on his front tire. An aged woman with a cane got up from a lawn chair and hobbled over with a lurching crab-like gait. Wilhemina Petru had sagging jowls, bulging eyes, and hair of an unnatural red. She wore a faded and dirty baseball cap slightly askew.

"I'm Willie," she said, her voice sounding like burlap rubbed on a cedar post. She extended her hand, steadying herself with the cane.

Nate shook her hand. "I'm the new vet, Nate Holub."

Willie squinted at him and tightened her grip. "We use Dr. Templeton…but I guess you'll have to do." She released his hand and reached up to scratch a hairy ear with a knobby forefinger, her eyes never leaving his. "We got a good one for ya."

Nate flexed his fingers to get the circulation back. He looked toward the barn, his throat suddenly dry. "You got her in the pen?"

Willie gave a little snort. "Nope, but she ain't going nowhere. She's down at the creek. You can't get your truck down there, but I'll drive us in my Mule." She motioned toward a four-wheeler parked near the house. "You can put your stuff in the back."

Nate walked back to the truck, trying to think of everything he would need—ropes, calf puller and chains, obstetrical sleeves, bucket, betadine, cooler with medications, needles, syringes. In several trips, he carried it all over to the four-wheeler and piled it in the back. Then he climbed into the seat beside Willie, who was revving the engine, both hands on the wheel, eyes fixed straight ahead.

She reached up and pulled her cap down tight. "Hold on."

The vehicle jerked into motion, and they shot off across the yard with the dog leading the way. They hit a cattle guard at full speed, causing Nate to bounce up and hit his head on the roll cage, then Willie followed a rutted overgrown trail down into the woods. Nate tried to reposition himself, looking frantically for something to hold on to, but each bump sent him scrambling. He ducked to miss a tree limb, but the next one slapped him across the face. He slid down in the seat and put his knees up on the dash to brace himself. Then Willie pulled to a jarring stop in the middle of a yaupon thicket.

"This is as close as we can get." She picked up her cane and pointed to her left. "The creek's over there."

Nate spit out a leaf and stumbled out of the vehicle. When he looked in the back, he was surprised to see everything still there. He started threading his way through the woods, following the sound of a man's voice. Maybe he would have some help.

He soon spotted an expanse of stagnant brown water through the leaves. Then he saw the cow—a black Brangus cross standing in the water up to her belly, all four feet stuck deep in the mud. The tip of the calf's tail extended from her vulva, indicating it was in breech position. The air was hot, still, and soupy, filled with a sweet sickly smell, the sound of buzzing flies.

A lean bearded man wearing a straw cowboy hat waved from the other side of the creek. "I'm Kenny Petru. This here is Justin." He nodded at a teenage boy shyly emerging from the shade of the creek bank.

Nate introduced himself, then returned to the four-wheeler to get his supplies, relieved that at least the cow was immobilized— no rodeo heroics needed. After piling everything on the bank, he slipped on obstetrical sleeves and drew up a syringe of lidocaine. He looked at the cow for a moment, then took a deep breath and waded out to her. The water came up to his knees, and it took effort to pull his feet from the mud with each step. When he grasped the cow's tail to give her an epidural, she swung her head around and almost hooked him with one of her long horns.

"She's a little salty, ain't it?" Willie chuckled as she took a seat on a tree stump. The dog sat down beside her.

Nate went back to the four-wheeler to get a rope, gritting his teeth. When he returned, he tossed a loop around the cow's horns, pulled it tight, and threw the end of the rope to Kenny and had him tie it around a willow tree. Now free to work, he gave the epidural, scrubbed the cow's vulva with betadine, and rinsed her off. When he reached in with his gloved arm, the calf felt swollen and gassy, tight against the dry walls of the uterus. It had been dead for some time—probably three or four days, maybe longer. The stench was overwhelming, and he breathed through his mouth to avoid the worst of it. He wondered if he should call Everett.

He waved a fly off his nose with his free hand. "The calf's pretty rotten. How long she been calving?"

"Rotten? What're you talking about? She just went missing this morning." Willie looked at Kenny. "Ain't that right?"

"That's right, Mama," he said. "She never showed nothing."

Nate's mind was racing. The usual remedy for this presentation was turning the rear limbs around and pulling the feet up into the birth canal, but that wasn't an option—there just wasn't enough room. And a C-section was clearly out of the question. A fetotomy was the only way to go. If he could cut off both back legs just below the hocks, he could put chains on the stumps and maybe pull the calf out. He had helped Everett with a fetotomy the week before—it was doable. Nate sloshed back to the bank and explained what he planned to do.

Willie leaned on her cane. "You sure it's dead?"

"No doubt about it."

Willie scowled, sighed, and looked away.

Nate walked back to the truck to get more supplies, not wanting to risk another ride on the four-wheeler. By the time he returned, he was out of breath, his shirt damp with sweat. He poured a gallon of lubricant into his bucket. Holding the bucket in place between his knees, he passed a plastic stomach tube into the uterus and attached the other end to a stomach pump. Then he operated the pump, stopping several times to redirect the tube, and covered the calf with the thick slimy lubricant.

"What the hell ya doing that for?" Willie said, standing and craning her neck. She stepped forward a few steps to get a better view.

"It's too dry in there. This lubricant makes it easier to work and will help the calf come out."

"I guess that'll cost." Willie shook her head as she turned around and sidled slowly back to her seat. "I never seen Dr. Templeton do such a thing."

Nate tied a long length of obstetrical wire to the end of an obstetrical chain. Reaching into the cow, he tried to get the chain around the calf's left rear limb. There wasn't much room to work, and the chain slipped just out of his grasp repeatedly. He stood there struggling, his arm in the cow up to his shoulder, starting to feel numb. The foul dank air made it hard to breathe. He shifted his feet, struggling to wrench his boots free. The mud was a dark, vile, formless thing—cruel and relentless—slowly pulling him and the cow into the abyss.

Just as he was about to admit defeat, to walk out of the creek in disgust and call Everett, Nate felt his finger slip through the end link of the chain. He pulled the chain out, and when he reached back in, he could feel the wire looped around the leg, just below the hock. This might just work.

He ran the free ends of the wire through a Frick speculum—a metal tube two feet in length—and then passed the speculum into the birth canal until it was firmly against the calf's leg. He recruited Kenny to hold the end of the speculum in place. Then he put on work gloves, wrapped the free ends of the wire around his hands several times, and using a back-and-forth sawing motion, he quickly severed the calf's leg. He pulled it out and tossed it onto the bank, just close enough to Willie for her to catch a good whiff of it.

The dog began sniffing on the leg, and Willie swung at him with her cane. "Ringo, git!"

The other leg went a lot faster. Nate reached in and looped chains around the stumps and then walked to the bank and retrieved the calf puller. He returned and set the puller in position, attached the chains, and started cranking. The calf slowly emerged, inch by inch, and when the hips came through, he knew he had it made. He gave a few more cranks and pushed down on the puller, and the calf slid out and hit the water.

Nate felt a warmth inside that surged out to his fingertips and down to his waterlogged toes. He smiled as he unhitched the chains from the puller and began tugging the calf toward the bank. When he was almost ashore, his right foot slid on the slippery creek bottom and he went backward with a splash. He got up quickly, his face burning, and wiped his muddy elbow on his wet jeans. He got the calf onto the bank and kneeled to remove the chains. When he glanced at Willie, she was leaning forward, her jaw set, her eyes steely.

"Now what?" she said.

Nate dropped the chains into the bucket and stood up. He paused, waiting for his head to clear, and then faced her.

Willie motioned to the cow with her cane.

Nate looked at the cow and then back at Willie, not sure what she was getting at.

"Whatcha gonna do now?"

Nate turned toward the cow. Her tail hung limply in the water from the epidural, flies still buzzing. She had sunk even deeper into the mud. He couldn't just leave her there, but what was he expected to do? He stood silently, looking down at his muddy boots.

"I can maybe get the tractor down here," Kenny said.

Nate removed his obstetrical sleeves and rolled them up. Of course. Why didn't he think of that? "Okay...sure."

The creek bank closest to the house was too thickly wooded to get the tractor close enough, but Kenny thought he could get down to the opposite bank. Using ropes to pull her out would be risky, but Nate remembered he had two broad nylon straps in his truck. He had seen Everett use straps to lift a downer cow with a tractor's front-end loader. They might work for this too. When Kenny left for the tractor, Nate walked back to the truck to retrieve the straps.

He returned to the creek and waded back out to the cow. With a lot of effort, he managed to get one strap behind her front limbs and the other in front of her back limbs. When Kenny arrived, he linked the straps together and attached them to the tractor with a chain. Kenny then idled the tractor forward, slowly pulling the cow from the mud like a cork from a bottle. Nate breathed easier when she was finally on dry ground.

After they unhitched the cow, she tried to rise but went back down, clearly exhausted. Nate flushed out her uterus and gave her injections of cortisone, an antibiotic, and tetanus antitoxin. Then he administered a slow intravenous infusion of a glucose and mineral mixture.

While he was discussing follow-up care with Kenny, Justin pointed down to the water. "Look." Nate turned in time to see a cottonmouth as thick as his forearm swimming toward the opposite bank, its head raised and its tail whipping through the murky water.

By the time Nate got into his truck and headed back to the clinic, it was late afternoon. He was wet, smelly, and bone-tired, but he was singing along with the radio. The cow looked good when he left. She'd be on her feet soon.

When he got to the clinic, he cleaned up his equipment, put on dry clothes, and then went into the office. Everett was at his desk and asked how it went. As Nate described what happened, Everett nodded along. "Nothing like jumping in with both feet. It'll just get easier from here."

Nate slept better that night than he had in weeks. The next day, he and Russell delivered another calf while Everett stayed at the clinic. Things were looking up. Following surgery that afternoon, he called Willie to check on the cow, hopeful she had changed her opinion of him for the better.

She answered after eight rings.

"Hi, Mrs. Petru. This is Nate Holub. How's your cow doing today?"

There was silence, then Willie cleared her throat. "Not so good. I knew I should've waited for Dr. Templeton."

Nate felt weightless, like he was plunging helplessly, the bridge he was building having collapsed underfoot. He leaned forward with both elbows on his desk and swallowed hard.

"What do you mean? She's still not up?"

"Up?!" Willie laughed. She paused, and when she spoke again, all trace of humor had left her voice. "My boy found her this morning in the creek…drowned like a goddamned rat."

Nine

After his talk with Tiny, Nate's thoughts never drifted far from Clarissa. She was a mystery, flitting in and out of his childhood memories like some lovely, rarely seen bird. One memory in particular kept returning to him, and he analyzed it again and again in hopes of uncovering a clue.

He remembered hauling hay with his father one summer afternoon. It must have been a lease pasture of Jerome's, a broad sloping field surrounded by a brush-entangled fence. Scarcely a breeze stirred that day, and the distant fields shimmered in the moist heat. The aroma of freshly baled hay filled the air.

The crew consisted of his father, Jerome, and a burly teenager hired for the day, and they were stacking the hay bales onto a flatbed trailer. Nate was too small to lift square bales but tall enough for his foot to reach the gas pedal, so his job was driving the truck. As he kept the truck lurching slowly forward between the lines of bales, his father and the teenager kept pace alongside the trailer, tossing the bales up to Jerome to stack. It was Nate's first time to drive, and he got a nervous thrill when the big truck surged forward with the lightest touch of his foot.

His father made him promise not to tell his mother. "When I was your age, I was already driving a truck and tractor both, but she don't see it that way. So this'll be our secret, all right?"

His father wore a straw cowboy hat and a long-sleeved shirt, dark with sweat. He grabbed the wires binding the hay with his calloused ungloved hands and tossed the bales with ease. When the trailer was loaded, they drove several miles to another farm, Nate and the teenager riding in the back of the truck. At a barn, Nate pushed the bales to the edge of the trailer while the others unloaded and stacked them. Then they returned for another load.

On one of their returns to the hayfield, Nate saw a white convertible parked just inside the gate, in the shade of a large tree, and when they got closer, he saw Clarissa sitting behind the wheel. She had placed a cooler of lemonade on the car's hood, and she got out and started filling plastic cups as they approached.

She wore faded jeans, sandals, and a white tank top, its shoulder straps covered by her thick chocolate hair. Drops of sweat glistened on her forehead, and wisps of hair at her temples were matted together from the moisture. Her eyes were the deepest blue, deep enough to drown in.

His father and Jerome took their cups and had a seat on the edge of the trailer, their feet dangling off, while Nate leaned back against the car hood, directly across from them. Clarissa took a red handkerchief out of her pocket and wiped the sweat and hay dust from Jerome's forehead. Then she complained about her foot hurting. When she leaned toward Nate to take off her sandal, her tank top drooped downward and her bare unfettered breasts came into view, quivering gently as she struggled with the sandal strap. She looked up and their eyes met, just for an instant, before he turned and began refilling his lemonade, even though his cup was half-full. He thought she had smiled, but he wasn't sure. He took a long drink and a few deep breaths before turning back around.

Later, Clarissa sat sideways on the trailer, leaning on Jerome with her feet propped up. She extended her leg and put her foot on his father's thigh. "My foot hurts, Denny. Tell me what's wrong with it."

His father's hat was off, his face grimy with hay dust. He picked up the pale foot with his rough dark hands and studied it carefully. The nails were painted bright red. "Lame, huh? I've treated a lame cow or two in my day. Looks like hoof rot to me. Hey Nate, I've got some medicine in the truck. You run and get it. We'll hold her down."

She threw her head back and laughed, and Nate remembered that laugh clearly—full-throated and high-spirited, bolting from her lungs like a wild animal uncaged. When she tried to pull her foot away, his father held on to it. She leaned forward and gave him a push, still laughing, kicking to free her foot, and he finally let go.

What was Jerome's reaction to this exchange? Did he sit sullenly, or did he laugh along? Try as he might, Nate couldn't remember.

One day during his lunch hour, Nate stopped by the Hadlow Public Library, which occupied the first two floors of the old

DeLeon County Jail, a towering structure of red brick and stone sitting a block off the courthouse square. The building resembled a castle, with parapets, turrets, and a central tower, needing only a moat and drawbridge to complete the picture. In the center of the third floor and extending up into the tower was an open space that originally contained the gallows. The third floor now housed a museum of DeLeon County history.

Nate remembered his father telling him about an escape from the jail one year. While everyone in town watched the county fair parade, a prisoner rappelled from a third-story cell window to the ground, using a rope of tied bedsheets. The man was never recaptured, and in his father's version of the story, the escapee rode in the parade in a stolen car, smiling and waving at the crowd.

A perky librarian named Latoya showed Nate where to find the archives of the *Hadlow Herald* and demonstrated how to operate the microfilm reader. Knowing the date of his father's death—April 16, 1975—he quickly found the article he was looking for. It was on the front page of the April 15 issue, in the bottom right corner, so small he almost missed it. The headline was "Accident Claims Life on Hwy 34," and it read:

"On the night of April 12, emergency personnel responded to a one-car accident on the bluff road. At approximately 10:30 p.m., a northbound 1972 Ford LTD convertible went off the road, broke through the guard rail, and plunged down the side of the bluff. The car caught fire, and the Hadlow Volunteer Fire Department was called to the scene. Traffic on the road was shut down for approximately three hours. Pronounced dead at the scene was Clarissa Holub, age 30, of Hadlow. Dennis Holub, age 41, of Houston was taken to Ben Taub Hospital with serious injuries, where he remains in critical condition."

The bluff. He knew it all along, at some level. The following week's *Herald* had both of their obituaries. After reading them, first his father's and then Clarissa's, he put his head in his hands and quietly wept.

Nate found it difficult to concentrate at work. There were so many questions, and he wasn't sure where to look for answers. He found himself longing for his old life in Houston. Maybe he had been unhappy there, but at least he could immerse himself in his work and not feel completely unequal to the task, like he did now. And in Houston, the past was comfortably buried, out of sight and out of mind, not rearing up its monstrous head to devour him whole.

Ten

October arrived, and the days were getting shorter. It was still very warm, but the suffocating heat of summer had eased, and some mornings felt almost cool. The pace at Hadlow Veterinary Hospital was picking up. Most calves were born in the spring, but some ranchers preferred fall calvings.

Everett and Nate met for breakfast one Friday morning at Rita's Cafe, which sat just off the southwest corner of the courthouse square. The cafe had booths along the wall, a few tables, and a row of black leather stools along a Formica counter, worn smooth from the sliding of countless plates and coffee cups.

Rita Blaschke was a short, buxom, fire hydrant of a woman. She wore her silvery hair curled into a bun and had a pair of turquoise horn-rimmed glasses with a neck chain. She ran the place by herself every morning, and her daughter Renee came in to help for lunch.

When Nate walked in, Rita was taking an order at one of the tables. He spotted Everett in the booth closest to the front, near a large window looking out on the street.

He slid into the opposite seat. "Hey, boss."

Everett looked up from his paper. "You look like you've been rode hard and put up wet."

"Busy night. I had a wire-cut horse for Roy Heath and a uterine prolapse at Delbert Rudloff's."

Everett studied him over his glasses. "Did you call Russell? Delbert isn't much help at his age."

Nate knew what he was thinking—this guy will never make it. He'll be back in Houston before Christmas. "No, I didn't want to bother him. I managed."

Everett folded up his paper. "Your decision. Don't hesitate to call him though."

Nate wanted to say that he could handle something as routine as a uterine prolapse. To change the subject, he asked about Leroy and Ruthie's dairy problem, which had been on his to-do list for weeks.

Everett sighed. "That's been a real thorn in my side. I was hoping you'd waltz in here and wave a magic wand over those goddamned Holsteins."

He shook his head and frowned. "I've tested the feed for everything under the sun. And something infectious doesn't make any sense, but I've looked for anything that might cause a chronic herd problem—BVD, Mycoplasma, you name it…all negative. There doesn't seem to be a common denominator. Something is fundamentally wrong on that place, but I can't get a handle on it. I'm starting to blame evil spirits. You know any good shamans?"

"Ruthie thinks the same thing. I'll see what I can do."

Rita walked up and refilled Everett's coffee cup.

Everett said, "Rita, I want you to meet Dr. Nate Holub, my new associate."

"Welcome." She looked him over, then leaned toward Everett. "Is he staying longer than your last one?" She cackled and slapped Everett on the back. "Now what can I get you two gentlemen to eat this morning?"

Everett said he would have the usual—the "ranch hand breakfast," consisting of three eggs, toast, hash browns, and sausage. Nate ordered a cheese omelet.

While waiting for their food, Nate looked out the window toward the town square, where two-story Victorian-era buildings surrounded a stately limestone courthouse. The Crown Theater sat on the corner, its ticket booth window boarded up and its red and gold crown badly in need of paint. He remembered seeing *Charlotte's Web* at the Crown with his father and sister—one of the few times Sarah made the trip to DeLeon County with them. Many of the square's buildings were vacant or occupied by antique dealers, interspersed with the odd real estate or legal office. It wasn't the same place he remembered from childhood. The only businesses he recognized were Ehrlich's Hardware, which was somehow holding on, and Chaloupka's Meat Market on the northeast corner.

"The square sure has changed," he said.

"You can thank Walmart for that," Everett said. "It's kind of fitting the downtown here is focused on antiques, don't you think? The whole idea of family-owned businesses is an antique, right along with American manufacturing."

Nate looked back at the square. What was it like when his father was a boy? Or during Viola's youth? It must have been the place to be on Saturday mornings.

"How do all these antique stores stay in business?"

"They mostly buy and sell from each other, I think. And of course, weekenders from the city like to come out to the quaint little town and buy a knickknack or two."

While eating, Everett introduced Nate to some of the cafe regulars. Skeeter Pilat was a wiry man of indeterminate age wearing grease-spotted coveralls and carrying no more than 120 pounds on his coat hanger frame. Skeeter was a genius with engines, working as a mechanic at the local tractor and farm implement dealership, but his real passion was competitive barbecuing. He owned a custom-made trailer pit, which he kept parked in his driveway and pulled to contests all over the state. The thing was built like a tank and had every possible contrivance, including a canopy with fluorescent lighting for cooking in the wee hours. Everett said it was probably worth more than his house.

Two stools down from Skeeter in a crumpled three-piece suit sat Garner Prescott, who had a law practice on the square. Garner was once DeLeon County District Attorney, a job he held for over a decade, but his career had been on a downward trajectory since then. His practice now consisted mostly of divorces, estate planning, and personal injuries. He was overweight with sad watery eyes and a racking cough brought on by decades of cigar smoking. Garner liked to pontificate to the cafe clientele about issues both large and small, exhibiting the eloquence that once served him well as a prosecutor. That morning the topic was one of his favorites—intellectually-challenged criminals.

"Here's a story that might interest you, Skeeter," he said, looking down at his newspaper. "Or maybe *horrify* would be a better word choice— 'DWI Sends Austin Man to Jail Following Weekend Pyrotechnics.'"

"So it appears that this particular gentleman, after a day of youthful high jinks at Lake Travis, which included the grilling of meat and the consumption of a significant quantity of alcohol, decides to take the party home, so to speak. He puts a barbecue pit full of hot coals into the back of his pickup truck and heads to the house. Unbeknownst to him, or to his equally inebriated girlfriend, the pit turns over in the bed and a trail of smoke begins emanating from the back of the truck. After traveling this way for some distance, the truck, now spouting flames, catches the attention of a highly observant police officer, who with some effort manages to finally get the man's attention at a stoplight. He and the girl scurry out, just before the truck is consumed by a fireball."

"What a dumbass," Skeeter said, as he extracted a piece of bacon from between his incisors with a toothpick.

Rita snickered as she wiped off the counter. "Garner, I imagine you've seen a lot worse."

"Indeed, I have." He turned in his stool to assess the potential size of his audience. "The effect of drugs on human behavior is a fascinating subject, simply fascinating. I could write volumes on it."

"Damn it, Rita. Now you got him started," Everett said, in a low voice only Nate could hear. Everett found Garner insufferable, but he was a good client, keeping a small herd of overly pampered Longhorn cattle and other assorted pets, so he tended to give him a long leash.

Garner sat back on his stool, leaning against the counter with his thumbs tucked under his vest. "I remember an incident back in '93, or maybe it was '92. I prosecuted a young illegal named Humberto Morales. It all started when Mr. Morales was at a bar, some shady establishment in Warrenville. There's a bar fight, and a police officer arrives on the scene to investigate, leaving his car's door unlocked and the keys inside. Mr. Morales, who's under the influence of a strong dose of cannabis and needing a ride home, gets in and drives off, despite the fact that his driving skills are somewhat rudimentary. He later claimed he didn't know the car belonged to the police, having somehow overlooked the siren on top and the word Police written in large letters on the side.

"So as he's driving through town at a high rate of speed, he starts hearing the dispatcher's voice on the radio, but he can't tell where it's coming from. He thinks the car is haunted, possessed by a 'fantasma,' as he put it, so he panics and drives through a red light, gets sideswiped by an eighteen-wheeler, and runs off the road into a drainage ditch. The car rolls a few times before landing upside down, but he crawls out and walks home without so much as a scratch. To the surprise of all, he had conscientiously fastened his seat belt before leaving the bar."

"Safety first," Everett said with a chuckle. Then, in a bid to head off a whole string of Garner's stories, he told one of his own.

"I've got a friend who's a vet in Dallas. He told me one night he was at his clinic alone, and these two rough-looking, tattooed dudes came knocking on the door with a pit bull that was all torn up from fighting. They reeked of marijuana. Being a kindhearted guy, he saw the dog needed help and let them in. He quoted them a price and asked for a deposit before getting started, and one of them reached into his pocket for his wallet and pulled out a knife instead. My friend didn't want stitches himself, so he spent the next hour or two sewing the dog up at knifepoint. The dog was so high from breathing the weed inside their car that it barely needed any sedation. So he finished the job and sent them on their way, but those clowns had a big surprise when they got back to their house…the police were waiting."

Before anyone could ask the question, Everett continued. "As they were leaving, he had asked them to complete a new client questionnaire, and of course one of them stopped and dutifully filled it out, making sure to include his correct name and address."

Nate smiled, but the smile vanished when he turned around and saw Duke Woller sitting in a booth in the far corner. He was sipping coffee, absorbed in his newspaper.

"It's the Duke himself," Everett said, keeping his voice down. "He doesn't come here too often."

"Russell told me about him. Big shot, eh?"

Everett nodded. "That family's got this town by the balls."

"Not just Duke?"

"Duke's got three sons. Leland is president of DeLeon County State Bank, among other things. Louis is a lawyer and our current mayor. The other one, Landon, lives in Houston. He's in the oil business, I believe."

"All L's."

"What's that?"

"All of their names start with L."

"Yep. Duke's real name is Lawrence. His wife is Lydia."

"How'd they get so rich?"

Everett emptied his coffee cup and set it down. "I don't know the whole story, but Duke's father was a ruthless son of a bitch… or so they say. That was R.J. Woller. I think their money goes back before him even, but he made them what they are today. R.J. did some wildcatting out in West Texas. He made a killing, then came back here and invested in land and cattle, then later branched out into other things. He was in politics for a while too—served a couple of terms in the state senate. Duke once had political aspirations of his own, apparently."

"Did you ever meet R.J.?"

"Nope. He died before we moved here."

When they had finished their breakfast, Everett tossed his napkin on the table. "Well, I better skedaddle. I've gotta be at Sandy Oaks by eight."

Sandy Oaks Ranch was one of their best clients, situated on five hundred beautiful rolling acres west of town. It was owned by Harlan Adams, a Houston real estate magnate. Russell's brother Jeremy looked after its two hundred head of registered Angus cattle. Nate had been to the ranch only once, when he had accompanied Everett during his first week.

"What's going on out there?"

"They're having a bull sale next week. I'm fertility testing thirty bulls." Everett slid out of the booth. "See you in a bit." He waved to Woller on the way out.

Nate resisted the urge to turn around. Since meeting Woller, he had gone over their conversation many times. Something about the man unnerved him, but he couldn't put his finger on it.

He finished his coffee and got up to leave. When he turned, he saw Woller watching him, faintly smiling. Nate waved and took a few steps toward the door. Then, on an impulse, he turned and walked back to Woller's booth.

"Good morning, Mr. Woller."

Woller put down his paper. "Morning, Nate."

"Do you mind if I join you for a minute?"

Woller motioned to the seat across from him. "Please do."

Nate settled into the booth, his palms moist on the vinyl seat cover.

Woller took his glasses off, slipped them into a leather pouch, and laid the pouch on top of his paper. "So, tell me, how are you adjusting to the pace of life in our little town? I suspect it's taking a bit of recalibration."

Nate nodded, feeling short of breath. "I'm getting there."

"You're not a stranger to Hadlow though. You must've come here as a child."

Nate nodded again. "Yes, many times. My father brought me on weekends." He watched Woller's face, looking for a reaction. Nate leaned forward, forearms on the table, and took a deep breath. "Did…did you know him?"

Woller's eyes narrowed. He picked up his leather pouch and put it in his shirt pocket. "Yes, Nate, I knew your father."

Nate waited for him to continue, but Woller just looked at him with that maddening frozen grin.

"I've hardly been back since he died. I'm still searching for answers, you might say." Nate shifted in his seat, wishing he hadn't brought up his father, that he hadn't approached Woller at all, that he had kept walking out the door. "I just found out the truth about his accident a few weeks ago. It was a bit of a surprise… to say the least."

Woller rubbed his chin, studying him. "You mean to tell me… that in all this time…you never knew what happened?"

"All I knew was he had an accident." Nate looked down at the table, then back up at Woller. "I didn't know Clarissa was involved."

"Your mother hid the sordid details from you, is that it?"

Nate nodded.

"So…escaping the rat race, as you put it, is not your only reason for returning here."

Nate shrugged.

"And I assume you know about my relationship with Clarissa? That's why you're talking about this with me?"

Nate shook his head slowly. "No. I just…had a hunch…that you might be able to tell me something."

Woller's expression turned suddenly contemptuous, the veneer of civility rubbed clean. He leaned forward, his eyes boring into Nate. "I'll save you some time. There's nothing more to learn. It's just a typical sad story—a drunk, and a whore, getting what they deserved."

Woller got up abruptly, leaving Nate staring at the empty seat, his jaw clenched.

Heading toward the door, Woller stopped and turned. "I know what I'm talking about, Nate. That whore was my sister."

Eleven

When Nate arrived at the clinic that morning, he saw Russell out front, busily stocking Everett's truck. He entered the office through the side door. Finding a laundry basket of socks, towels, and underwear on his desk, he dropped it on the floor and collapsed into his chair, still thinking about his conversation with Woller.

Everett walked in, sat down at his desk, and began rummaging through some papers. "This is a big job today. I'll need Russell. Can you hold down the fort?"

"Sure, no problem."

"It may be quiet. There's only a couple of spays on the book so far."

Ana ran into the room. "Daddy, Daddy, Olivia ate all the pancakes!" She climbed onto Everett's lap, put her arms around his neck, and gave him a woeful look.

"That's not very nice of your sister," he said.

"Mama says I have to eat Cheerios."

Everett frowned, puffing out his lower lip. "Cheerios? That won't do at all, Buttercup. Let's go see if we can rectify this situation."

"What's rec-ta-fly?"

"Make it better."

As Everett carried Ana into the kitchen, Nate felt a twinge of nostalgia for the days when Emma and Marianne were that age. He checked his email and then sat staring at his computer screen, too tired to move. He was habituated to lack of sleep, but the late-night calls had left him more fatigued than usual.

Irene appeared from around the corner, gingerly carrying a steaming cup of coffee. "I saw your receipts. You were busy last night. I bet you can use this." She carefully set the cup on his desk.

"Thanks. I didn't expect to see *you* today."

"Jennie's out sick." Irene leaned lightly against the side of his desk, her arms folded across a green flannel shirt.

Nate was more surprised by the coffee than her presence in the office that day. He picked up the cup. "We've got some surgeries today?"

"Two dog spays. I also just got a call from a woman with a sick cat. She'll be coming by a little later."

"What's wrong with it?"

"She said he's vomiting."

"That's what cats do." Nate smiled wanly and took a sip of coffee.

Hadlow Veterinary Hospital didn't operate on a strict appointment schedule like his old clinic in Houston. Appointments were encouraged, but drop-ins and drop-offs were frequent, making things completely chaotic at times.

"It looks like just you and me today," he said. "Hopefully, we can keep our heads above water."

Irene wore no makeup, and Nate noticed a hint of freckles on her cheeks. This was the first time she had made any effort at conversation. His questions typically received a yes or no answer and not much more. She now seemed chatty by comparison, but she still had the same numb, detached expression she was wearing the first day he met her. He had learned she had an eight-year-old son named Zach.

He leaned back, cradling his coffee cup in his lap. "How's school going?"

Irene looked at her feet. "I don't know. Okay, I guess."

Nate wondered about her age. He guessed mid-thirties. "I hear you're studying to be a nurse?"

She nodded.

"My mother's a retired RN. Worked in Houston for forty years."

"I'm going for my LVN. It's not too bad—just two years. The hardest part is the drive. It's over an hour one way." Her nose twitched, and she reached up and adjusted her glasses with a forefinger. She had on her wedding ring.

"Is it tough going back to school after so long?"

She hesitated.

Nate regretted asking the question, but luckily, the phone rang. Irene turned to walk back to the waiting room, and he followed her, stopping to look out the window while she answered the phone. A truck and trailer were backing up slowly to the loading chute.

Ready or not, the day was afoot. He took a couple of gulps of coffee and walked back to the office to get his coveralls.

The truck and trailer belonged to Randy Krupala, owner of one of Hadlow's barbershops. He had taken the day off to work on the family farm, and one of his cows needed its horns tipped. Nate helped him unload the cow into the circular collecting area. Then he swung around a large gate, funneling her into the alley leading up to the squeeze chute. After getting her in the chute, he turned around in time to see Everett driving off. Russell gave him a faint wave from the passenger seat.

One of the cow's horns was curled and growing into the side of her head, and the skin around the horn tip oozed pus. After restraining the head, Nate quickly and painlessly sawed the horn tip off with a length of obstetrical wire, and then he did the same on the other side to make the horns symmetrical. Another truck and trailer pulled up as he was cleaning the skin wound. When the driver got out and started walking his way, Nate recognized him as one of the Lubojasky brothers.

Harold Lubojasky and his identical twin brother Harvey lived on neighboring farms out on the Warrenville highway. Their hatred for each other knew no bounds and seemed to have its origin in a dispute over their father's will, but it probably went back much farther. They hadn't spoken to each other in fourteen years.

When describing them, Everett said, "Those two cats are polar opposites. Harvey's as friendly as a politician on Election Day, while Harold's got the personality of a diamondback rattlesnake. I'm not sure how to explain that dichotomy from a scientific standpoint, but I'm convinced those two are worthy of study, and there's probably a geneticist or psychologist somewhere who would jump at the chance." Everett went on to say he had done everything possible to run Harold off, but he kept coming back, probably because no other vet in a fifty-mile radius would let him through the door. The brothers not only looked and dressed alike, they also drove similar dark blue trucks, so telling them apart could be difficult. Nate had met Harvey, but not Harold.

The man wore sunglasses and a green cap. He had a dark tan and short black hair. With his luck, Nate knew it had to be Harold.

"Hey there, Mr. Lubojasky. What can we do for you today?"

"Who the hell are you?"

Harold, of course.

"I'm Nate Holub, the new vet."

The thin hard line of Harold's mouth didn't budge as they shook hands. "I've got some heifers that need brucellosis vaccinations. Can you handle that?"

Nate turned around and walked back to the cow, taking a deep breath, telling himself to stay calm. "I'm just about done with this one, and then we'll get your calves unloaded."

He sprayed the cow's wound with an antiseptic and let her out of the chute. While getting her back onto the trailer, Nate noticed two cars parked at the clinic and saw Irene walking his way.

"How much longer are you going to be?" she said. "The cat's here, and there's a parrot that needs a beak trim."

"I'll be in right after I get these calves done." He wanted to get rid of Harold as soon as possible.

"These are my best replacement heifers," Harold said as Nate ran them into the alley. "Be gentle with them."

Nate sighed as he walked over to open the trailer gate, making no effort to hide his irritation.

There were eight calves, and after working each, Nate released them into a small holding pen adjacent to the chute. It all went smoothly. Then, right after Nate caught the last calf in the head gate, Harold yelled, "Oh shit!"

Nate looked to his left and saw calves exiting the pen through an open gate. He ran over and chased three of them back, but the other four were free and running toward the highway.

Harold sprinted to head them off, his cap flying off. "You fucked up now!"

Nate couldn't remember leaving the gate open. After latching it, he started to follow Harold, but he stopped and ran back to the chute to put down his bottle of vaccine. He glanced at the calf in the chute and saw that her head had slid lower in the head gate and her eyes were rolled back—she was choking!

He rushed over and released the head gate, frantically holding her head up. "Breathe, goddamn it. Breathe!"

After an agonizing moment, the calf's eyes fluttered, and her nostrils flared with a breath. She got to her feet slowly, then staggered over to join the other three in the holding pen.

Nate mumbled a quick prayer as he ran out of the barn to see where the escaped calves had gone. They had spooked and split up when Harold chased them—two continuing toward the highway, and the other two going in the direction of the house. Harold reached the front gate first, and he stood there and waved his arms to turn the calves back toward the barn. Nate hurriedly unlatched and swung open a panel of the nearest pen, and then he walked toward Harold, yelling for him to start pushing the calves his way, down the fence line. Working together, they managed to get both calves penned.

As they went to look for the other two, Irene came out of the clinic. One of the calves stood in the back corner of the lot, and the other had disappeared behind the house. Nate asked Irene to close the front gate. Then Harold went after the calf in the corner, while Nate looked in the backyard.

When he rounded the corner, Nate saw the calf standing on the patio next to Daisy's cage. She took off in the opposite direction but slipped on the concrete, and as she struggled to get her footing, one foot caught the edge of the cage, causing it to totter sideways and tumble down with a crash. The door popped open, and the iguana raced out.

Nate cursed and ran after him, but he tripped over a potted plant and landed hard, banging his knee on a steppingstone and ripping a hole in his coveralls. He looked up and saw Daisy's long tail disappear into the tomato plants in the garden.

He got up, hobbled after the calf, and managed to get her turned around. He pushed her down the fence line toward the other calf, and once the calves were together, they settled down. Nate and Harold drove them back to the front, then Nate opened the pen and prevented the penned calves from escaping while Harold and Irene ran the other two in.

Nate wiped his face on his shirtsleeve and handed Harold his cap. "Sorry. I thought that gate was closed."

"You're damned lucky we didn't lose any. Help me load them up, so I can get the hell out of here."

Nate reminded him one calf hadn't been vaccinated, so they ran them all back through the chute. When the calves were finally back on the trailer, Nate returned to the backyard to search for Daisy, but he couldn't find him. He walked back around to the front of the house, just as Harold was pulling his truck and trailer onto the highway.

Nate changed out of his coveralls and tried to catch up in the clinic. While Irene was restraining Elwood the Parrot for his beak trim, he escaped her grasp and flew around the exam room, squawking loudly, and landed on the top medicine shelf. Nate tried to get a towel over the bird, and he got bit on the thumb—deep enough to draw blood—and when he jerked his hand back, he knocked over a large bottle of vitamin B12, which fell and shattered, spilling the thick amber liquid all over the counter and floor. Elwood's owner, Marjory Thompson, finally coaxed him down with a cracker.

A steady stream of customers kept Nate and Irene hopping all morning, and they had no time to eat lunch. When Nate was halfway through his second dog spay in the afternoon, he heard a commotion in the waiting room.

Irene rushed in. "We've got a dog. It's been hit by a car."

Nate removed his gloves and asked her to keep an eye on the anesthetized dog.

He went into the waiting room and saw Hector Trevino cradling the injured dog, a poodle named Roxie, in his arms. Nate carried her into the exam room and placed her gently on the table. A quick exam revealed she was in shock and had a broken tibia. He grabbed a bag of fluids from the bottom cabinet and tossed it in the microwave to heat up. Irene went to the kennel to get an electric blanket and IV stand, while Nate inserted an intravenous catheter in a front limb and taped it in place.

When they had the fluids flowing and Roxie warming on the electric blanket, Nate walked back to the waiting room and gave Hector an update. Then he put on a new pair of surgical gloves and tried to finish the spay.

Irene monitored Roxie, leaving periodically to attend to customers in the waiting room. As Nate started the last layer of sutures, Roxie's breathing suddenly got heavier. He walked over and checked her gums—they were white. Her abdomen looked distended, and when he touched her cornea, she didn't blink.

Hector stood as Nate walked into the waiting room.

"I'm afraid it looks bad. She's got internal bleeding. I'd have to do surgery to stop it, but it's too late for that. I'm really sorry."

Hector nodded and lowered his head. Nate went back into the exam room and told Irene she could go back to her desk. He put on another fresh pair of gloves and went back to work on the other dog. By the time he finished suturing, Roxie had stopped breathing.

At the end of the day, Nate sat at his desk and fretted about what he might have done differently. If he had detected the bleeding sooner, surgery might have saved her. On the other hand, how would he have managed it with his only surgery table and anesthesia machine in use? Would he have been able to find and stop the source of the hemorrhage anyway?

Audrey bounced in from the kitchen. "Hey, looks like you've had a rough day."

Nate wondered what pill she took to give her so much energy. Dealing with adolescents all day had to be at least as tiring as veterinary practice. Whatever it was, he wished he had a prescription.

"It's been a crazy day. Like a busy Saturday morning, only all day long." He gave her a quick recap of the day's highlights.

"Oh, dear. Well, don't worry about Daisy. He's gotten out before. We always find him."

Irene walked in. "I guess I'll be going. I need to pick up Zach. I think we're finally caught up."

"I believe we are," Nate said. "Thanks for all your help today."

"It's been interesting. I like days like this. I don't know why. I guess I like staying busy...and the challenge of it."

"An adrenaline junky, eh?" Audrey said. "You picked the right career then."

"I guess so. But after working here, human medicine might seem pretty tame."

Nate tried to smile. Unlike Irene, he hated days like this. At quitting time, he was only satisfied if he had helped every animal he worked on, and doing the best job possible was more difficult if time was a factor, if he couldn't give every patient his full attention. After seventeen years, a big gap still existed between his expectations and the harsh reality of veterinary practice. And sadly, the move to DeLeon County had made the gap even wider.

Twelve

Only a faint crimson glow lay on the horizon by the time Nate got to the house. He fed Roscoe, heated up a microwave dinner, then sank into his recliner. He stared at the blank screen of his television, still unplugged because he hadn't called the satellite company. His legs ached from being on his feet all day, his right knee was bruised and swollen from his fall while chasing Daisy, and his bandaged thumb throbbed from the bite inflicted by Elwood.

Before he could take a single bite of chicken lo mein, his phone rang. He cursed loudly, startling Roscoe, and fumbled in his pocket for the phone. It showed *Raymond Holub 261-484-7237*. What the hell?

"Hello?"

"Hey cousin," Wink said. "Hope I didn't catch you in your bubble bath. I need a calf pulled."

Nate squeezed the phone tightly, resisting the urge to throw it across the room. He got the directions and said he would be right out. He put the phone back in his pocket, leaned his head back, and closed his eyes, Wink's voice echoing in his head. He tried to will himself into motion, but his legs wouldn't cooperate. It seemed an impossible task—getting up, walking out the door, driving the truck, facing Wink and his goddamned cow. Every molecule in his body rebelled.

Suddenly, he felt something wet. He opened his eyes and saw Roscoe with his feet up on the chair, licking his hand. When Nate snapped his fingers, Roscoe hopped onto his lap and started licking his face.

"Okay, okay." He wrapped his arms around the wiggling dog, trying to hold him still. "You trying to cheer me up? Or do you just want the chair for yourself?" He lifted Roscoe and put him on the chair as he stood, reaching down and giving him one more pat. Then he put his dinner in the fridge and headed for the door.

The cow was at a lease pasture only a couple of miles away. When Nate got there, Wink's son Garrett opened the gate for him. A barn and pens sat close to the road. Nate pulled up and parked next to Wink's truck, which had the engine running and the headlights on to illuminate the pen. He got out of the truck and walked over to Wink, who was leaning on the fence, watching the cow between the slats. Wink had on an untucked SVEC work shirt and a camouflaged cap advertising Vrabel Feed and Seed.

"She's been at it all afternoon," he said. "I called Dr. Templeton, and he said *you* were on call. It's getting to where that man don't want to work anymore."

Nate bit down on his lip hard as he turned and walked back to the truck to get his ropes. When he returned, he saw Wink inside the pen, trying to get the cow into the alleyway.

"I'd rather not put her in there, Wink. I'll use ropes on her. If she lies down in the alley, we're stuck."

"Ropes, huh? Okay, doctor, you do it your way."

Nate glared at him as he uncoiled his rope. He damn sure would.

After Wink stepped through the gate, Nate walked over to the corner of the pen and climbed up on the fence. When the cow saw him, she took off in the other direction. He tossed the rope, and it landed miserably short.

Wink snickered. "This might take a while. Bring me a beer, Garrett. I'm gonna watch the rodeo. Should've brought some lawn chairs."

After a few more attempts, Nate managed to drop the rope over the cow's head as she ran by. He got a couple of wraps on a post and tied off the rope with a half hitch. He picked up his second rope, and using the casting method Everett taught him, he soon had her on the ground. Nate had Garrett hold the rope taut while he went for his supplies. He had a bad feeling about this one—no feet were showing.

He returned, slipped on obstetrical sleeves, and cleaned the cow's vulva. When he reached into the birth canal, his suspicions were confirmed—the calf was still in the uterus, and he wasn't certain which part of it he was feeling. He found the backbone, then an ear, and he realized all four limbs were facing forward and out of reach. He closed his eyes, his face contorted. Another one of Everett's "interesting" calf deliveries. Son of a bitch.

Nate lay there struggling, his arm inside the cow up to his shoulder. The only sounds were the hum of Wink's truck engine, the chirping of crickets, and the cow's heavy breathing. Sweat dripped off his forehead and burned his eyes. Wink and Garrett looked down at him, watching his every move. He tried to find a foot. Then he pulled on the ear, trying to turn the head around. After a few minutes, he could barely feel his arm. Desperation grew within him, whispers becoming shouts, cursing him for believing he could do this kind of work.

He finally stood. "The calf's in a weird position, Wink. The legs are all facing forward, and I can't get a grip on them. I think the calf's dead." He wiped the sweat from his forehead and looked down at the cow grimly. "If she was on her other side, it might help. Can you give me a hand?"

With some effort, they rolled her over. The weary cow made no attempt to rise. When Nate checked the calf, he found he could move the head toward him and reach one elbow, but he was unable to extend the limb. Putting his finger in the mouth elicited no response.

He stood again. "The calf's definitely dead. The only safe way to get it out is with a C-section. I'm not comfortable trying anything else."

Wink's eyes shifted from the cow to Nate. "If it's dead, why can't you cut it up? I've seen a vet do that before."

"The calf's too far in there. A fetotomy would be dangerous. I'm not going to try it."

"How much money we talking about?"

"Around three hundred, maybe a little more."

"Shit." Wink muffled a laugh. "Have you even done one before?"

"Yeah, I've done one."

It was partially true—he assisted Everett with a C-section not long after starting the job—but he dreaded the prospect of doing his first solo one in those conditions, with Wink breathing down his neck.

Wink took off his cap and scratched his head, scowling. "With cattle prices what they are, I can't afford spending a lot of money, especially with some greenhorn vet. If it goes wrong, I've got nothing to show for it but a big bill and a dead cow."

Nate looked at Wink wearily. He stumbled slightly as he shifted his weight from one foot to the other, his knee aching. "Well, it's your decision."

Wink turned his head and spat. "I'll just put a bullet in her." He put his cap back on, turned abruptly, and walked away.

Nate stared down at the cow until Wink was almost out of the pen. "Hold on…wait! There's one more thing I can try."

He walked to the truck and returned with a head noose and some other supplies. If he could get the noose around the calf's neck, he might be able to pull the head toward him far enough to reach the front feet. First, he pumped some lubricant into the uterus, and then, after much struggle, he got the noose around the neck and tied an obstetrical chain to it. He attached the other end of the chain to the calf puller and took a few cranks. When he rechecked the calf's position, he could feel the head slowly moving up into the birth canal. With a few more cranks, he could get a firm grip on the left forelimb just above the carpal joint. If he could get the leg turned and grab the foot, he might have a chance. The carpus was tight against the uterine wall as he pulled. He kept steady pressure on the leg as it inched slowly toward him. Suddenly, it surged ahead and he felt the two claws of the calf's foot.

Nate's arm felt numb again. He pulled it out and shook it, flexing his fingers and elbow. When he reached back in to find the other forelimb, something felt soft and spongy. He became suddenly nauseous when he realized what he was feeling. He pulled out his arm quickly. Even in the poor lighting, blood showed clearly on the obstetrical sleeve—a lot of blood. He ripped the sleeve off, balled it up, and threw it hard to the ground. He leaned forward, his forearm on the cow's hip, feeling dizzy.

"What's the matter?" Wink said.

Nate had his eyes closed, and his hands were trembling. He rose slowly and turned to face Wink.

"Her uterus tore."

Wink looked down at the cow and then back at Nate. "How the hell did that happen?"

"I was trying to turn the foot around…and it just tore. If we do a C-section, I can suture the tear, and she'll have a good chance of making it. That's the only option."

Wink let out a long sigh, shaking his head. Then he fell silent. Nate studied his face, but it was hard to read in the dim light.

"No sir," he said finally. "You've done enough already. I'll take it from here. You can just pack your shit up and get the hell out of here." He turned and started walking toward his truck.

"But Wink, wait…I'll pay for it myself."

Wink stopped and turned. "I said no. Now get the hell out!"

Nate started to explain that if he had agreed to a C-section earlier, this never would have happened, but Wink had already left the pen. He removed the ropes angrily and tossed them over the fence. The cow lifted her head but did not try to get up. He took his calf puller and bucket full of chains to the truck and threw them in the back with a loud clatter.

Nate saw Wink walking back into the pen and started to follow him, but he stopped when he saw the rifle in his hand. Wink strode up to the cow, leaned over, and put the end of the barrel against her head. Nate turned away and braced himself, but the sharp crack of the rifle still made him wince. He steadied himself against the side of the truck, feeling queasy. Then he climbed into the cab, shakily started the engine, and drove off as fast as he could.

After getting back to the house, he stood in the shower for a long time, until the hot water ran out. He ate a few bites and then lay on the couch, staring up at the ceiling.

When sleep finally came, he dreamed he was working on Wink's cow, but during the day and in the cattle pen at the Holub farm. Marianne and Emma sat on top of the fence, looking down on him as he worked. He stood and walked over to them and explained what he was doing. Emma pointed, and he turned. A man walked up to the cow, his back to them, and shot her with a rifle. A pool of blood collected on the ground around her head as her legs jerked. The man turned to face them, and Nate was shocked to see his father, his eyes sad and questioning.

Nate woke with a start. The windows held a glimmer of early morning light. The ceiling fan whirred softly, as a cow in the pasture bellowed for her calf. He lay there motionless for some time, exhausted and utterly dispirited, trying to summon the courage to face the day.

Thirteen

Nate felt a pleasant chill in the air when he stepped out of the house that morning. The first cool front of the season had just passed through, bringing some badly needed showers. Roscoe seemed to like the change as well. He had an extra wag in his tail as he hopped off the porch and sniffed the damp ground.

The pace at work was steady, but not as frenzied as it could get on Saturday. Nate welcomed the slower tempo after the hellish day he just experienced.

Small animal work occupied most of his time. He had the usual array of vaccinations, skin problems, and suture removals. He did a recheck on a dog with a broken leg—it seemed to be healing well.

Late in the morning, David Petras brought in a coughing dachshund. When Nate drew blood and examined a drop under the microscope, the telltale squiggle of larval worms made the diagnosis of heartworm disease, but he did an antigen snap test to confirm it. He recommended bringing the dog back in on Monday for treatment, but David was hesitant when told the cost.

Just before noon, Tina Anders and her teenage daughter April brought in a sick cat named Buster. Feeling a greatly distended bladder, Nate diagnosed a urinary obstruction. Tina agreed to leave Buster at the clinic over the weekend for treatment. With Irene's help, Nate sedated him, passed a urinary catheter, and drained the bladder. Then he sutured the catheter in place, inserted an intravenous catheter in a front limb, and started a slow IV fluid drip.

Irene had a gentle way with animals, and Nate enjoyed working with her. In her hands, even the most intractable cat or dog seemed to calm down.

Everett often let owners hold their animals during vaccinations and other procedures, but Nate always tried to get help from one of the staff. An experience during his first year in practice had taught him the importance of proper restraint. He leaned down to examine the front paw of a seemingly friendly German shepherd, while the owner made no effort to restrain the dog. When Nate finished the exam, the man looked surprised. "I can't believe he didn't bite you. He hates vets."

Nate had the weekend off, and he was leaving for Houston that afternoon, so he walked out to the barn to discuss Buster's treatment with Everett. The radio was tuned to the local station, which played polkas on Saturday mornings. Everett was finishing up a cosmetic dehorn on a show steer. Over the sound of accordion and trumpets, he said, "You take it easy this weekend. I'll do my best not to kill your cat."

Nate drove into town. He was late for lunch with Ruthie. They were meeting at Chaloupka's Meat Market, which occupied the first floor of a two-story building on the square.

The hardwood floor creaked as Nate walked in, and a small bell on the door jingled. The room was long and narrow with a meat display case at the front, tables in the middle, and pits in the back. Fans extended down from the tall, pressed tin ceiling. The brick peeked out on the faded walls, unadorned except for a couple of dusty deer heads, an unplugged neon Pearl Beer sign, and a few unframed yellowing photographs. The odor of smoked meat permeated every square inch of the place.

This had been his father's favorite place to take him for lunch on Saturdays, and everything was just as Nate remembered. He half expected to see his father sitting there waiting for him, but instead it was Ruthie, happily chatting with someone at a neighboring table. He greeted her and apologized for being late.

They walked up to the counter in the back and waited in line. Behind the counter stood brick pits with massive metal doors raised and lowered with pulleys, the wall behind them darkened from decades of smoke. There was no menu in sight.

When it was their turn, an elderly, gum-chewing man at the cash register nodded at Nate. "What can I getcha?"

Nate ordered a few slices of brisket and a half link of sausage, coleslaw, and potato salad. A portly bearded man in a greasy apron speared the meat off the pit, sliced it on a cutting board, and put it on a sheet of brown butcher paper. The other man added a small cup of sauce, two slices of white bread, and more cups containing the sides. When Nate and Ruthie had their food, they filled cups with iced tea and found an empty table near the front.

After getting seated, Ruthie said, "Pardon me for saying it, but you look like hell, Nathan."

"I'm just tired. Had some after-hours calls this week. I've been meaning to take another look at your cows. I'll try to get out there next weekend."

"Don't worry about that. I don't know what you can do that ain't already been done." Ruthie laid a slice of brisket on a piece of bread, poured some sauce on it, and folded the bread over. "Like Mama used to say, it'll all come out in the wash."

"Have you seen Grandma lately?"

"I go out there every Monday and cook her supper. She's gotten to where she don't hardly cook for herself. I bring her food to last the week. And then we usually take her to church on Saturday evening when she feels like going."

Nate was so wrapped up in his own problems, he didn't realize how much care Viola needed. He vowed to go see her more often, even if it meant crossing paths with Wink.

"Her mind is still sharp, and her medicine is working good," Ruthie said, "but she's getting so frail. I've asked her about moving into that assisted living place, but she won't listen. She's about as muleheaded as you can get."

Ruthie paused to take a sip of tea.

"I caught her out in the garden the other day at noon when it was already over ninety. I told her, 'Mama, you can't be out here in this heat,' and you know what she said? She said, 'I used to chop cotton all day long when I was pregnant with Dennis and with Jerome strapped to my back. Don't tell *me* about no goddamned heat.'"

Ruthie took a sideways glance, worried somebody might have overheard.

Nate remembered what Ruthie had told him about Viola's childhood—the drunken father, the abuse, the growing up fast. He had always assumed her upbringing was no different than others of her generation—harsh and ascetic by today's standards, but otherwise unremarkable. He tried to recall everything he wanted to ask Ruthie, but he was tired, his thoughts jumbled.

"Ruthie, tell me about Uncle Alois. I seem to vaguely remember his farm. Everett said he had a daughter living with him?"

"Alois's daughter is Tilly. Matilda is her name, but she's always gone by Tilly."

Ruthie paused to say hello to a couple walking by on their way out. When they were gone, she leaned toward Nate. "That's Sally Wehmeyer. Her daughter Gina is the same age as Margaret. She was diagnosed with cancer a few months ago, poor thing. She's taking chemo in Houston every week."

Nate wasn't sure if it was Sally or Gina who had cancer, but before he could ask, Ruthie went on. "So anyway, nobody in the family ever talks to Alois. Nobody else talks to him much neither. He lives on his place there and comes to town only long enough to buy groceries or whatever. He's a strange one, but you know they say he was mostly normal before the war."

"What happened to him?"

"I don't know. He had a rough time of it, I guess."

Nate envisioned Alois with helmet on, hunched down in a landing craft, headed for the beaches of Normandy, bullets whistling overhead and ripping the water around him. "He must be pretty old by now. Is he about Grandma's age?"

"Something like that. I've talked to him maybe three or four times in all these years, if you can believe it. Your daddy and Jerome both knew him better than I did. They used to haul hay for him and help him with his cattle every now and then. He carried the mail for years." Ruthie leaned forward, her arm on the table. "There are all sorts of crazy stories about Alois running around this town."

Nate put down his fork. "What kind of stories?"

Ruthie frowned and shook her head. "Nothing worth repeating. He just wants to be left alone. People just don't know how to deal with someone like that."

Nate racked his memory for any trace of Alois. "I don't remember ever seeing him."

"You probably never have."

"So what's the story with Tilly?"

"You know, Nathan, that poor girl's never been right. I'm not sure what you'd call her…autistic, I guess it is. They had her in school for years until she kicked a teacher one day. Knowing the teacher, he probably deserved it. They sent her off to some special school in Austin for a while. Alois doesn't let nobody around her. I don't know what's gonna happen to her when he's gone."

"Nobody checks up on them?"

Ruthie shooed a fly off her potato salad. "Alois has a daughter older than Tilly. She lives out of state. I guess she calls him, but I don't know. Maybe she even comes to visit. I've tried going by there a few times, but he won't answer the door for me."

"About how old is Tilly?"

"She's younger than me. Let's see…she was younger than Sammy too. Probably mid-fifties?"

"And what happened to Alois's wife?"

"She died probably twenty years ago or more. Miriam was her name. Nice lady. Died of stomach cancer, I think it was."

The crowd had thinned out and there was now little danger of being overheard. Nate took a swallow of tea, scooted his chair up slightly, and leaned forward. "Ruthie, while we're talking family secrets, I have something else to ask you about."

He paused and studied her face, his pulse quickening. "I was never told much about Daddy's accident." He took a deep breath, held it, and slowly exhaled. "Mom never told me…about Clarissa."

Ruthie brought her napkin up and wiped her mouth, avoiding his eyes. She folded it carefully and placed it on the table.

"Ruthie, they were having an affair, weren't they?"

The color left Ruthie's face. She looked down at her plate and then to either side. She reached across the table and grasped his arm. "It's true. I thought your mother had probably told you by now. Before the funeral, she told me and Mama she didn't want you finding out. You were such a young fella then."

She released his arm, picked her napkin up, and dabbed the corner of her eye. "I'm sorry, Nathan. I'm truly sorry."

"You don't have to apologize. How long did it go on?"

She put her elbows on the table, rested her chin on her folded hands, and closed her eyes. "I really don't know. It could've been only months, but I guess it could've been longer."

"Did you know about it? Did Jerome?"

She opened her eyes and shook her head. "I didn't know. I'm not sure about Jerome, but I think he must've known. Clarissa had a reputation. That wasn't the only time she cheated on him, not by a long shot. She was a wild one. Broke Jerome's heart. It nearly killed him losing her and Dennis like that. I guess maybe it did in a way. He was never the same. Mama neither."

"Who was driving?"

"They figured Dennis was driving and got thrown out. Neither had their seat belt on. I don't think they could tell for sure."

"Was he drunk?"

Ruthie gave a quick nod and looked away, tears flowing down her cheeks.

Nate sighed and slumped in his chair. Sunlight streamed through the front window, and a coat rack by the door cast a long shadow across the hardwood floor. He watched the reflections made by passing cars in the meat display case.

Ruthie reached out and held Nate's arm again, firmer this time. "Listen to me, Nathan. Dennis loved Jerome, and I know it made him sick inside. And God knows he loved you and your sister. I believe he still loved your mama too. I really do."

Nate imagined his father had been caught in a self-destructive loop fueled by his desire for Clarissa and for alcohol and wasn't strong enough to break free. He meant no harm, but harm he had done, immense harm to everyone who loved him. Nate was angry—not just at his father, but at the senseless tragedy of it all.

When they had finished eating, they walked outside and lingered on the sidewalk.

"I'm glad we had this talk," Ruthie said. "It's not good to keep things bottled up. Not good at all."

Nate gave her a hug and wiped a tear from his eye as they parted. He watched her as she walked down the street, and then as she drove slowly around the square. He got into his car and headed out to his house, stopping only long enough to pack a bag and pick up Roscoe, and then he was on Highway 34 north, driving fast, needing to put DeLeon County far behind him.

The sky was still overcast from the front that pushed through early in the morning, and to Nate it felt like the dark shadow of the past, casting its pall across the land, pervasive and inescapable. There seemed little hope of ever seeing the sun again.

Driving eastward on the interstate, Nate descended to the coastal plain and the human footprint on the land became gradually more apparent. Development spread outward from the city like the tentacles of some insatiable beast. Wide swaths of two-story brick homes crowded the horizon, each a climate-controlled cocoon on its six thousand square feet of irrigated and chemical-saturated San Augustine. Farther in, strip malls, big box stores, gas stations, and fast-food restaurants lined the freeway. Auto dealerships flew giant American flags over acres of glittering vehicles, while immense billboards hawked everything from airline fares to Scotch whiskey to strip clubs. The vehicles on the freeway built up from a trickle to a torrent, and then to a raging river—oversized pickup trucks and massive SUVs driving bumper to bumper at high speed, impatient to get somewhere and heedless of the consequences, all rushing pell-mell into oblivion.

The air turned acrid, smelling of diesel exhaust. Nate felt short of breath and tightened his grip on the wheel. The flow of vehicles suddenly slowed to a crawl, and he almost rear-ended the car in front of him. He was in the middle of a four-lane freeway, and the vehicles were closing in, smothering him. He had spent countless hours on Houston freeways, but now it somehow seemed unfathomable.

"Traffic shouldn't be this bad, Roscoe. Not on a Saturday."

Roscoe gave him a sympathetic look from his perch in the passenger's seat. A truck behind him honked, and Nate jumped. Traffic was moving again. He drove on, not breathing easier until finally exiting the freeway two miles later.

He planned to spend the night with his mother before visiting the girls on Sunday, but he first went by and checked on his house. The front yard was overgrown, although not as bad as he expected. He mowed the grass, hoping this was the last time it would need mowing until spring, and then he edged along the street. The house was a mess when he moved out, so he tried to do some cleaning, but his heart wasn't in it. The place demoralized him, and he couldn't wait to leave.

Nate ate dinner with his mother that evening on her patio. When she asked him about his new life, he tried to be positive. He didn't want her worrying, so he didn't mention Willie Petru, Harold Lubojasky, Wink, or his brush with Tiny's cow.

When they had finished eating, she took their plates inside and brought back glasses of wine. It was dark by then, and moths circled the dim glow of the porch light. On the drive in, he had decided to ask her about the accident, even rehearsing what he would say, but his resolve evaporated. His exhaustion from the last few days didn't help.

"Have you seen the girls lately?" he said.

She frowned. "Not as much as I'd like. Your ex-wife is a real bitch, but I guess you know that well enough. I took them to the zoo a few weekends ago, the first time I'd been there since you and Sarah were little. But most weekends they're running around too much. And she won't bring them here. I have to go get them."

This wasn't surprising. Caroline and his mother had never been exactly chummy. The mention of his sister reminded Nate he needed to send her his new address.

"Have you talked to Sarah lately?"

"Not for a couple of months."

Nate detected a touch of bitterness in her voice. Sarah was married to a career military man. She had three kids, ranging from seven to fourteen, and the family had moved from one air force base to another over sixteen years, most recently to Qatar. His mother and Sarah had been at odds since her troubled adolescence. Sarah fell in with a rough crowd and barely managed to finish high school. Other than Christmas cards and the very rare phone conversation, Nate had no contact with her. He wished they had a better relationship.

After a few more minutes of halting conversation, his mother said, "It's getting a bit chilly. I think I'll go inside."

Nate followed, wishing he hadn't mentioned Sarah.

They spent the rest of the evening quietly. His mother read a novel, while Nate half-heartedly tried to watch a baseball playoff game and paged through a magazine. He couldn't keep his mind off his lunchtime conversation with Ruthie. If his mother noticed he was distracted, she didn't mention it. There was a palpable tension in the room, but neither of them would acknowledge it.

They took the dogs for an early walk the next day, enjoying the cool morning air. With few cars out and the Victorian homes lining the streets, it was easy to imagine what the neighborhood looked like back in its heyday. The Heights was once on the edge of town, a fashionable area for the city's up-and-coming, connected to downtown by streetcar. Like so many old neighborhoods, it suffered from neglect during the post-war era as families moved to the suburbs. Gentrification over the past couple of decades had brought many of the old homes back from the brink.

Nate left Roscoe with his mother for the day and picked up the girls just before noon. After stopping for lunch at Sal's, they headed south to Galveston. The island had been a favorite spot for family outings when the girls were younger. Nate thought the water might be too cool for swimming, but he told the girls to bring their swimsuits anyway. Marianne rode in the front and talked the entire trip, while Emma stared out the rear window.

When they reached the island, they first explored some shops on The Strand. Nate remembered his father telling him about their Holub ancestors arriving in Galveston from Europe. The city was one of the largest in Texas before the hurricane of 1900 almost wiped it off the map. A few downtown buildings survived the storm, and as they walked the streets, Nate wondered if any of them were standing when those early Holubs stumbled off the boat.

They got back in the car and drove down to Seawall Boulevard and the beach. The water was surprisingly still warm, and Marianne stripped down to her bathing suit and was soon crashing into the surf, urging Nate and Emma to join her. Nate hadn't even brought his trunks, and Emma just frowned.

Nate took off his shoes and socks, pulled up his pant legs, and walked up to the water. The wet sand felt good on his feet. Emma reluctantly followed, and they started walking along the water's edge. The briny sea air echoed with the shrieks of gulls and the laughter of kids farther down the beach.

Nate stopped and looked at Emma. "Everything all right? You're being really quiet."

Emma looked down, rubbing her big toe on the opposite heel, holding his arm for support. "You know me, Dad. I'm the quiet temperamental one."

They started walking again, and Nate looked over his shoulder at Marianne. He began to yell to her not to go out too far, but he hesitated, knowing she was an excellent swimmer. He turned back to Emma. "So how's your mother doing?"

Emma was squinting at a fishing boat bouncing over the waves far on the horizon, and the squint became a scowl. "She's turning positively weird, Dad, I swear. She obsesses over things so much."

"Like what?"

"First, it was our clothes. She thinks we can't be seen wearing anything less than designer labels. She takes us to the Galleria about every other weekend. Marianne likes to shop, but you know me, I'd rather be anywhere than the mall. And now, it's my friends."

"What's wrong with your friends?"

"It's like they're not good enough for her or something. She's threatening to put me in a different school. She's flipped since the divorce, Dad. She really has."

"Aren't you still friends with Allison?"

"Allison? We changed schools, remember? Plus, she moved to Florida last year. I know a couple of girls from the cross-country team."

"They're good kids?"

She rolled her eyes. "They're just nerds like me. We go to movies or just hang out mostly."

Nate wished he had been keeping up with her social life better. Their email and phone conversations were mostly about her classes and cross-country meets. He was worried about her grades slipping since the change of schools. She had always been an A/B student but was making Cs in algebra. He should have been asking about her friends as well. She could be running around with drugged-out crazies for all he knew, getting tattoos and body piercings, dyeing her hair green.

Nate looked back again to check on Marianne, but he couldn't see her. Taking Emma by the hand, he turned around. "Come on, we should head back and see about your sister."

He picked up the pace, looking nervously at the waves until he spotted her and saw she was safe.

The fragility of life terrified him, at least where his daughters were concerned. The line between happiness and despair is razor-thin, and all it takes is a sudden shift in the wind or a moment of inattention by the driver in the other lane to turn life upside down instantly.

He turned back to Emma. "And dare I ask…what about boys?"

Emma scowled again. "Can't help you there, Dad. You need to talk to my fair sister. She has that market cornered."

Nate cringed. *Oh God, just help me get through these next few years.*

They walked back, sat down on the sand, and put their shoes back on. Sunlight shimmered on the gentle swells beyond the surf. Marianne was playing with some kids who were body surfing with inflatable rafts. They let her ride one, and she shrieked when she took a spill, her limbs flying wildly into the air. Nate laughed and glanced at Emma, but she was sulking.

He brushed a strand of hair from her eyes. "You sure you're okay?"

She turned her face away.

He gently pulled her chin toward him and saw tears running down her cheeks. He put his arms around her and pulled her close. "Don't cry, honey. Please don't cry."

He rocked her softly, her head against his cheek, watching the ebb and flow of the surf on the dark wet sand. "What is it? What can I do?"

She pulled away and looked up at him with wet eyes, sniffling, and shook her head. Then she leaned back against him and took his hand in both of hers. "This is enough."

He wrapped his arm around her shoulder. He wanted to keep holding her, to protect her from a cold uncaring world, but he felt powerless to do so, as though she were on a boat headed over a waterfall while he watched helplessly from the shore.

After Marianne finished her swim, they left the beach and went to Moody Gardens. One of Marianne's friends had told her about the penguin exhibit, and she wanted to see it. The penguins' antics made even Emma laugh, and Nate was glad to see her mood improve. They watched an IMAX movie about the Grand Canyon and then went to Gaido's for some seafood.

On the drive back to Houston, Marianne again rode in the front. Nate couldn't believe how much she had changed in the few weeks since the move. Her hair looked darker, her face fuller, her movements less awkward and more self-assured. They were growing up so fast.

He turned down the radio. "So what's this I hear about boyfriends?"

Marianne turned around and glared at Emma. "Well...despite what you may have been told, there are no boyfriends. I have some friends who happen to be boys, but that's all."

In the rearview mirror, Nate saw Emma roll her eyes. He hesitated, shifting in his seat. "You uh...just be...um...you know—"

"Dad, don't worry. Mom has given us 'The Talk.'" Marianne mimed quotation marks. "She's on top of this stuff, she really is." She patted him on the shoulder reassuringly. Then she pointed at him and laughed. "You're blushing. Look Em!"

Nate rubbed the back of his neck. "Uh, no I'm not. Just got a little too much sun today."

They drove on in silence. On their left, the sun was low on the horizon, and soft golden light lay over the coastal salt flats. A gentle north breeze stirred the marsh grass, creating ripples along the water's surface. A great blue heron stepped gingerly in the shallows, patiently eyeing the water for fish and crab, while a flock of newly arrived geese rose from a distant inlet and became lost in the sun. Development was still relatively light along this stretch of the interstate, the threat of hurricane flooding having kept all but the most intrepid developers at bay. As they drove north, however, those few remnants of the once vast coastal marsh gave way to an inland sea of housing around La Marque, Dickinson, and League City.

Nate pondered his role in his daughters' lives. Even before the divorce, he felt them slipping away, moving just beyond his grasp, to a place where he wasn't really needed or maybe even welcome. That feeling intensified after the divorce, and his reach for them had started feeling more like a desperate lunge. But Emma had shown him he was still needed, that he still had a role to play. He knew he had to visit more often. He also had to bring them to DeLeon County once his spare bedroom was furnished and the house tidied up.

Assuming he lasted that long.

They passed the exits for Clear Lake and were soon immersed in the cacophony of the city. It seemed like he had been gone much longer than a few weeks. Houston had been his home all of his life, but it now felt strange to him, the chaotic buzz of the place unsettling. He felt disconnected…adrift…unable to get his bearings.

On the interstate driving back that evening, somewhere west of Houston, Nate realized his life was balanced between two very different worlds, just as his father's had been. Maybe they shared something after all.

Then later, as he neared Hadlow, it dawned on him how different their situations really were—for his father, one of those two places had felt like home.

Fourteen

Life in DeLeon County had developed a rhythm by mid-October. The long hot summer had finally ended, and football season was in full swing. Store windows throughout town were painted with slogans to cheer on the local high school heroes—the Hadlow Armadillos.

When Nate got to the clinic one Friday morning, he walked into the waiting room and saw Irene sweeping the floor. She wore a purple sweater over her usual flannel shirt.

"Hey, Irene. Jennie in Vegas for a three-day weekend?"

She stopped sweeping only long enough to look up. "No, just taking the day off."

Try as he might, Nate had yet to make her smile.

He checked the appointment book. He was scheduled to go to Henrietta Kovar's house right after lunch to vaccinate and deworm some dogs. When he had told Everett about the appointment, he said, "Henrietta? You better take Russell and be prepared for anything. I've had some real rodeos out there."

Everett planned to recheck Myrtle Hamilton's lame horse that morning, and then he was headed out to Sandy Oaks to palpate cows.

Nate turned to Irene. "How's Zach doing?"

Irene had started opening up a bit in recent weeks. She had told him Zach was having trouble in school. Since her husband Clint's death, Zach had been prone to angry outbursts. He had a fight with another kid at school recently and was suspended for three days. Nate also learned that Irene moved to Hadlow from Austin that spring to live with her mother, who had lupus and was frequently bedridden.

Irene walked over to the reception desk. She rested her arm on the counter and frowned. "There haven't been any more fights, but his grades still aren't very good. I try to help him, but I can't spend as much time with him as I'd like."

Nate leaned on the counter, his legs crossed behind him. Now that Irene was standing close, he could see how tired she looked. Instead of the usual ponytail, her hair cascaded down her shoulders, flaming like a sunset. She twirled a strand of it around her finger.

"Hang in there," he said. "Once he meets more friends, he'll start doing better. It's always tough for the new kid."

"Yeah, I guess so."

Irene's eyes were hazel. There was kindness in them, maybe even a hint of playfulness beneath the layers of worry and grief.

Nate felt impulsive. "Hey, is Zach a football fan? Everett invited me to the big game tonight. Why don't you meet us there?"

Irene shuffled her feet, looking down at the countertop. "I don't know."

"Come on. It might do you both some good."

"Maybe."

Nate gently grasped her shoulder, feeling the plush sweater, her soft hair on the back of his fingers. "You really should come. It'll be fun."

Irene fidgeted and ducked her shoulder, and Nate quickly withdrew his hand. She turned and went back to sweeping, and he walked toward the office, his face burning.

That morning was as busy as any Nate had experienced. The town buzzed with energy about the game, and people were on the move, running their errands. With Everett on the road, Nate struggled to keep up. Trailer after trailer pulled into the drive. Between the large animal jobs, Nate ducked inside to catch up while Russell waved the next trailer back to the loading chute. They had a cow with a cervical prolapse, calves to vaccinate and dehorn, and a cow with an abscess on her jaw.

While Nate was lancing the abscess, Russell said, "Don't look now. Mr. Sunshine is here."

Russell could tell the Lubojasky brothers apart better than Nate, and Nate grimaced when he realized Harold had stepped out of his truck and was walking their way.

"Hey there, Harold," Russell said, grinning. "Isn't it a great day to be alive?"

"Where's Dr. Templeton?"

Nate was flushing the abscess with a large syringe of saline. "He's out on the road. Won't be back until after lunch. Can we help you?"

Harold scowled and shook his head. "I got a lame cow…bad lame. Dr. Templeton needs to see her. She's one of my best cows."

Nate bit his lip. Of course she is. Bovine royalty, no doubt. "We'll put her in the pen. He can take a look at her later this afternoon."

"Later this afternoon? You said he'd be back right after lunch."

"I'm not exactly sure when he's getting back, but he's got some surgeries to do after lunch. He'll get to your cow when he gets time."

"Surgeries? What…some mutt needs its balls cut off?" He laughed. "Shit, I thought that was *your* job."

Nate turned his back on Harold as he drew up an antibiotic injection. He took a slow deep breath.

Harold hesitated, then stormed back to his truck. He sat down in the cab with the door open and made a phone call.

"Don't let that asshole get to you," Russell said.

Nate tapped the cow's neck several times rhythmically with the back of his hand before popping the needle in. He attached the syringe and gave the injection. They got the cow back on the trailer, then Nate went inside while Russell helped Harold unload his cow.

In the office, Nate slipped off his coveralls and went into the bathroom to clean up. A few people were waiting—a woman with an itchy cat and an elderly couple with a dog needing its anal glands expressed. It was just past noon by the time he finally caught up.

Nate and Russell headed to Henrietta's house after stopping for lunch at El Guapo, a Mexican restaurant on Highway 34 North. She lived eight miles from town on Holloway Creek Road.

On the way, they drove through "The Flat," a low flood-prone area near the river where many of Hadlow's poorer residents lived. Sagging ramshackle houses lined the streets, and rusting wheelless cars sat in overgrown yards. Shady dirt side lanes snaked back into wooded areas where other homes hid from view. They passed a public housing development of tan brick duplexes with paint peeling from the eaves and screens falling off the windows. The only businesses were a barbershop, a couple of bars, and a funeral parlor. Nate had never been through this part of town and seeing the despair of the place did nothing to improve his mood.

They pulled up at Henrietta's a few minutes later. Her trailer sat back in the woods, not quite level, the yard strewn with rusty appliances, concrete statuary, bags of aluminum cans, broken-down lawnmowers, and a moldy bathtub or two.

Over the din of barking dogs, Russell said, "Doc, I sure hope your tetanus shots are up to date."

They got out of the truck and approached warily, following a winding path through the junk. Nate knocked on the sagging screen door. After a long wait, Henrietta waddled out, wearing a faded pink t-shirt, baggy green shorts, and tall rubber boots. She had thick eyelashes and bushy brown hair starting to gray.

Nate introduced himself.

"Hello there," Henrietta said, ignoring his outstretched hand, reaching instead for a can of insect repellent in a plastic crate near the door. "I'm afraid we've got a bit of a tick problem. You might need some of this." She started applying it and disappeared in a cloud of spray.

Nate and Russell looked at each other and shrugged, deciding to take their chances.

They followed Henrietta across a carport and then down a path around the back of the trailer. Dog pens were set up randomly in the woods, most obscured by vegetation. Some had concrete floors, but most were dirt. Nate didn't know how many German shorthaired pointers Henrietta had, but it sounded like no less than a hundred.

"I hope you brought plenty of vaccine," Henrietta said. "I've got three litters of pups and some adults that need their annuals. I used to do all this stuff myself, but I've got arthritis so bad now I can hardly get going some days. I lost two of my best dogs to lepto a few years back, so I don't trust the store-bought vaccines anymore."

In each pen Nate and Russell entered, they had to sidestep piles of feces. Many of the dirt-floored pens had deep pits where the dogs had tried to dig out. More than once, they tripped over exposed tree roots. The dogs were excitable, and Russell had trouble catching and holding them. Henrietta provided a running commentary while they worked.

"This is Günter's Ghost. We call him G.G. He's out of Aldabella, sired by Baron von Wagenbach. I used to show his mother. He's a jumper. That's why I've got his pen covered. The rascal was jumping on top of his house, then out of the pen."

One large pen they entered had three young males. "These are littermates I've held on to, but I've got one of them sold to a breeder in New Mexico. They'll make good studs. They're great-grandsons of Durango, a littermate of Theodora, who won best of class at Westminster in '97. I need a heartworm test and health certificate on Jupiter. He's the lighter one there in the corner."

The excited dogs ran around the pen, leaping up on Nate and Russell with muddy paws. Nate set his cooler containing vaccine, dewormer, syringes, and ice packs on the ground along the side of the pen. Russell caught Jupiter and held him while Nate kneeled to give him a quick physical exam. When he did so, he felt something soft and wet on his knee.

"Jupiter's got the look everybody wants right now," Henrietta said. "See that slope to his shoulder? The broad chest? Those big nostrils? That's what the judges like. Isn't he a dreamboat?"

"He sure is," Nate said as he stood and shook the feces off his pant leg.

Russell held off the vein on Jupiter's front limb. As Nate bent over the dog, trying to draw a blood sample, one of the other dogs jumped on his back and started humping him. He felt the dog's breath on his ear, drool running down his neck.

"Poindexter, you stop that!" Henrietta said.

She grabbed the dog by his scruff and pulled him off. Jupiter lurched, pulling the needle out of the vein, and the leg started bleeding. Nate held off the vein with a cotton swab and waited, but the bleeding wouldn't stop. While pulling more swabs out of his pocket, he heard an odd sound and looked to his right. Behind Henrietta, Poindexter had his leg raised and a stream of urine flowed into the open cooler.

"Doesn't Jupiter have the most beautiful eyes you've ever seen?" Henrietta said. "Almond-shaped is what the judges look for. Round eyes won't do you any favors. And look at those feet. See how they're webbed, and how the toes are arched? Aren't they gorgeous?"

"Yes ma'am," Nate said, wishing Jupiter's leg would stop bleeding. When it finally did, they managed to get the blood sample from his other leg.

By the time they vaccinated and dewormed all three dogs, and then thirty more, it was getting late, and Nate's patience was stretched thin. One dog had escaped the pen, and they had to hide a sedative tablet in a piece of cheese to get it recaptured. A couple of dogs growled at them and needed muzzling, and another cut its leg on a loose wire and needed sutures.

Tired and sweaty, Nate finally plodded back to the truck with his urine-soaked cooler, scratching a tick bite, dog barks ringing in his ears. He filled out Jupiter's health certificate, then walked back to the trailer.

Henrietta sat on the carport with her boots off and her bunioned feet propped up, cradling a can of diet cola, looking entirely too pleased with herself.

Nate handed her the paperwork, eager to get back on the road. "Thank you, Ms. Kovar."

Henrietta took the papers and laid them on a cluttered table nearby. "That wasn't bad at all." She took a gulp of her drink, burped, and wiped her mouth with the back of her hand. "It went a whole lot better than usual."

Nate went to his house after work to eat and shower before heading back for the game. The Hadlow Armadillos played their home games at Spenrath Field, located in a residential area in the middle of town. An old brick building nearby had been the high school in his father's day, now converted to the school district administration building.

When Nate found a parking spot along a side street and got out of his car, he heard the band playing the national anthem. Moths swirled in the glow of the stadium lights as he headed toward the music. Once he reached the stadium, he paid for his ticket at the booth and walked over to the edge of the home stands.

Spenrath Field was an older stadium of quirky design. The home bleachers were only ten rows high and stretched from goal line to goal line. The press box was on the visitor's side, where the stands were taller but not nearly as broad. The home crowd wore the Hadlow High colors of navy blue and gold, while the visitors sported the red and white of the Wiley Mules.

The game was standing room only, and Nate wished he had arrived earlier. He looked for Everett and Audrey and finally spotted Audrey waving at him from the top row, wearing a blue

Hadlow sweatshirt. She motioned that she had a seat saved for him, so he carefully made his way up to join them.

"About time you got here," Everett said as Nate sat down next to Audrey. "Don't you know this is for the district championship? You gotta get your game face on, son." He reached behind Audrey and punched Nate in the shoulder.

Olivia sat between Everett and Audrey, and Ana was on Everett's lap. Irene and Zach were nowhere in sight.

A woman to Nate's left cursed and then a roar rose from the visitor's side. He looked up to see a Wiley running back racing down the far sideline with the closest Hadlow defender ten yards behind. When he crossed the goal line, the Wiley band broke into their fight song as their cheerleaders did tumbles and cartwheels down the field.

"Not a good start," Audrey said, shaking her head. "They beat us 44-10 last year at their place, but I'm hoping we can make a better game of it this year. This is a huge rivalry. It's always the biggest game of the year."

"Any of the players students of yours?"

"A lot of them I've had. I teach freshmen and sophomores mostly. There's only four or five I have this year."

Olivia grabbed her arm, trying to get her attention. "Mama, I want some popcorn. Please?"

"Not now, honey. We'll get some later."

Everett leaned toward Nate. "How'd it go out at Henrietta's?" He had left for a farm call before Nate and Russell made it back to the clinic.

"It was like you said—a rodeo. One thing you forgot to warn me about is the ticks." Nate reached down to scratch a bite on his ankle, wishing he had taken Henrietta up on her offer of repellent.

"Ticks, huh? That's a new one. I've never gotten ticks out there, but I did get stung by yellow jackets once. Henrietta is a real piece of work."

The game was intense, but Nate had trouble paying attention. He looked for Irene, scanning the crowd, checking both entrance ramps. Touching her that morning was a mistake. God, what was he thinking?

Wiley had the bigger and faster team, and they surged forward, threatening to blow the game open, but then Hadlow battled back.

Just before halftime, a Hadlow cornerback jumped in front of an errant pass and ran the interception back for a touchdown, giving the home team a narrow halftime lead.

Nate walked to the concession stand to get a drink. Spectators stood along the fence surrounding the field. Seeing Russell with a couple of his friends, Nate stopped to chat and compare tick bites. Then he continued toward the far end of the field. When he spotted Wink leaning on the fence and talking to another man, he looked straight ahead and walked a little faster.

In line at the concession stand, Nate felt a tap on his shoulder. He closed his eyes and gritted his teeth. Oh shit, Wink had followed him. He turned around, but instead of Wink, it was Harold Lubojasky.

The evening had just gone from bad to worse.

Harold extended his hand. "Dr. Holub, how are you?"

Nate looked at him suspiciously, trying to keep his cool, their exchange that morning still fresh on his mind.

"Are you enjoying the game?" Harold said.

"Uh, yes…I am."

"Hope we can hang on. That Wiley running back is tough. You know he's only a sophomore? Probably has college recruiters camped out on his lawn already." He chuckled.

Nate nodded. Maybe Harold's not as bad as he thought. Maybe this was his way of apologizing.

"Hey Mike," Harold said to a man walking by with a tray full of drinks.

The man stopped and bobbed his head. "How's it going, Harvey? Haven't seen you in a while."

Nate shook his head and sighed. Harvey…of course. What an idiot. He turned back around. It was almost his turn in line.

On the way back to his seat, Nate saw Wink still in the same spot, his back turned. He walked by briskly, spilling some of his drink. Just when he thought he had it made, Wink yelled, "Dr. Holub!"

Nate stopped and turned slowly.

Wink stumbled up and put his arm around his shoulder, the man he had been talking to at his heels. "Dr. Holub…I want to introduce you to someone."

Nate smelled alcohol on his breath.

Wink motioned to the man with his free hand. "This here is Mr. Anthony Cervenka. The two of us go way back. We were classmates, ain't it Tony? I was just telling Tony what a fine vet you are. I told him how lucky we are to have you bring such high-powered medicine to us poor ignorant country folks."

Nate glared at Wink, his heart racing. He turned to Tony and shook his hand. "Excuse me. I've got to get back to my seat."

"Aw, don't rush off. I was hoping you could tell Tony here how you helped me out the other night. It's a helluva story."

Nate clenched his fist. He took a deep breath, turned, and walked away.

Wink followed him a few steps and patted him on the back. "Don't be a stranger, cousin."

Wink's laughter followed Nate back to the stands as the Wiley band finished its halftime show. When he reached his seat, he looked down at his hands—they were trembling. He suddenly felt very tired. Irene had still not shown up. He should have stayed at home.

As the game continued, the prospects for a Hadlow win grew dim. The frustration in the stands was palpable as Wiley slowly and methodically wore down the home team. The Armadillos could muster only one touchdown in the last two quarters. The final score was 41-28.

While leaving the stadium, Nate looked out on the field and saw the Hadlow team kneeling in a circle around their coach, some with their heads down, their faces streaked with tears. This game meant everything to those kids, and for the seniors, there was finality to the outcome and no chance of redemption.

Nate talked to Everett and Audrey for a few minutes outside the stadium, and then he walked back to his car. The night had turned a bit cool, so he zipped up his jacket as he made his way through the parking lot and crossed the street.

When he reached the lonely side street where he had parked, he saw a man's shadowy figure leaning against his car. He and the stranger were the only two people on the street. The man coughed loudly, a guttural cough emanating from deep in his lungs, and as Nate approached the car cautiously, Wink's face emerged from the darkness.

Nate's anger from earlier in the evening returned. "Wink, I don't know what the hell you're up to, but I'm—"

"Don't get all riled up, cousin. I ain't hurting your car."

Now close enough to see Wink's face clearly, Nate saw he was very drunk. He leaned against the driver's side door with a beer in his hand. His left eye flickered as he pushed himself away from the car and stumbled forward a few steps.

Nate said, "Listen, Wink. I'm sorry about how things turned out with your cow, but sometimes a C-section is necessary. If you'd just let me—"

Wink waved him to a stop. "Shit happens with cattle. Believe me, I've fucking seen it all."

He took a swallow of beer, swayed from side to side, and then cocked his head, bleary-eyed. "You know I used to help the old man pull calves. Helped him all the time. Whenever he needed me, there I was. Not that I had a choice in the matter." He snickered. "Yeah, I've seen things I'd rather forget, things that would curl your fucking toes. Pulling calves with tractors, shit like that. *God almighty.*"

Wink shook his head slowly, looking down at his boots. "I remember one time at the farm. We were chasing this wild old bitch out in the pasture. Couldn't get her in the pen, but the old man got a rope on her somehow. It was in the winter. Cold as shit. I must've been twelve or thirteen, something like that. Goddamn it was cold."

Wink took another swallow of beer. He looked down the street. Nate followed his gaze and saw a cat lurking in the dismal glow of a streetlight.

"The old man gets a rope on her, and he gets it wrapped around a tree. And he tells me 'You hold this rope. If she starts to choke, you give her some slack.' So I took the rope. I wasn't gonna argue with him. Then when he walks up behind the cow and grabs the calf's feet, that crazy-ass bitch runs around and around the tree. She damn near runs me over a couple of times. I'm trying to hold this rope, and it's burning the shit out of my hands, and he's yelling at me not to let go."

Wink paused, staring down the street again, and stumbled sideways.

"Then she starts to choke. And he yells at me— 'Give her slack! Give her slack, goddamn it!' But the rope is wrapped up and I can't get it loose. So you know what he does? He runs up, grabs the rope, and gives me a backhand across the face so hard it knocks me on the ground."

Wink drained the rest of his beer, crushed the can, and threw it hard against the curb. The thin metallic clink of can on concrete hung in the air as he leaned in close, his beery breath in Nate's face.

"That's how I got this." He flashed a mirthless smile and pointed at a broken tooth on the lower right side of his mouth.

Nate looked into Wink's eyes and swallowed hard.

Wink lurched a step backward. He turned his head and coughed loudly. "Well cousin, it's been fun reminiscing about the good old days, but I better get on home. Otherwise the wife might think I'm not being respectable."

He stumbled off down the street in the direction Nate had come, stopping once and turning around. "You know what? That fucking cow was all right. Thank God for that."

Nate watched him until he almost reached the intersection.

"You okay to drive, Wink!?"

Wink's laugh echoed in the cool night air. "Don't worry about me, cousin!" He laughed again, but coughing cut it short.

As his dark form moved away, Nate heard him whistling. The tune sounded familiar, but he couldn't place it.

Nate got in his car and sat there in a daze, not sure what he was feeling, or if he was capable of feeling anything at all. All he knew was that he was exhausted. He fumbled with his keys before finding the right one, then started the engine. As he drove by the stadium, the song Wink had been whistling came to him. It was the Wiley High fight song.

It would stay with him for days.

Fifteen

Autumn comes quietly in South Central Texas. After surviving the long brutal summer, trees are too weary for flashy displays of color. The leaves of post oaks and pecans turn various shades of brown before swirling away in the north wind, while live oaks flatly refuse to recognize such a season, discretely dropping their leaves when the new growth arrives in the spring. There *are* a few patches of color—the golden yellow of cedar elms and hackberries and the occasional brilliance of a sumac—but modesty is the general rule.

The post oak leaves were starting to change as Nate drove out to the farm on Sunday morning. He was on call that weekend and driving his work truck. As he crossed high above the jade waters of the Soledad and headed up the bluff road, his thoughts were on his father, and his mother, and Jerome, and Clarissa, and the whole damnable set of circumstances that had ripped the fabric of his family apart.

Every time he drove along the bluff, the magnitude of what happened there weighed on him, urging him to stop and look around. As he slowly made the sharp turns, he wondered which curve had been the site of the accident. What caused it? Where were they going that night? Were there any witnesses?

There was so much he didn't know, yet he was afraid to dig too deeply.

The sky was partly cloudy with large patches of blue. October rains had diminished the drought and brought life back to the countryside. New grass had emerged, and stock tanks were almost full again.

Nate slowed as he approached Alois's house. On a sudden whim, he pulled into the lane and stopped just beyond the cattle guard. The house was to his left, only partially visible, enveloped in the gloomy shade of tall pecans and cedar elms. He edged forward slowly, scanning the porch until the white screen door came into view.

The house was simple and unadorned, bare except for a few surviving patches of olive paint under the eaves. Hackberries stood very close, appearing to hold the structure up. Vines wrapped around the corner porch pillar and climbed onto the roof. The house looked less like a neglected man-made structure than a part of the land itself, sprouting from the soil like some wild thing.

Something about the place made him uneasy. He felt a yearning… so intense…so visceral as to be almost painful.

Disconcerted, he backed out of the lane and drove on, crossing the bridge and turning at Viola's mailbox. The yaupons along her lane were thick with small crimson berries. Three deer darted in front of him, their white tails vanishing like ghosts into a dense growth of cedars.

Nate found Viola sitting on the front porch in her rocking chair, her eyes closed. A cat lay curled up in her lap, and she held a folded newspaper against her chest. The cat jumped down and disappeared under the house when Nate got out of the truck.

Viola's eyes opened and flickered as they focused on him. She looked even thinner and frailer than she had on his last visit. She was withering away, life seeping from her like water from a dying spring.

Nate sat down at her feet on the edge of the porch. "Hey, Grandma. Sorry to wake you."

"Just resting my eyes."

"Did Ruthie take you to church last night?"

"No, I wasn't feeling too good. Upset stomach. I'm better now." She squinted as she looked down the hillside toward the creek. "Ruthie's got better things to do than pack her old mama around. They got cattle problems."

"Yeah, I know. I've been trying to help them. It's unusual. Every test we do comes back normal."

"Sounds like my doctors. I give 'em hell, but they're doing what they can. Some things ain't so simple, I guess."

They sat quietly, listening to the lively chatter of a chickadee. Nate looked down toward the creek bottom, surveying its broad leafy expanse, wondering what secrets lay hidden there.

"Grandma, when's the last time you talked to Uncle Alois?"

Viola looked down at her lap and brushed off a cat hair. "I couldn't say."

"A long time?"

She nodded.

"It seems odd he keeps to himself so much. Don't you think?"

"He's always been that way."

"Ruthie told me she thought he changed after the war."

Viola shrugged. "Cap used to say he was always a little different. He wasn't around much before the war."

"Where was he? Didn't he live around here?"

She looked down at her hands, tracing the deep creases of her right palm with her left thumb. "No, he ran off, about the time we got married."

"Ran off? Why'd he do that?"

Viola shook her head. "Like I said, he was always different. Had his own ideas."

Nate sensed irritation in her voice. "Where did he run off to?"

Viola glanced at him, her lips tightening. "Those were hard times. He joined the CCC. Worked out west…all the way out to Arizona. Never came home until after the war."

"Where was he during the war? Europe?"

Viola shook her head.

"The Pacific?"

She nodded. Then she started rocking, and Nate took it as a signal to move on to another topic.

They sat in silence, the floorboards creaking beneath the rocker.

"I brought a fishing rod," he said finally. "I thought I'd try my luck at the creek, if that's okay."

Viola's rocking slowed. "You can fish whenever you want. Nobody's been fishing down there for years."

"Daddy used to take me fishing."

She reached up and adjusted her glasses. "He always did like to fish. Hunt too."

Nate turned and looked up at her. "Daddy would also take me squirrel hunting along the creek. And I went deer hunting with him a few times."

Viola continued rocking. A mockingbird hopped about the yard, raising its wings to scare up insects.

"What about Grandpa? Was he much of a hunter?"

"No, he never was. Cap was funny that way. Never liked to kill nothing, not even the hogs at butchering time."

Nate leaned back against a porch pillar. "Daddy and I never deer hunted here at the farm. It was a place in the river bottom. There was a camp house. I remember one time Daddy, Jerome, Wink, and I all spent the night there and got up early the next morning to hunt. I shot a deer that day, the only one I ever shot. I guess I lost interest in it after that."

Viola stopped rocking and shifted in her chair, uncrossing one leg and then crossing the other. "That was the Wilbert Orsak home place over by Turner's Bend. The boys used to make hay for Wilbert, and he'd let 'em hunt. He was the County Commissioner for years. Had a son the same age as Sammy...they were good friends."

A limb of the big live oak groaned as it swayed in the wind. Viola rested her cheek on her palm. The newspaper fell off her lap, but she didn't seem to notice. Nate picked it up and tried to hand it to her, but she was staring off toward the creek, her eyes glistening. He placed the paper on the chair at her side. She finally reached over slowly and grasped it with a shaky hand.

"I better go in. Been out here long enough."

Nate helped her up. He followed her into the house, and they sat down at the kitchen table. He tried to get the conversation going again but soon realized it was hopeless. He asked if he could do anything for her before he left, and she said he could fill the wood box near her kitchen stove from the pile by the back door.

After doing that, he made several trips to the woodshed to replenish the pile. Then he walked over to the garden and did some weeding around the tomato plants. A few small tomatoes were just starting to form among the tender green leaves.

When he finished in the garden, Nate returned to his truck and retrieved the fishing rod and tackle box he purchased at Ehrlich's Hardware earlier in the week. He walked down the hillside and opened the gate leading into the bottom hayfield. Crossing the field, he imagined it planted waist-high in cotton, the bolls open and fluffy white, his father and his siblings and Viola and Cap, all trudging along, backs bent, pulling cotton sacks behind them, casting long shadows in the afternoon sun.

At the end of the field, he stopped in the shade of a massive pecan that predated any Holub footstep on the place. Nate remembered a story his father used to tell—he and Jerome being left in a makeshift playpen under the pecan while Viola worked in the field. She operated a mule-drawn riding cultivator back in those days, and his father's first memory was sadly watching her recede from view as she worked the cultivator, then happily seeing her return up the next row, the heartbreak and joy played out over and over again.

Nate recognized the pecan, but the creek bottom looked different, much thicker with brush than he remembered. He crawled through a barbed wire fence and then picked his way through a dense thicket of yaupons and briers, heading in the general direction of the water. Twice he ran into an impenetrable wall of vegetation and had to backtrack and try a different route. By the time he reached the creek, he was sweating and had scratches on his arms and a tear on his shirtsleeve.

Pettus Creek was slow-moving and murky, flowing between high earthen banks, the sky overhead hidden by the interlocking branches of sycamores, pecans, and cottonwoods. Piles of logs and drift slowed the water's flow to a crawl in some places.

Nate made his way carefully along the muddy bank, wishing he had worn rubber boots. Turtles basked on partially submerged logs where sunlight poked through the foliage, and they slipped quietly into the water as he approached. He was ever watchful for snakes, a precaution drilled into him by his father at an early age.

Looking for something familiar, he finally came to a spot he recognized—a wide bend where the creek hugged the high bank on the opposite side, forming a deep pool of sluggish water. The near bank was broad and sandy with clumps of tall grass and piles of drift. The water was mostly in shadow, but sunlight flooded the bank. A large sycamore rose from the opposite bank, its trunk encased in thick intertwining grapevines.

Nate sat on the trunk of a fallen cottonwood near the water's edge, the mud at his feet thick with animal tracks. A dragonfly landed on a limb of the cottonwood, then zipped away erratically toward the opposite shore, getting lost in the shadows. A cloud of tiny feathery insects whirled silently and landed on the water in unison, floated downstream for a short distance, then rose to do the same ballet again and again. In quiet pools, water striders skated rhythmically across the water's surface, leaving gentle ripples in their wake. The water made no sound as it slid slowly by, and if Nate closed his eyes, the only clue to his whereabouts was the scent of damp leafy decay that permeates such places.

There was no trace of a human presence on that creek bank, and the perplexities of the world seemed distant. Here was life at its most basic, seething and raw, played out on a grand stage. As Nate became immersed in his surroundings, a memory came bubbling to the surface, a memory from the simpler days of his childhood, when life was full of wonder and promise, when he was not yet burdened by his responsibilities or imprisoned by his fears.

He and his father once shared a fall afternoon at that bend in the creek. They sat on a tree trunk with a tackle box and a cooler on the ground nearby. His father sipped a beer and held a glass jar containing grasshoppers they had caught earlier in the afternoon. He wore an untucked, long-sleeved gray shirt over a white t-shirt, and his face had a growth of dark whiskers. The afternoon sun backlit the sycamore on the opposite bank, and the wind softly stirred its amber leaves, occasionally sending one on a long, slow, meandering descent. Splinters of sunlight passed through the leaves and danced at their feet. Nate held the fishing rod anxiously as the red and white bobber sat on the surface of the dark water, the line taut against the creek's gentle flow.

"You be ready now," his father whispered. "Them old cats don't play around."

Nate gripped the rod a little tighter.

His father leaned forward. "I've caught fish bigger than you in this creek. I came along so you don't get pulled in."

As he predicted, it didn't take long for the fish to find the bait. The bobber jerked once and disappeared suddenly beneath the water's surface, leaving barely a ripple. Nate gulped and yanked the rod upward. He stood up, knocking over the tackle box, and started reeling excitedly.

"You got him! Hold on!" his father said.

Nate fought the fish with everything he had, thinking he had a record-breaker. He imagined a picture of himself posing with his monster catch in the *Hadlow Herald,* but when the fish surfaced, it was a small yellow cat, only about a foot in length. His father reached down, grabbed the line, and pulled the flopping fish from the water. He stuck his thumb in its mouth and held it up proudly at arm's length.

"This is a fine fish, son, a fine fish." Seeing Nate's dissatisfaction, he added, "You know I was just joking earlier. The fish in here don't get much bigger than this." He gave Nate a wink and a smile, instantly changing his disappointment into triumph.

They caught one more catfish from the pool, a smaller fish they released, and then the fish stopped biting. His father wanted to cook their catch right there, so he told Nate to collect some wood while he walked back to the truck to get a few supplies.

"If you go to pick up a piece of wood and it moves, don't pick it up," he said.

When they had a fire going, he pulled out his pocketknife and showed Nate how to clean the fish. He tossed the guts into the grass. "Some old coon's gonna have a feast tonight."

While Nate washed the fish off in the creek, his father cut some green yaupon branches and whittled them down to make skewers. He sliced the fish into small pieces, placed them on the skewers, and sprinkled them with salt and pepper. When the fire had burned down, he stuck some forked yaupon limbs in the ground beside the fire and laid the fish skewers on them, just above the coals.

The afternoon had turned cool. They sat on the ground, enjoying the warmth of the fire. His father opened another can of beer and handed Nate a can of soda. He told Nate that when he was a boy, Viola sent the kids to the creek bottom to pick dewberries, wild plums, and mustang grapes. Cap always came along when they picked grapes because they grew high in the trees and could only be reached with ladders. He said he never ate store-bought jelly until he moved to Houston. They picked up pecans every fall, and in the winter, he and Jerome went coon hunting on cold moonlit nights. They chased the hounds up and down the creek for miles, sometimes following the creek all the way to the river.

He told about the time a hound climbed up a leaning tree after a coon and got stranded there. They found her halfway up, looking down at them and whining pitifully. His father climbed up after her, but the dog was too big to carry back down safely, so Jerome went back to the house to get a rope. When he finally returned, his father fashioned a makeshift harness and slowly lowered the dog to the ground. By this time, the coon had made a break for it and was long gone.

His father turned the fish periodically, checking to see if it was done with his pocketknife. When it was ready, they slid the pieces off the skewers and ate hungrily in silence, avoiding the sharp slender bones. It had a wonderful smoky flavor. Everything was in shade by then except the top of the sycamore, its white bark luminous in the late afternoon sun. Sitting there with his father, Nate felt safe and content. He didn't want it to end. He wished they could camp there and wait for all of the night creatures to emerge.

The raucous cry of a blue jay brought Nate suddenly back to the present. The bird flew over him from the opposite bank, and when he looked up, something caught his eye in the thick brush around the sycamore's base. The lighting was poor, but he saw the face of a young girl. She had a tangle of long blond hair and peered down at him from between the branches.

Nate stood up. He felt dizzy and closed his eyes, waiting for his head to clear. When he opened them, the face was gone.

"Hello?" he said.

There was no answer, only a slight rustling of leaves in the wind. He walked down the bank, trying to get a better view, then stopped and listened. He went back up the creek, still looking, before returning to the cottonwood. He picked up his fishing rod and began making a few half-hearted casts, scanning the woods while he reeled.

Had he imagined it?

It was certainly possible. Anything was possible.

The fish weren't biting, and Nate was in no mood for fishing anyway. The sky was clouding up, and the bottom was suddenly darker, less hospitable. Retracing his path, he made his way back to the hayfield. He leaned back against the pecan tree for a few minutes, unsure if he should stay or go, feeling both stabbing nostalgia and creeping fear.

He finally walked back up the hill, his steps ponderous. The terraces in the field rolled down at him like crashing waves. He stopped on top of one and looked back toward the creek, listening to the lonely call of a meadowlark. Then he turned and continued as the house towered above him, a silent sentinel, watchful and impenetrable.

The past had never felt more out of reach.

Sixteen

The sky had turned overcast by the time Nate made it back to the house, and he wondered if rain was in the forecast. He checked the weather radar and saw a band of thunderstorms moving in slowly from the northwest.

After answering an email from Marianne, he sent Emma a message asking how she did on her algebra test. Marianne had been bugging him to start texting, but he still needed to update his phone plan.

Nate then walked out to the barn with Roscoe to check on one of Bruno's cows. While feeding the cattle early that morning, he noticed one cow standing away from the group with her head down, breathing heavily. He had walked her into the pen and examined her, discovering she had a fever, harsh lung sounds, and a swollen udder, firm and hot to the touch. When he called Bruno and told him one of his cows had mastitis and pneumonia, Bruno told him to do whatever was needed, so Nate milked the infected quarter—getting out thick globs of pus—and infused it with an antibiotic. Then he gave her an intramuscular antibiotic injection and left her in the pen. He was relieved to see the cow looking much better now, nibbling on the hay he had left her.

As he walked back to the house, Nate stopped and stared ruefully at the corner of the yard near the tool shed. It was already too late to plant a fall garden. Perhaps in the spring, if he was still around.

After eating lunch, Nate sat back in his recliner with Roscoe at his side, enjoying the breeze coming through the open window. Comfortable in his chair and savoring the country quiet, he dozed off, but a phone ring cut his nap short.

"Nate? This is Leroy. We got a dead cow. Can you come out and take a look?"

Nate sat up, rubbing his syes. "Sure, Leroy. She's been sick?"

"This one's been doing poorly for a few days. Yesterday I thought she was looking better, but Darrell just found her dead."

"I'm on my way."

The problem on the Kollatschny dairy had been eating at him for weeks. He scoured his textbooks and the Internet for anything that might explain it. After reviewing all of the testing Everett had done, he decided it had to be something toxic or nutritional, but the feed they were using was a commercial feed, and there were no reports of similar problems in herds elsewhere. Leroy and Ruthie grew their own hay, and Nate had it analyzed for nitrates, mycotoxins, and toxic plants. The well water had been checked for pesticides, herbicides, and mineral imbalances. Everything came back normal, and he was running out of ideas.

On the drive to the dairy, Nate's thoughts turned to Irene. Her failure to show up at the game had been more upsetting than his interactions with Wink. She didn't show up at work on Saturday morning either, having called Audrey to say Zach was sick with a stomach virus. Maybe that explained why she hadn't come to the game. Or did it? It was probably just an excuse to avoid him.

By the time he pulled up at the dairy, a bank of dark clouds loomed in the north. Nate saw a flash of lightning and heard a low rumble of thunder. He was getting his supplies out of the truck when Darrell approached from the direction of the milking parlor. He looked like a younger version of Leroy—short and muscular, almost chubby—and his walk was brisk and purposeful.

"Stan the Man," Darrell said.

Nate smiled at the memory of his childhood nickname. His mother was pregnant with him when his father watched the St. Louis Cardinals play the old Colt 45s in Houston. It was near the end of "Stan the Man" Musial's long career, and his father was so enthralled with Musial that he had insisted on naming his first child Nathan Stanley Holub. His mother didn't know why he was so adamant about the name until years later, and it became a family joke.

"How've you been, Darrell?"

"Doing good." He looked at the sky over Nate's shoulder. "Looks like you're bringing us some rain."

"I hope that's all I'm bringing. Those clouds look pretty bad."

"Yeah, looks like a blue norther. Let's try to get this done before we get wet. The cow's over here in the sick pen."

Nate collected his supplies and followed Darrell over to the pen. "Where's Leroy?" he said, trying to keep up.

"He's inside. Should be out in a minute."

As Darrell opened the gate leading into the pen, the wind suddenly picked up. It blew out of the north and had a bite to it. The cow lay on her side with her abdomen distended and froth coming out of her nose. Nate looked down at the cow nervously as he put on his gloves. He hadn't performed a necropsy on a cow since school, but if he just thought of it as a really large dog, he could probably muddle through it.

He noticed the neck and brisket area were swollen and doughy to the touch—pitting edema. Taking his knife, he made an incision through the skin inside the forelimb and then extended it through the muscle until he could push the limb up over the back. He did the same with the rear limb, and after connecting the two skin incisions, he cut the subcutaneous tissue and reflected the skin up and out of the way.

Then came the moment of truth—cutting through the body wall. He made a shallow incision behind the ribs, and then tentatively made his incision longer and deeper, going through the muscle layers. As he cut, his confidence grew. This was a mammal, after all, with the same basic anatomy as a dog or cat. He continued cutting, more boldly now, and suddenly an explosive gush of pungent rumen gas and fluid shot up into his face. He staggered backward and shook his head, blowing bits of rumen content out of his nose. He wiped his face on his shoulder and tried to smile it off.

He took a deep breath and continued, extending his incision and exposing the abdominal organs. Then he opened the thoracic cavity, cutting the ribs with a pair of tree loppers, and clear yellow fluid poured out. The heart looked enlarged, and when he opened the pericardial sac, fetid fluid with thick clumps of stringy yellow fibrin came out. As he started to remove the heart to examine it more closely, his glove snagged and tore on something hard. Not bothering to change gloves, he reached down, located the object, and cut it free. After looking at it, he started breathing easier. He turned to Darrell, just as Leroy came hobbling up.

"Did you find something?" Leroy said.

"Good news and bad. I can tell you why this cow died, but it doesn't explain your other problems. I found this in her heart."

He held up a three-inch wire, slightly bent on one end. It was a textbook case of traumatic reticulopericarditis, or hardware disease.

Leroy took the wire from Nate and inspected it.

"So how did this get into her heart?" Darrell said, after Leroy handed him the wire.

"It penetrates the stomach wall…the reticulum actually. Then it goes through the diaphragm here and right into the pericardial sac."

"You know, we've had this before, years ago, back when we used baling wire on our hay," Leroy said. "Daddy always put magnets in every cow, but we stopped doing that a long time ago. I guess we still got pieces of wire lying around." He scratched his chin, frowning. "I'll be damned."

"She's been off feed for a few days," Darrell said. "But we figured she was just like some of the others. She never looked real sick."

"Cows are tough," Nate said.

"You got that right." Darrell's words were almost drowned out by the boom of thunder, which was much closer now. A few raindrops started falling.

"We better get inside," Leroy said. "Nate, you come in and ride out the storm."

Nate took his blood-soaked instruments back to the truck. After rinsing and stowing them away and washing up himself, he started toward the house. The wind was chilly, and he picked up his pace as the rain began falling harder. As he neared the porch, he suddenly felt the hair on his arms stand up. Then a brilliant flash and deafening crack made him stumble and drop to his hands and knees. He crawled onto the porch, stood up shakily, and then leaned against the wall of the house. He moved along the wall to the door, fumbled with the knob until it opened, and entered as quickly as he could.

Ruthie rushed over to him. "Are you okay, Nathan?" She put her arm around his waist and walked him over to the kitchen table. "That was a close one."

His legs felt wobbly. He sat down and leaned on the table.

"You look white as a sheet," Darrell said.

Nate took several deep breaths. "I uh…I almost…I think I almost got struck by lightning."

"Jesus!" Ruthie said. "Y'all should've come in sooner, Leroy." She wiped his wet face off with a dish towel. "You sure you're okay?"

Nate nodded.

"Well shit, Nate," Leroy said.

"Nobody's fault but my own," Nate said.

"You know that Krupala boy got struck by lightning on the golf course last year," Ruthie said. "Didn't kill him, thank God, but it sure could have."

Darrell sat down next to Nate. He looked at Ruthie. "Remember that time Grandma lost those heifers? How many was it? Four?"

"Six!" Ruthie slapped the table, and Nate flinched. "They were under a tree in that little trap by the pens. Dropped 'em all dead where they stood. Must've been about ten years ago. You remember that, Leroy?"

"Yeah, I do. I hope we didn't lose any just now." Leroy walked over to the bay window and looked out toward the cattle pens. Rain was coming down so hard that visibility was poor, and it was loud on the house's metal roof.

"Mama's had some tough luck with her cattle," Ruthie said. "Some years it just don't pay to be in the cattle business. I wish she'd go ahead and sell 'em. She can't get out and check on 'em like she used to, and Wink can't tell her nothing."

"I was by the farm this morning," Nate said. "I'm getting worried about her. She was sitting out on the porch, and she could barely get up by herself. I'm afraid she might fall."

Ruthie nodded. "I asked her again last week about moving to town, but she said we'd have to carry her. She won't go on her own. I call her every day, but she ain't always by the phone. I'm getting her one of those necklaces, you know the kind where if she falls down and can't reach the phone she just has to push a button to call for help."

"Good idea." Nate looked down at his hands. The color was coming back to them. "I think I understand how she feels. I guess if you live in a place for so many years, you don't want to leave it."

He knew the farm meant more to her than just familiar surroundings. It must have been vital in a way he could scarcely imagine. She had invested her life in that land and in the children she bore within those walls, three of whom lived only in her memory. The farm validated her life in a way some generic apartment in town never could.

"One more thing I've been wondering, Ruthie. Could Grandma be depressed...I mean clinically?"

Ruthie frowned. "You know, Nathan, I've asked her doctors about that, more than once, but they say no."

"She's been tested?"

"Yeah, she has. I think whatever her problem is, there ain't no medicine for it."

Ruthie made a pot of coffee and put out some oatmeal cookies, and the four of them spent the next hour sitting around the kitchen table. The Cowboys game was on in the living room, and Leroy got up occasionally to check the score. They reminisced about the family get-togethers held on the farm when Nate and Darrell were kids. Those gatherings would include Holubs, Kollatschnys, and sometimes a few of Viola's relatives from the Skrivanek side of the family. The women would be in the kitchen, while the men congregated out by the barbecue pit, drinking beer and swapping stories. The meal usually consisted of barbecued chicken and sausage, along with boiled potatoes, green beans, rolls, fruit salad, deviled eggs, and sweet tea. For dessert, there was banana pudding, pecan pie, and kolaches—poppy seed, cheese, and pear. The kids ran wild outdoors, playing hide and seek, football, and baseball.

It was during one of those gatherings that Viola scolded Nate and Darrell for their indiscretion with the pears. Nate reminded Darrell about it, and they had a good laugh.

The rain slowed to a drizzle and finally stopped. Leroy and Darrell went outside to check on the cattle, while Nate watched them from the bay window.

"Ruthie, when Daddy and Clarissa had their accident, do you remember who investigated it? I mean, who was first on the scene? Was it the sheriff?"

Ruthie looked up at him from the table and scowled. "Why are you still worrying about that? There's nothing to be gained by it."

Nate turned to face her. "I just need to know. And then I'll put it to rest. The bluff is outside the city limits, right? So it probably wasn't the town police. It must have been the sheriff. Or maybe the DPS?"

Ruthie sighed. "Well, the sheriff back then would've been Arno Scruggs. I believe he's still living, but I wouldn't swear to it. He was sheriff for a long time. He's a good man, old Arno. His wife died young. He raised them three kids alone, and they all turned out pretty good."

Nate walked over and sat down beside her. "There's something else. I talked to Duke Woller a while back. I never knew Clarissa was from such a prominent family."

Ruthie nodded. "She was the black sheep of the Woller family, that's for sure."

"What did they think about her marrying Jerome?"

"They didn't like it at all. Jerome was quite a bit older than her and from a nobody family. I bet it burned old R.J. up. She didn't care. She did what she wanted."

"Duke really hated her, it seems."

"She was an embarrassment to the family, running around the way she did. You know Duke ran for office one time…state representative or something. They say she showed up to one of his campaign meetings drunk and raising hell, cussing him out for something. They had to carry her off." Ruthie chuckled. "He doesn't like our family to this day. If I pass him on the street, he won't so much as say hello."

"Why would he hold a grudge against *you*?"

"That's just the way some people are."

"What about Wink?"

"No different."

"When R.J. died, did Wink get anything?"

Ruthie shook her head sadly. "Not one red cent. It's a damn shame, ain't it? With all the money those people have?"

The back door opened, and Leroy came back in.

Ruthie said, "Hey Leroy, Arno Scruggs is still living, ain't he?"

"Arno? Yeah, he's in the nursing home. I talked to his boy Mark a while back at the feed store. Said he's not doing too good, but he's hanging in there. Got a bad liver, I believe. Why you asking?"

"Me and Nathan were just talking about old times, and his name came up."

"Well, I need to be getting back," Nate said. He stood and hugged Ruthie. "Thanks for the hospitality. Sorry to keep you from your football game, Leroy."

"Ah, he doesn't care about that game," Ruthie said. "He sleeps through it every Sunday."

"Ain't that the truth," Leroy said.

"Sorry for making you miss your nap then."

"Thanks for coming," Leroy said. "Hey, before you leave, there's something I need to talk to you about."

He put his arm around Nate's shoulder and walked him toward the door while Ruthie started cleaning off the table. He lowered his voice. "I just want you to know I've heard Wink is badmouthing you around town. Saying you killed his cow."

Nate turned, and they walked out the door, stopping on the front porch. "I experienced that firsthand on Friday night…at the game. His cow needed a C-section, and he wouldn't let me do it. So I tried to get the calf out, and the uterus tore. He still refused the C-section, and then he shot her."

Leroy shook his head. "You don't need to explain yourself to me. I've known Wink all his life. I know he can be a hothead."

Leroy followed Nate out to his truck. After Nate climbed into the cab and started the engine, he said, "Thanks again. Sorry for calling you out in a thunderstorm."

Nate smiled feebly. "No problem. That lightning about scared the piss out of me though. I think someone's trying to tell me something." He put the truck in gear. "You take care."

"You too, Nate."

Driving back down the lane, Nate considered how dangerous his life had become. First Tiny's cow, now this. He had never experienced such close calls before. What was next?

Before turning onto the county road, he stopped and looked to the northwest. A silvery line of cloud stretched over him like a blanket pulled away from the horizon, leaving sky of a perfect crystalline blue. Streaks of sunlight angled down from the western edge of the cloud bank, glistening the landscape. The distant hills glowed vividly, every feature of the land sharp and unmistakable, every tree, barn roof, and fence post scrubbed clean. The cold purifying rain had seemingly washed away the world's ills—all of the hatred, greed, and ignorance—leaving a shining, more hopeful place. Nate lingered there, wanting it to be true, if only for that brief precious moment, a vision to return to in the hazy days to come.

Seventeen

When Nate arrived at Rita's at six thirty on Tuesday morning, Everett was already in his customary corner booth. It had become a routine for them to meet for breakfast on Tuesdays, using these times together as a sort of staff meeting. Although they shared an office, Everett much preferred the relative peace and quiet of the cafe.

"Morning," Everett said, as Nate slid into the booth. He was already on his second cup of coffee and perusing the sports section of the *Chronicle*. "Get this, the average salary for pro baseball players is $2.82 million. The *average*. For standing around spitting and scratching their crotch. Can you believe that shit?" He shook his head and tossed the paper down in disgust. "I should've spent more time playing ball and less time studying back in my formative years."

Rita walked up with a cup of coffee for Nate and took their orders.

"What about you?" Everett said. "They still talk about the Holub brothers around here. You play any ball yourself?"

"No, I didn't inherit the baseball gene."

Everett took a sip of coffee. "I was a decent third baseman, but I couldn't hit a curveball to save my life."

Garner Prescott turned in his stool to address the handful of cafe regulars. "Did any of you watch that show last night about the southern sasquatch? Some believe the southern wilds of this country are inhabited by a large hairy beast of immense proportions, a cousin, as it were, to the more familiar creature of the Pacific Northwest. They claim to have recorded eyewitness accounts from North Carolina to Texas. They even have casts of footprints, but the evidence isn't convincing if you ask me. I've spent a lot of time perched in deer stands in the wee morning hours, and if such a creature exists in our fair county, I have not witnessed it."

Skeeter Pilat swiveled his stool toward Garner, scratching his chin. "You know what, Garner, I spotted something like that last summer. It was right here in town, over on Hilburn Street. I was about to call Texas Parks and Wildlife, but then I realized it was Tiny Sebesta, mowing the yard with his shirt off."

Rita chuckled as she refilled the coffee maker. "Isn't there an old story about some kind of a wild man down in the river bottom?"

"Ah yes, I think you are referring to the *Wild Woman of the Soledad,*" Garner said, "back in the antebellum period. She would sneak into cabins at night, stepping over the inhabitants' sleeping dogs, and take food, always leaving half of it behind. She'd also borrow tools, axes and so forth, and always return them polished and in perfect condition. This went on for years, and the story took on mythical qualities. When they finally tracked her down and treed her one day, 'her' turned out to be a 'him,' an escaped slave who'd been brought over from Africa relatively recently. His long hair had fooled them into thinking it was a woman, you see. The poor fellow was sold back into slavery and died a slave, if I remember correctly."

"I'm with you, Garner," Everett said, "if sasquatches were roaming around this county, some old boy would have one mounted in his living room by now."

"Unquestionably. The temptation would be far too great. But perhaps we should consult the local taxidermists, just to be sure."

Rita brought their food. Between bites, Nate told Everett about his necropsy at the dairy.

"Hardware, huh?" Everett said. "I haven't seen a case of that in years. I'm surprised we don't see more of it with all the junk on these old farms. I did have a case of lead toxicity last spring though, over at Curtis Matocha's. He had a cow that was circling and acting blind. I thought she might be rabid. When I did the post, I found little bits of metal in her reticulum. I finally put two and two together and asked Curtis if he had any old batteries around the place, and sure enough, we found a battery she'd been chewing on. I sent some kidney to the lab, and the lead level was sky high."

Everett took a bite of his scrambled eggs. "Any progress with Leroy's herd problem?"

Nate sighed as he put down his coffee cup. "No. It's pretty frustrating. Nothing adds up."

"Join the club. Those damned Holsteins made me pull out what little hair I have left."

They continued eating, Everett reading the paper and Nate staring out the window. Since Sunday morning, he hadn't stopped thinking about the girl in the creek bottom. Who was she? The more he thought about it, the less certain he was that she was real. Lack of sleep and a play of the light probably made him see something that wasn't really there.

When they had finished eating, he said, "Do you know of any families with children living around my grandmother's farm?"

Everett leaned his elbow on the table. "Children? No. Why do you ask?"

Nate shook his head, wishing he hadn't brought it up. "Ah, it's nothing. I was out at the farm on Sunday, down at the creek fishing, and I thought I saw a girl watching me from the woods."

"A girl?"

"A young girl, maybe eight or ten."

Everett narrowed one eye at him. "I don't know of any kids around there. But I don't know everybody."

"I probably just need to get my eyes checked."

Nate tried to smile it off, but Everett wasn't smiling. He was studying him in that cool, calculating way of his, probably trying to decide if he should start looking for a replacement. Nate wondered if Wink's "badmouthing," as Leroy put it, had made its way to him yet. In a town this small, it was just a matter of time. Nate hadn't told Everett about Wink's cow. He wished he had.

Garner walked over. "Since the veterinary brain trust is here, I thought I would ask for some free advice." He pulled up a chair and sat down heavily.

"Free advice? I'm not sure about that, Garner," Everett said, tapping his watch. "Billable hours, you know."

Garner coughed loudly into his coat sleeve. "Touché, my good man, touché. But as you know, I am always available to dispense legal advice to my friends, *pro bono.*"

Everett and Nate looked at each other knowingly. Over the years, they had both given out enough free advice to friends, and non-friends alike, to fully fund retirement accounts. They listened as Garner described the way his cat Milo drank water. He would lie down by the bowl, dip his paw in the water, and then lick his paw. Garner wondered if this meant Milo was sick.

Everett started to answer, but he paused and motioned to Nate.

"Well, I've seen cats do that before," Nate said. "If he's drinking more water than usual, you might bring him by so we can draw a blood sample and check his urine. He might have diabetes or a bladder infection. But if he's otherwise healthy, it's probably just normal for him."

Everett nodded. "Cats are a strange bunch."

"Strange indeed. I thank you." Garner stood halfway up, but then he sat back down. "Oh, I just remembered another odd thing he does. Doris and I will be sitting in the living room, and some nights Milo will start making this horrible yowling sound and then go tearing around the house, leaping onto the furniture, trying to climb the walls, and so forth. Sometimes he'll come close to us, get up on his tippy toes with his back arched, and with his hair standing up, and he'll do this little dance, hopping sideways toward us with this wild look in his eye."

Garner stood and demonstrated the dance for them, to the amusement of everyone in the cafe. "Yes, it's quite comical, but also a little frightening." He sat again. "What do you make of it?"

Everett grinned. "Garner, that's just Milo trying to tell you that, in essence, he's still a wild animal, and if only you were smaller, or he was bigger, you'd be dinner."

Garner blinked at Everett, then turned to Nate.

"Some cats do that little dance when they're playing," Nate said. "It's sort of a mock aggression type thing. Nothing to be concerned about."

"Very interesting, very interesting indeed. Well again, thank you. I'll tell Doris she can stop worrying. Perhaps you gentlemen need to open a side business in animal psychiatry."

"Sometimes I think this town is in dire need of more psychiatric help," Everett said as he stood to leave. "And not just for the animals."

Later that morning, Nate called Mark Scruggs to ask if he could visit his father Arno at Shining Oaks Nursing Home. It seemed the proper thing to do. He didn't want to just show up unannounced and start asking questions.

When he explained who he was and why he wanted to talk to his father, Mark seemed confused at first, but then accommodating. "You can come by around six this evening or any day this week if you'd like. I'm there at five thirty every day after work. I'll tell him you're coming. He won't mind…he loves company. But he has good days and bad. Hopefully you'll catch him on a good one."

Shining Oaks was on the southwest side of town, a sprawling brick building on a rise overlooking the river bottom. When Nate entered Room 116 in the east wing that evening, a man about his age with short-cropped hair was leaning over a hunched figure in a wheelchair. Nate knocked lightly, and the man turned and walked over with an outstretched hand.

"Nate? Mark Scruggs. He perked right up when I told him about you. I have to run. Please try not to stay too long. He tires out easy."

They walked over to Arno, who had dozed off.

"Daddy, here's Mr. Holub, the man I told you about?"

Arno's eyes opened and blinked a few times. Gray liver-spotted skin hung loosely from his long face. He was bald except for unruly tufts of silvery hair around his ears. A pair of glasses perched on a broad fleshy nose.

"Hello there. What was the name again?" His voice was deep and resonant, much heartier than his appearance suggested.

"Nate…Nate Holub. It's nice to meet you, Mr. Scruggs."

"Call me Arno. Holub, you said? You any kin to Viola?"

"I'm her grandson."

Mark put his arm around Arno's shoulder. "Daddy, I gotta go now. Kelsey has a volleyball game. I'll see you tomorrow. Take care now."

Arno waved to his son as Nate pulled up a chair.

"I knew Cap well," Arno said. "A good man. And Viola and I go back a lot of years. How's she getting on?"

"She's hanging in there. Still out on the farm."

"Good for her. She's a tough old bird. Some people find her… how should I say…a bit cantankerous. But I've always liked her."

He coughed, a breathless wheezing cough that left him unable to talk for a few seconds.

"People like her are a dying breed. Chiseled out of the old rock, I guess you could say. I read about Jerome passing. Damn shame. So you'd be Dennis's boy?"

"That's right."

Arno coughed again, worse this time, and Nate asked him if he wanted some water. He pointed at the sink, unable to talk, and Nate got up and filled a paper cup. Arno took a sip of the water with a quivering hand.

"Appreciate it. I didn't know your daddy very good. Only talked to him once or twice. Friendly fella. A helluva ballplayer."

"That's right," Nate said, relieved Arno had retained his memory. "Maybe Mark told you why I wanted to talk to you. My dad died in a car accident. It happened on the bluff in 1975. I've never known the details. I thought maybe you were involved in the investigation?"

Arno lifted his glasses and rubbed the inside of his eyes with thumb and forefinger. He brought his hands back down, blinked a few times, and swallowed. "You know, Nate, I was sheriff for twenty-six years, and in that time I saw some bad accidents. I still have nightmares…after all these years. Your father's accident wasn't the only one I saw along the bluff road. One time three kids were killed coming home from a dance late one night. That was the worst, no doubt. I had to call the parents."

He shook his head slowly, then fell into a long silence.

When his eyes started to droop, Nate put his hand on his arm. "Arno, do you remember any details…about my father's accident? Could you tell who was driving?"

Arno took another sip of water. "We couldn't tell. Your father was thrown well clear of the car. The car caught fire, and we had to get a fire truck up there. It was a real mess. The girl was burned too bad to recognize, poor thing. Ah hell, what was her name now…?"

"Clarissa."

"Ah yes…Clarissa." He drew out the name, seeming to relish the sound of it. "R.J.'s daughter. How could I forget? What a dish that one was." He lowered his head slightly and peered at Nate over his glasses. "If you don't mind me saying."

Nate held back a smile. "Not at all. They were going north? Toward town?"

"That's right. We finally got some concrete barriers put up along those curves. There was nothing but flimsy wooden guardrails back then, if you can believe it. Had to fight with the state for years before they finally decided to do it."

"Were there any eyewitnesses?"

"Not that I can remember."

"Where would I find the official report? At the courthouse?"

Arno nodded. "Should be at the courthouse or the courthouse annex, I would think."

Nate saw he was struggling to stay awake. "Well, Arno, thank you for answering my questions. You've helped a lot. I'll let you get some rest now."

When he stood to leave, Arno was staring at the wall and rubbing his cheek. "You know, something about that case always puzzled me. Oh hell, now what was it…?"

Nate sat back down and waited.

"Now I remember. Don't ever get old, son. Sometimes I can't remember the names of my grandkids, and then the next minute I'll remember the name of some old gal I took to the homecoming dance sixty years ago." He rested his chin on his palm and stared dolefully at the floor.

After a long pause, Nate said, "So, what was it…that puzzled you?"

Arno shook his head as he snapped out of his daydream. "Skid marks."

"Skid marks? What about them?"

Arno leaned forward. He opened one drooping jaundiced eye wide and fixed it squarely on Nate. "There weren't any, least as far as I could tell."

Eighteen

Winter has a cadence in South Central Texas—gray periods of damp and cold separated by flawless sunny days, crisp and invigorating. The pastures are a patchwork of yellow and gold sprinkled with emerald fields of ryegrass and oats. Woodlands are bare on top and green below, crimson berries adorning the yaupons until thinned out by hungry birds.

Nate immersed himself in his work over the winter months. He often treated cows with grass tetany, a condition resulting from low magnesium. Affected cows developed a staggering gait and went down, and the treatment consisted of a slow intravenous infusion of a mineral solution.

Grass tetany cows could be aggressive, so getting the head restrained was often challenging. Once Nate got a rope around the cow's neck, he placed a loop around her nose to make a halter. Then he wrapped the rope snugly around her hock to keep the head turned back, allowing easy access to the jugular vein. After threading a long needle down the vein, he stood by the cow's side and slowly dripped the fluid, watching her jugular pulse to assess the heart rate. Administering the solution too rapidly could be fatal, so patience was critical.

The treatment took twenty minutes or more, giving him a chance to have a leisurely chat with the rancher. When the bottle was finally empty, he ran a second bottle quickly into the abdominal cavity. After removing the rope, he and the rancher stood back and waited. The recovery was often dramatic, with the cow getting up and stumbling off within minutes. Quick cures are rare in medicine, and the rapid recovery was a joy to behold.

Throughout the winter, Nate liked to sit on his front porch on cold mornings with a cup of coffee. He watched the first light slowly animate the eastern sky and then creep over the landscape, creating a kaleidoscope of patterns, shades, and colors. The sun glistened the frost on the bare hackberry limbs as it leisurely dispelled the chill from the air. Those mornings could be poignantly quiet, with the only sounds the melancholic calls of a rooftop dove, the thump of Roscoe's tail on the porch floorboards, and the distant cawing of crows as they stirred from some hidden roost.

During those peaceful mornings, Nate was free to think, to contemplate this new world and the viability of his place in it. He often felt a gnawing sense of isolation, and sleep continued to elude him. He finally got a prescription for a sleeping medication, but it caused headaches and left him feeling groggy, so he quit using it. Then he tried various herbal and homeopathic remedies for insomnia, but none seemed to help.

On weekends off, Nate visited his daughters, and he spent more time on Houston freeways than he liked. The girls' schedules were so busy that he could often see only one at a time. Emma seemed to be adjusting to her new school, but Nate got the impression she was unhappier than she would admit, and her grades still worried him. Although he hated doing it, he called Caroline to talk about her. It was the first time they had spoken since the move.

"Nate, it's just Emma being Emma," Caroline said. "You know how she is. She'll snap out of it." She then started questioning him about his job. "The girls tell me you've got quite the life going out there–driving a truck, living on a ranch, riding horses, being some kind of a cowboy."

"They exaggerate…a lot."

"That's quite a change. I didn't know you had it in you."

There's a lot you don't know about me, he wanted to say. Hearing her voice again saddened him, and he realized that at least on some level, he still loved her.

"So…everything's working out?" she said, ending an awkward silence.

"Yeah, I like it here." He tried to sound convincing.

"Well, that's great, you deserve to be happy."

"I have to go now. Just let me know if Emma needs anything, or Marianne for that matter."

After hanging up, he realized he hadn't asked her how she was doing. He imagined she was happy, finally living the life she had always wanted—exciting husband, swanky home, stylish friends. She had often said how much she hated their cramped, outdated, three-bedroom house. "I am so tired of this place. Why can't we move?" And she couldn't understand his lack of interest in a social life. "Face it, Nate. You're a hermit. You'd be happiest living in a monastery somewhere in the Himalayas." She had to drag him to dinner parties and her hospital's annual Christmas party. Nate tried to endure them as best he could, listening to her insufferable coworkers talk about their new five thousand square foot home or their timeshare in the Caymans.

On those winter weekends in Houston, Nate sometimes stayed with his mother on Saturday nights before seeing the girls on Sunday. On one of those visits, in late January, they were sitting in the living room after eating out, Nate on the recliner, his mother on the couch with her laptop. The tension had built up over his last few visits and had finally reached the breaking point. He leaned forward with his elbows on his knees, staring at the floor.

"Is something wrong?" she said.

He rubbed the back of his neck and took a deep breath. "Mom, there's something I've been wanting to talk to you about."

She took off her glasses and closed her laptop. "What is it?"

Nate walked over and sat down beside her. He looked down at his hands, chewing on the inside of his lip. Then he studied her face, looking for a clue that she knew what was coming, but she betrayed nothing.

"I found out about Daddy's accident. I know what happened."

She blinked a few times, then sank back into the couch with a sigh, seeming to shrink into the upholstery. She closed her eyes, and the anguish crossed her face like a dark cloud. Her eyes welled with tears. "I wanted to tell you before you moved out there...I really did."

Nate leaned in closer. "Did you know about Clarissa? I mean... before the accident?"

She reached for a handful of tissues from a box on the end table. She wiped her eyes and then balled up the tissues tightly. "No. I suspected it though."

"Why?"

She sniffled. "I don't know. Your father changed. His drinking got worse. He was just...different somehow. Sadder maybe."

"Did anyone else know? Jerome? Grandma? Did anyone say anything afterward? At the funeral?"

She shook her head. "It was a surprise to everyone, from the little I could gather. But if Viola knew anything, she wouldn't have said. Not to me anyway."

Nate's memories of the funeral included the dark church, the casket draped in flowers, the gray windswept cemetery. He couldn't remember seeing his mother and Viola together that day.

"Why did you two never get along?"

She looked up at him with bleary eyes. "She never accepted me. I guess she thought I wasn't right for your father."

Nate remembered the story of how his parents met. She was working in the front office at the factory, a summer job during college. He brought up completed work orders every day and fell in love with her at first sight. They came from different worlds—he straight off the farm, she the daughter of a Montrose-area obstetrician. She was aloof at first, but he charmed her, slowly wearing down her defenses.

His mother closed her eyes tightly, then she opened them, staring down at her crumpled tissue. "Sometimes I think it wouldn't have mattered who your father had married, Viola would have treated her the same."

"Why?"

"I don't know. I don't think she was overly possessive or anything like that. There's just always been a deep sadness about her. She needed your father after Cap died, not just to help keep the farm going, but emotionally as well. Then when she lost Sammy, her dependence on him grew that much more."

"I know what you mean…about the sadness."

"It wasn't as bad when we first got married. I can even remember her laughing."

Nate tried to imagine Viola's laughter, the sound filling the Holub farmhouse and echoing down the hillside, chasing the shadows away.

His mother dabbed her eyes, then she looked at him. The pain was still visible after so many years. "You know it's strange, but I don't even think of Clarissa as the main problem between your father and me. There was a lot more to it than that."

Nate returned to DeLeon County that Sunday feeling a mixture of emotions. He was relieved that the barrier between him and his mother was finally breached, but questions about his father still haunted him. That week, he dug up the accident report at the courthouse. The file included drawings and photos taken at the scene, allowing him to locate the curve where the accident happened. There were photos of the smashed and burned car, but thankfully, none of Clarissa's charred body. The report made no conclusions about the lack of tire marks on the road.

One day during lunch, Nate parked at the top of the bluff and walked down to the site of the accident, the first sharp curve to the left as the road started its descent. It came after a straightaway, and it seemed reasonable that a heavily intoxicated or distracted driver might fail to use the brakes before it was too late. Woller was probably right—there was nothing more to be learned. Then again, his father and Clarissa had both driven that road countless times and knew the risk, so the lack of skid marks was puzzling.

Nate climbed over the concrete barrier and carefully peered over the side of the bluff. Looking down at the rocks below, he suddenly felt queasy and had to step back and brace himself against a tree. He closed his eyes and gripped a limb tightly with both hands, so tight the bark burned his palms.

What happened that night would never be known. The only witnesses had been the wind, rocks, and trees. He climbed over the barrier and trudged back up to his car.

Irene filled in between Christmas and New Year's while Jennie went on a skiing trip to Ruidoso. Everett was also gone that week, taking the family to visit Audrey's parents in Corpus Christi. Everett's absence made Nate uneasy, but having Russell around helped. Irene left Zach at home with her mom, but she worried about him constantly. Her mom's lupus was flaring up, making her too fatigued to watch him very closely.

During those relatively quiet unhurried days, Nate often found himself pulled from his office to the front desk like a bee to a flower. He tried not to say or do anything that might give away his feelings, but he imagined Irene could see right through him. She had become much easier to talk to, but she remained moody. There was the occasional smile—weak and obligatory—and that was an improvement, but he longed to make her truly smile, an unbridled smile of joy.

Late one afternoon, Irene helped him transport an anesthetized dog from the surgery table to the kennel following a spay. They wheeled her on a gurney. She was a large black Lab, and it took both of them to lift her and put her into one of the bottom cages. In the close confines of the cage, their shoulders and arms touched as they adjusted the dog's position. Nate had never noticed Irene wearing perfume before, but he smelled it then. When the dog was in place, and their shoulders were still touching, Nate froze and held his breath, waiting for her to move away from him, but hoping with every ounce of his being that she wouldn't. And for a brief agonizing moment, she didn't.

They stood and looked at each other. Nate felt the blood rushing to his head, pulsing in his ears. Irene looked down as he stumbled backward. Without a word, he turned and walked outside hurriedly, gulping huge breaths of cool winter air.

Nate visited Viola on Sunday mornings during his weekends on call. Wink never came by the farm then, and Sunday emergency calls were rare before noon, so it was the ideal time to visit. On the way there, he would pick up some kolaches or strudel from Kubena's Bakery, which was the only place in the county that made them correctly, according to Viola. During those visits, Viola ranged from reticent to completely aloof. Nate could occasionally get her talking about the past, but her mood would take a turn for the worse if he asked about one of her sons. He didn't dare bring up the accident.

When conversation stalled, Nate went down to the creek, always with the pretense of fishing. He headed straight to the bend where he and his father had fished. Sitting in the soft sand with his back to the cottonwood, he idled for long periods, even on the coldest mornings, absorbing himself in the wildness and becoming a part of the landscape. One morning, he was startled when a bobcat emerged cautiously from the woods, walked soundlessly to the creek, and lowered its head to drink. When it looked up, their eyes met, and Nate held his breath, close enough to see the water dripping off the animal's face. On another occasion, in early March, a ruby-throated hummingbird landed suddenly on a twig only inches above his head. The bird sat perfectly still for only a second, glittering in the bright sunlight like an iridescent jewel, then vanished into the ether as quickly as it had appeared.

Nate realized that life's most stirring, exquisite moments are often the most fleeting, be it an unexpected encounter with a wild creature or the paralyzing electricity of a woman's touch.

Although he felt compelled to start going to Mass again, Nate found the pull of the creek much stronger. There, amid so much life, so much wonder, he felt as close to finding meaning as anywhere else.

He sensed his father's presence in that quiet place they had shared, and by lingering there, he thought he might somehow come to a better understanding of him.

Nate watched for the woodland nymph he saw in the fall, but she failed to make a return appearance. He finally decided she had been a dream or a product of his overwrought state of mind. Then, one morning in early spring, as he walked up the creek on his way back to the house, something caught his eye in a partially dried-up creek channel. He stopped, kneeled, and traced its outline with his finger. There, in the soft dark mud, was a perfect human footprint, solitary and delicate, about the size that a young girl might make.

Nineteen

The days gradually began to warm and lengthen as the countryside woke from its winter slumber. Springtime meant calving season, the busiest time of the year at Hadlow Veterinary Hospital. The phone rang constantly, and Nate and Everett were on the road, crisscrossing the backroads of DeLeon County.

Calf deliveries made up the bulk of their farm calls, but many other problems came with the season—prolapses, retained placentas, mastitis, cows with nerve paralysis, calves that failed to nurse, and calves with diarrhea, pneumonia, and broken legs. Nate came home exhausted every day, only to be called out again in the evening.

Russell accompanied him on most calving calls. Everett told him, "Until you get your first C-section under your belt, you better take Russell along."

Nate's first solo C-section had been worrying him. The one he assisted Everett on back in September was done at the clinic with the cow standing in the squeeze chute. Doing one in the field was more challenging.

It didn't take long for the opportunity to arise. One morning in early March, Nate and Russell were returning from treating a grass tetany cow when Jennie called in on the truck radio.

"Tippy Wiedenfeld's got a first-calf heifer that needs help. He's trying to get her in the pen."

"Okay, we're on our way," Nate said.

"Tippy's got a bad habit of putting his bull out on his heifers too early," Russell said. "We had to cut out two for him last year. You'd think he would've learned his lesson by now."

The Wiedenfeld farm was ten miles northeast of town, close to the community of Hostka, which consisted entirely of a tiny Czech Brethren church and an old store that had been closed for decades. They drove over a cattle guard, then followed a long winding lane to a tidy gray house. After pulling up to the barn around back, they were relieved to see the heifer standing in the pen, but Russell groaned when he saw her small size and the disproportionately large hooves protruding from her vulva.

"Shit, here we go again," he said.

As they got out of the truck, a man approached from the direction of the house. He was slight of build and sinewy, with black horn-rimmed glasses, closely cropped white hair, and skin the color and texture of mesquite heartwood. He had a mild limp, but his movements were otherwise brisk and nimble. Nate judged him to be in his late sixties or early seventies.

"John Wiedenfeld," he said, his breath smelling of pipe smoke, "but they all call me Tippy."

Nate introduced himself, and by the time he made it over to the pen, Russell had the heifer roped and tied snugly to a post. They soon had her cast, and Nate did a quick exam to confirm what he already knew—the calf was wedged so tightly in the birth canal that trying to pull it was out of the question. After cursing his bad luck, Tippy agreed to a C-section.

Nate administered a sedative and gave an epidural, then they rolled the heifer on her right side. Russell tied both the front and rear limbs to posts so she was stretched out and unable to rise. Then Nate clipped the hair on her left flank, injected a local anesthetic in the shape of an L around the incision site, and scrubbed the area thoroughly with betadine. He opened a surgical pack and donned obstetrical sleeves and a pair of sterile surgical gloves.

It wasn't hot, but sweat beaded on Nate's forehead as he kneeled over the heifer. He took a deep breath, then made a vertical incision through the skin and began incising the muscle layers carefully, worried about cutting too deeply and opening the rumen, as he had during the necropsy at the dairy. Tippy stood behind him, watching closely.

"Were those beehives I saw as we were driving in?" Nate said, trying to relieve the tension.

"Yep. My granddad had bad rheumatism. The doctors couldn't do nothing for him. But one of his neighbors told him to get some bees. He started eating the honey, chewing on the comb, and letting 'em sting him once a month, and the rheumatism went away, just like that. He kept doing it and never had a sick day in his life. Lived to ninety-two. My daddy did the same and lived to ninety-six."

Russell said, "Hell, Tippy. At that rate, you'll make a hundred."

Tippy tilted his head, giving Russell a puzzled look. Then he broke into a raucous cackling laugh. "This boy's got a good head for numbers, ain't it?" He slapped Russell on the back. "A hundred indeed."

As Tippy continued cackling, Nate exposed the glistening white peritoneal lining. He made a nick in it with his scalpel and then extended the incision to open up the abdominal cavity, relieved the rumen was out of harm's way. He reached in and pulled the uterus up into the incision, as he had watched Everett do. When he incised the uterus, one of the calf's back limbs quickly came into view. He lengthened the incision, put down his scalpel, grabbed both of the calf's hocks, then pulled the calf up and out of the heifer's abdomen in one swift motion.

Nate held the calf up for a few seconds, its eyes blinking and nostrils flaring, letting the fluid drain from its mouth and nose. Then he dragged it over to a patch of grass in the corner of the pen. The calf seemed sluggish, and Nate realized it was sedated from the shot he had given the cow. He went to the truck and returned with an injection to reverse the sedative. Shortly after receiving the shot, the calf sat upright and shook its head.

"Looks like he's gonna make it," Nate said. "It's a nice-looking bull calf."

Tippy grinned. "A bully. I'll be damned."

Nate put on a new pair of gloves and began suturing the uterus, glad the hardest part was over.

"You know, I get a little sick at the stomach watching this kind of thing," Tippy said. "I saw too much during the war I guess."

Thinking he meant Korea, Nate started to mention his father was in the service at that time.

"I was in the Third Army under Patton," Tippy said. "All the way through France and into Germany."

Nate glanced at Tippy, glad he hadn't opened his mouth.

"Was Patton like they show him in the movies?" Russell said.

"Worse. That was one crazy bastard. We was almost as scared of him as the goddamned Nazis."

After finishing the uterus, Nate started suturing the body wall while Russell chatted with Tippy about the war.

Tippy said, "You know it's funny how things happen. One day around camp, I started talking to some prisoners that was being moved behind the lines. They was just kids, you know…homesick…wanting the war to be over so they could get back home to their sweethearts. So we're talking, and my company commander comes by. He stops and listens for a while, and then he pulls me over and says, 'Private, where'd you learn to speak Kraut?' I told him I learned back home on the farm, in Texas, that I learned German before I did English, and he says, 'Well shit, we could use another translator.' So from then on, I was a translator. Just like that. Kept me out of the fighting."

Tippy squinted down at the heifer, scratching his chin. "*Sprechen der Deutsch* might've saved my life. Half of my old squad was killed or wounded before it was all over."

Nate finished suturing the body wall, then began closing the skin in a continuous interlocking pattern. When finished, he took his surgical supplies back to the truck. He returned and gave antibiotic and oxytocin injections, then Russell removed the ropes, tapped the heifer on the side, and urged her to rise. She sat up, looked around, and eventually staggered to her feet. They got out of the pen and watched as she walked over to the calf and sniffed him, then began licking him off in earnest.

They walked back to the truck. Tippy pulled a pipe from his pocket, filled it with tobacco from a small pouch, and lit it with a match. While watching Nate and Russell wash up, he said, "You know I had back surgery a few months ago. I'm doing a lot better now, but I was slowed up there for a while. When I was in the hospital, this nurse came by one day to give me a bath, a good-looking young blond."

Tippy chuckled, then paused to take a long draw on his pipe.

"She helped me sit up and untied my gown and let it fall down to my waist. She sponged me all over, and I've gotta admit, I was enjoying it pretty much. Then she pointed down to my privates and said, 'You need me to wash down there, or can you do it yourself?' I acted all helpless, you know, and I told her I didn't have the strength for all that. So she helped me get out of the bed, and when she pulled my gown off, my little old pecker was standing there waving at her. She looked at me, all surprised, and I had this big smile on my face. I said, 'Well, it looks like something still works.'"

Tippy started cackling, and he laughed so hard he put his hands on his knees to keep his balance.

Nate and Russell looked at each other and grinned.

When Tippy finally caught his breath, he added, "I might be pushing ninety, but I ain't dead yet."

Twenty

In late March, Darrell's daughter Amanda was marrying Cody Pruitt, a boy she had met at UT-San Antonio. It was the perfect occasion for Emma and Marianne's first visit. Marianne had been bugging Nate for weeks. "When are we going to ride horses on your ranch, Dad?"

He worried his "ranch" would be a major letdown for them, so he tried to lower their expectations as much as possible in the weeks leading up to the wedding. What little spare time he had was spent readying his extra bedroom. He purchased twin beds, a large area rug to cover the scuffed and dingy hardwood floor, wall hangings to strategically place over the holes, and curtains with a bright floral pattern to hide the unsightly window frames.

Ruthie was thrilled when Nate told her the girls were coming, and even Viola seemed pleased, or maybe he just imagined the shadow of a smile crossing her face when he gave her the news. Both of them had seen the girls only once, when he brought them for a visit when they were four.

Amanda and Cody picked a good day for the wedding. The weather was nice that Saturday, a calm cool morning followed by a warm breezy afternoon. Nate picked the girls up at nine, and on the drive back to DeLeon County, the roadsides billowed with bluebonnets, Indian paintbrush, phlox, evening primrose, dandelions, squaw-weed, and prairie spiderwort. The post oaks, hackberries, and cedar elms sported their tender new leaves, while the more cautious pecans were still bare. The live oaks were a brighter shade of green as new growth replaced the old.

They stopped by the clinic when they reached Hadlow, and Nate gave the girls a quick tour. Several vehicles were parked at the house, but it was quiet out at the barn. The hydraulic squeeze chute fascinated Marianne.

"This is way cool, Dad," she said when he let her operate the levers.

He explained how the chute could be turned on its side to examine or trim a cow's feet.

"Trim their feet? You mean like a pedicure? Did you hear that, Em? Who knew cows needed pedicures?"

Emma rolled her eyes.

Nate went by the kennel to check on one of his patients, a young golden retriever named Pajamas. He had performed surgery on the dog the previous day, repairing a broken femur. He carried Pajamas outside, placed him in a grassy area, and examined the surgical site carefully.

"How'd you fix it, Dad?" Marianne said as Emma kneeled and started petting the dog.

"I used what's called an intramedullary pin," Nate said. "It's a metal rod that goes into the marrow cavity of the bone. I also put a couple of pieces of wire around the bone at the fracture site to hold it together."

Emma looked up at him. "And all of that stuff stays in there?" It was the first time she had spoken unprompted since leaving Houston.

"The wire does, but the pin comes out. You can feel the end of the pin right here, under the skin," he said, showing them. "When the bone is healed, I'll make a small incision, grab the end of the pin with some pliers, and pull it out."

"Whoa, Dad, you do some wild stuff," Marianne said.

"It doesn't get infected?" Emma said. "I mean…at the spot where you pull the pin out?"

Nate shook his head. "I'll put a suture to close the skin incision. Young dogs like this heal quickly." He smiled. They knew so little about his work. In Houston, he had rarely taken the time to show them.

After returning Pajamas to the kennel, they stopped by the reception desk. Two clients sat in the waiting room, and Everett talked to another in the exam room. Irene was on the phone, looking at her computer monitor.

"We received that check on March 7." She tapped her finger on the side of the keyboard. "Your balance is now $107.32." She looked up at Nate, shaking her head. "Okay, that sounds good… uh huh…right…yes ma'am."

Nate watched her intently. Her ponytail rested on her shoulder, henna on blue flannel. A few wayward strands of hair curled along the side of her neck, just below her ear lobe, pink and delicate.

"Okay…yes… thank you. We'll be looking for it…okay… goodbye." She sighed as she put the phone down.

"Hey, I know you're really busy," Nate said, "but I just want you to meet my daughters."

Irene stood as he made the introductions. The door flew open, and a woman entered with a rottweiler on a leash. The dog lunged forward, dragging the woman with it. The leash got tangled around Emma's legs, almost tripping her. Nate got her untangled and then turned to Irene. "We better get out of the way. I hope it settles down some." He gave her a smile and a wave as they walked out.

They ate lunch at Rita's. While getting back in the car afterward, Nate turned to see Duke Woller standing on the sidewalk in front of the cafe, looking at him with his familiar smug grin.

"Girls, I'll be just a minute." He walked over to Woller.

Woller nodded toward the car. "Your kids?"

"Yes. My twin daughters."

Woller nodded. "In town for the weekend. That's great. So how are you faring, Nate?"

"Okay, I guess."

"I hear that maybe you're starting to catch on?"

Nate looked down at the cracked sidewalk, then back up at Woller. "I believe so. Yes."

"Good, good. The cattle of DeLeon County rejoice. By the way, how's that *search for answers* coming?"

Nate hesitated. "I've been too busy at work lately to worry about anything else."

"Glad to hear it. Well, enjoy the wedding."

Woller patted him on the shoulder and walked to the door of Rita's. With his hand on the doorknob, he turned. "Nate, one more thing. Take my advice—don't be held prisoner by the past. It can be a cruel warden." He waved and entered the cafe, still smiling.

Nate got into the car and slammed the door a bit harder than he would have liked. As he started to back out, he realized he hadn't mentioned the wedding. Or that the girls were visiting from out of town. He stopped and stared at the restaurant's plate glass window, gritting his teeth.

He drove out to his house, trying to forget about Woller. When they were just outside the city limits, Marianne said, "That Irene seems nice, Dad."

He glanced at her out of the corner of his eye. "She is."

"Is she single?"

Nate gripped the steering wheel a bit tighter. "Single? Uh, yeah."

Marianne turned and grinned at Emma, then turned back around. "I think you're sweet on her."

"What makes you think that?" he said, his ears getting warm.

"The way you acted around her." She laughed as she turned to Emma again. "It was cute."

"I think you have a really good imagination." He looked in the rearview mirror and saw Emma peering out the window, smiling.

They soon arrived at the house, not a second too soon. "Here we are." The car rattled over the cattle guard as he pulled into the lane.

If the girls were disappointed by his "ranch," they were tactful enough not to say so. He first showed them the house.

"You leave your windows open while you're gone?" Marianne said. "Won't somebody break in?"

"I don't worry too much about that out here. I don't have much to steal anyway."

Marianne pointed at the propane heater in his living room. "What's this?"

He explained how the house didn't have central air and how he used fans in the summer and space heaters in the winter.

"These heat the whole house?"

"More or less."

They went outside and walked around the yard. He showed them the windmill and water tank. "This is where my water comes from."

"What do you mean?" Marianne said.

"Well, the windmill pumps it out of the ground, and it gets stored in this tank. Then it flows into the house through this." He pointed at the pipe.

"Pumps it out of the ground?"

"Where do you think water comes from, nitwit?" Emma said.

"Out of the faucet, I don't know. How it gets there is not my problem."

"Let's be nice," Nate said.

Emma frowned and shook her head.

They walked over to the barn and pens. Nate poured a few cubes in the feed trough, and a cow strolled over from the pasture.

They watched as she started eating, her long tongue reaching out to grab the cubes.

"Can I pet it?" Marianne said.

"I doubt she'll let you," Nate said. "She's not *that* tame."

Marianne reached out, and the cow backed up several steps. "I see what you mean." The cow then raised her tail, and a big pile of wet feces plopped noisily to the ground. "Well that's kind of rude."

Emma said, "She's showing you what she thinks of you. Cows are smarter than I thought."

Marianne glared at her.

As they walked over to his truck, Nate explained how it was calving season and how busy he was with deliveries. He got his calf puller out and showed them how it worked.

"So how do you use this if they won't stand still?" Emma said.

He explained how he used ropes to cast them or worked on them in a squeeze chute. He went on to explain some of the complications that could occur. When he started to describe how a fetotomy was performed, Marianne said, "Okay, Dad, too much information."

"I guess you're right."

They got in the truck, and he took them on a drive around the place. Roscoe rode on Emma's lap, his head out the window. They went by the stock tank below the house and into the back pasture, which was on a lofty hill with a broad view. Bruno was a hands-off rancher, and the pasture had seen little management in recent years. It was covered with native grasses and overgrown with doveweed. The only trees stood along the fence lines and around the ruins of an old house sitting on the highest part of the property.

"Don't you get lonely out here?" Marianne said.

Nate stopped the truck near the old house in the shade of a stunted post oak. "Well, I don't spend much time here. On most days, I don't get home until after dark." When he saw the concerned look on her face, he added, "And I have Roscoe to keep me company."

"So…are you happy?"

Nate gazed out over the rolling hills. The pastures were resplendent in the midday sun, verdant new life bursting from the earth at every seam. The wind was gusty on that lonely hilltop, and it rippled the deep green foliage of the cedars along the fence line. In the field beyond, thick stands of bright yellow coreopsis were sprinkled with pink evening primrose and purple winecups, all tossing gently in the wind. The air was sweet and fresh, echoing with the faint twitter of birdsong, still holding a hint of the morning's chill.

He finally looked at his daughters. "Yes," he said, almost too softly to hear. Then he repeated it, louder and with all the conviction he could muster. "Yes...I am."

The music had already started by the time Nate and the girls arrived at the church. A young woman was singing "Love of My Life" to a piano accompaniment.

St. Anthony's was imposing for a small-town church—a Neo-Gothic edifice of red brick with vaulted ceiling, towering stained glass windows, faux marble columns, and Stations of the Cross in ornate wood frames with painted gold inscriptions in Czech. White lilies and blue hydrangeas adorned the altar. The festive mood helped offset Nate's misgivings about the place.

The procession began with the bridesmaids, dressed in powder blue dresses, escorted by the groomsmen in black tuxedos. Cody stood at the altar, shuffling his feet and nervously adjusting his collar. As everyone rose for the bride's entrance, Nate caught a glimpse of Viola in the front row, being helped to her feet by Ruthie. She had on the same gray dress she wore to Jerome's funeral.

Nate tried to imagine what was going through Darrell's mind. Amanda was the oldest of his four kids, and it had to be agonizing for him. Nate turned and looked at Emma and Marianne. It seemed like he had gone to sleep one day and woke to find them changed from toddlers to teenagers overnight. Another such nap would put them well into their twenties, children no more, independent and no longer needing his guidance. His life was hurtling forward at breakneck speed, faster and faster now that he had reached the summit and the momentum was carrying him down the other side. He wasn't sure what awaited him at the bottom—a slow, painful, sputtering slide or a spectacular gruesome crash. Neither alternative was pleasant to think about.

The reception was at the Knights of Columbus Hall, a rectangular metal building on the west side of town. The tables had covers of white plastic decorated with strips of blue ribbon, jars of potpourri, and candles. A table along one wall had snacks—chips, crackers, cheese, fruit—while other tables held a large bowl of punch and the bride's and groom's cakes. At the bar, men filled pitchers of beer from kegs, while others took the pitchers and filled plastic cups, struggling to keep up with the demand.

Gifts were piled high on a table by the entrance. Childhood pictures of Amanda and Cody sat near the guestbook, and one picture caught Nate's eye. Amanda and her three siblings sat on the front porch of Ruthie's house, barefoot and carefree. Amanda must have been around nine or ten, and she held her baby sister on her lap. Another sister lovingly held a cat, while her brother had his arm draped around a white floppy-eared dog.

Not long after they entered the hall, Everett and Audrey walked up. "So these must be the famous Holub twins," Everett said.

"That's right," Nate said. "Just back from their world tour."

Everett chuckled, then introduced himself and Audrey to the girls. "Are y'all enjoying your visit so far?"

Marianne nodded. "Dad took us by the clinic, and then he showed us his ranch."

"Ah heck, I must have missed you."

"Yeah, we just dropped by for a few minutes," Nate said. "You were busy."

"Is this your first Hadlow wedding, Nate?"

"I remember going to one when I was a kid…vaguely." Nate looked around at the crowd. "This is a much bigger wedding than I expected. There are more people here than were at the church."

Everett laughed. "This is pretty typical. They basically pull out the phone book and invite everybody in town. Most prefer the reception to the wedding though. Can't say I blame them."

Audrey frowned at him. "It was a beautiful ceremony."

"If you say so," Everett said. "I thought it was twice as long as necessary. Nate, did you know that one of the major motivations behind the Reformation was shorter weddings?"

Audrey punched him in the shoulder.

"It's true." He winced and rubbed his arm.

"Let's go look at the cakes, dear. It's wonderful to meet you two." Audrey smiled at the girls.

Everett glanced back over his shoulder as she led him away, giving them his best henpecked husband look.

"Now you know what I have to put up with," Nate said.

"They're pretty funny," Marianne said. "Wow, I can't believe all of these people. Where are Aunt Ruthie and Grandma Holub?"

"Probably still taking pictures at the church. They'll be along in a minute."

They walked over to the refreshment table, and while waiting in line, Nate spotted Wink standing by the bar, talking to Harold Lubojasky.

Marianne sensed the sudden change in his mood. "What's the matter, Dad?"

Nate turned and smiled at her. "Nothing." He was determined not to let Wink, Harold, or anyone else ruin the day.

When they had their drinks, Nate suddenly felt emboldened. Maybe it was his newfound confidence at work, or the fact he had his daughters by his side, or a combination of both, but whatever the reason, he decided a frontal attack was the best strategy.

"Come on, girls. I want you to meet somebody."

He led them across the hall and greeted Wink and Harold heartily. As he introduced Emma and Marianne, he noticed that Wink looked different. His face appeared haggard, his eyes subdued. The air of impudence Nate had come to expect was missing, and when they shook hands, Wink's grip lacked its usual strength.

"It's good to finally meet you," Wink said to the girls, smiling.

Harold gave only a slight nod.

"Where do you two go to school?" Wink said.

"St. Gabriel's," Marianne said. "It's a Catholic school in Houston."

Wink nodded and smiled again. Something about Wink's face caught Nate's attention. He couldn't decide if it was a flash of dimples he had never noticed before or a play of the light on his shadowy face. He couldn't put his finger on it.

Wink turned to Nate. "Hey cousin, I need you to come out and look at my bull. He's got a big lump under his ear, maybe an abscess or something. You want to come out, or should I bring him in?" He turned his head and coughed loudly.

Nate hesitated. "Uh, sure Wink…any time. It'd be best to bring him to the clinic so we can work on him in the hydraulic chute."

"Okay. I'll see if I can get him loaded next week."

Nate looked at Wink warily. What was he up to? Was he just playing nice for Emma and Marianne's sake?

Harold patted Wink on the back. "Hey man, I'll catch you later." He turned and walked off without a word to Nate or the girls.

When Harold had disappeared into the crowd, Wink leaned toward Nate's left, away from the girls, and whispered, "Just between you and me, I can't stand that son of a bitch."

Just then, the wedding party arrived with much fanfare. Nate and the girls walked in the direction of the hall entrance. Nate spotted Ruthie leading Viola toward the main table, a large U-shaped arrangement in the center of the hall. He waited for them to get seated, then led the girls over.

"Well, looky here. Who are these pretty young ladies?" Ruthie said. She stood and grabbed one of them with each arm and hugged them both. "Boy, you've grown." She turned to Viola. "Mama, Marianne and Emma are here. I don't even know which one's which. Let's see, you must be Emma."

Emma nodded, smiling.

Viola reached out, and the girls leaned down and hugged her. She had a white lily pinned to her lapel.

"Y'all sit down," Ruthie said. "I gotta go check on the food. Lord, this wedding's gonna kill me."

Nate pulled up chairs in a semi-circle around Viola. "Grandma, it's been a long time since you've seen these two. Do you remember them visiting way back when?"

Viola nodded. "It was in June. We ate with Ruthie in town, over at that Mexican place that's closed down now."

"That's right. You don't forget a thing, do you?"

"It's a curse."

Nate stood up. "Can I get you something to drink?"

"Beer would be good."

He smiled at the girls. "Okay, I'll be right back. You three can get caught up."

While making his way to the bar, Nate ran into Garner Prescott, who asked him about his latest feline problem—Milo had started eating Doris's houseplants. Nate advised him to make sure none of the plants were toxic, telling him there were websites listing the toxic ones. He also mentioned a spray with a bitter taste that might discourage him from chewing on the plants. Garner thanked him.

"We're still working on the plans for that new psychiatric ward," Nate added.

"Excellent news. Perhaps I'll donate to the cause in exchange for naming rights. We'll call it the Milo Prescott Center for Animal Mental Health."

When Nate returned with Viola's beer, Marianne was telling her about a trip to Bolivia she would be taking with a school group that summer.

"…and it's supposed to be air-conditioned, but the group that went last year said the AC was broken. They said it was like *so hot*. Can you imagine? And they said to pack plenty of insect repellent. There's no malaria where we're going, but they have these little biting flies that are supposed to be horrible. And we can only take what we can carry in a backpack. Nothing electric. No hair dryer. No phone even. Can you believe it?"

Viola sat passively, watching Marianne over her glasses with mild curiosity. Meanwhile, Emma sat with her elbows on her knees, staring down at the floor.

The meal consisted of barbecue brisket and sausage, boiled potatoes, sauerkraut, green beans, peaches, and iced tea, all prepared by friends of the family. After the meal was finished, the dance floor was cleared, and the Tommy Netardus Band set up on the stage at one end of the hall. Bearded stocky Tommy played the accordion, while other band members played guitar, trumpet, saxophone, and drums. Tommy announced that the grand march would soon begin, and couples started filing outdoors to line up. Nate and the girls sat with Viola at a table near the wall.

"Dad, what's the grand march?" Marianne said.

"I'm not exactly sure." He looked at Viola for help, but she hadn't heard the question. "I guess we'll find out."

Ruthie came shuffling up. "Come on, Nathan. You gotta be in the grand march." She took him by the arm and pulled him to his feet. "You need a partner though. Maybe one of the girls?" She looked hopefully at Emma and Marianne.

"I'll do it," Marianne said.

Nate looked at Emma, but she was looking down at her phone. "Okay, we'll be right back."

Ruthie had them line up just inside the hall doors, near the front of a long row of couples. "Just do what everybody else does," she said.

Nate and Marianne traded dubious looks.

The band kicked off a rollicking polka. Some in the crowd began whooping with the beat as the line of couples started strolling down the middle of the dance floor, led by an elderly couple, who were the designated leaders, followed by the bride and groom, the wedding party, the parents, other family members, and then everyone else. When the line reached the end of the floor, the couples veered off, left and right, alternating, and came back around the sides to where they had started. The opposite couples came together to form rows of four, arms linked, and then they did the same thing to form rows of eight.

The groom's parents, from Fort Worth, looked as bewildered as Nate and Marianne. Nate imagined it would be a lot more fun if he had consumed four or five beers, like some of the more exuberant participants. The band smoothly transitioned to a different song, then Tommy started singing in Czech— *"A já sám, vždycky sám, své koníčky osedlám…"* —and people started singing along. Nate craned his neck to look for Emma and was surprised to see her and Viola deep in conversation.

The rows of eight came together to form rows of sixteen. When these rows were lined up across the floor and stationary, the lead couple led the front row on a snaking course between the other rows, the end person on each row grabbing the hand of the last person, eventually forming one long train, which then wrapped around the outside of the dance floor, making a large circle. Then the lead couple faced each other and held hands above their heads to make a tunnel, and each couple that went through did the same, lengthening the tunnel, couple by couple.

Marianne laughed wildly as she and Nate went through the tunnel. After everyone had gone through, the lead couple then went back in the other direction, reforming the long train that wrapped around the dance floor. The wedding party then broke off to form an inner circle, surrounding Amanda and Cody for their first dance. While the couple two-stepped to a slow country ballad, the wedding party circled them, hand in hand, periodically collapsing in on them with yells and laughter. For the next dance, the wedding party joined the newlyweds. When that song was over, Nate led Marianne back to their table.

"Well, that was sort of fun." He sat by Viola, who was against the wall opposite Emma. "It looks like you two have hit it off."

Emma leaned forward. "Earlier, Grandma Holub was translating the song they were singing. Something about saddling horses. Right?"

Viola nodded.

"That was cool. Then she told me she and her sisters used to ride a mule to school. She said three of them would ride at one time. And their school had only one room, and all the grades were together. Isn't that crazy? Oh, and Grandma Holub, what was that other thing you told me in Czech? About the kolaches?"

"Bez práce nejsou koláče."

"And it means…?"

"Without work, there are no kolaches."

Ruthie and Leroy came up and sat down. "Mama, can I get you anything?" Ruthie said.

Viola shook her head.

"You probably want to be getting home before too long, ain't it?"

"I'm all right," Viola said, but she looked tired. Her eyelids drooped, and she leaned on the table for support.

They sat and listened to the music and watched the dancing. Nate tried to enjoy himself, but hanging over the wedding was the specter of the Kollatschny's cattle problem. The wedding must have cost a small fortune, and he knew they could ill afford production problems on the dairy.

Nate got up later to get drinks for himself and the girls. When he returned, Wink was sitting in his seat.

"Gramma, you ready to hit the road?" Wink said.

She nodded, and he helped her slowly get to her feet. Everyone else got up, and they all met at the end of the table, on the edge of the dance floor.

"Grandma, I've gotta take the girls back early tomorrow," Nate said. "I wanted to bring them by the farm, but we'll have to do that next time."

Viola nodded, and he sensed her disappointment.

As the girls said their goodbyes, Nate whispered to Ruthie, "Is Wink sober enough to drive?"

She leaned toward him. "I'll make sure."

After helping Wink take Viola out to his truck, Ruthie returned and sat down by Nate. "He seems sober enough."

"He looks sick. Do you know what's wrong?"

Ruthie shrugged. "He hasn't told me nothing."

"He doesn't look well. And he's acting peculiar…for him anyway."

The crowd thinned out, and the band packed up around eight o'clock. The lights were lowered, and a DJ took over, playing alternating sets of country and rock. Shoeless kids raced around the hall, sliding on the dance floor in their socks. In an aisle between tables, Nate taught Marianne how to two-step. He had learned how to dance in college, when Caroline talked him into taking lessons with her. When Marianne felt confident enough, they danced to a couple of songs on the dance floor.

Nate looked at Emma hopefully when they came back to the table. "Okay gal, now it's your turn." But despite his coaxing, she wouldn't budge.

Later, Nate sat with the girls, Ruthie, and Leroy while the Cotton-eyed Joe was played. As they watched the dancers, Nate said, "I remember being at a wedding like this when I was a kid, but it's pretty fuzzy."

Ruthie said, "Let's see, that would've been what, the late sixties? Or early seventies? It could've been anyone, but if it was someone in the family, it was probably Isabel. She married Joe Havelka sometime along then."

"Isabel?"

"Alois's oldest…Tilly's big sister. Joe got drafted. When he came back from the war, they moved out of state. They've lived all over the place. He's some kind of a salesman, I think. They were in Memphis, last I heard. He may be close to retiring, if he ain't retired already."

Nate wanted to stop by Alois's farm. He felt the pull of the place every time he drove by. What were Alois and Tilly like? He had imagined lives for them—Alois puttering around the barnyard, feeding his chickens, calling them by name, Tilly sitting in a dark room lit by a narrow shaft of sunlight, rocking the days away, stirring up swirling motes of dust.

"What does she look like?" he said.

"Isabel? She's got—"

"No, no, I'm sorry. I mean Tilly."

"Oh, Tilly. She makes *me* look tall. Takes after her mama. She was small too. Even shorter than Emma here and thin as a fence post."

"What color hair?"

"She always had long blond hair that she wore in braids, but I haven't seen her in years. Why you wondering?"

Nate slammed his fist on the table, causing everyone to look up in surprise. He shook his head slowly. "I'm such an idiot."

"What is it?" Ruthie said.

"Last fall I was down at the creek, at Grandma's, and I thought I saw a young girl watching me from the woods on the other side. Later I decided I'd imagined it. But then this spring, I saw her bare footprint along the creek bank." He paused, shaking his head again. "I just now realized it's got to be Tilly."

Ruthie smiled. "That could be. She always did run the woods like a wild Indian. Never wanted to wear no shoes neither. I remember one time she got on the school bus barefooted. I must've been in high school, and she was probably in second or third grade…something like that. Our bus driver, old Mr. Priesmeyer, told her she had to have shoes on or he wouldn't let her ride. She gave him a funny look, backed off the bus real slow…then shot off into the woods like a jackrabbit."

Twenty-One

Nate had the girls out of bed and on the road early the next morning. One of Marianne's school clubs was having a car wash fundraiser, and she had to be there by nine.

Nate chalked up their visit as a success. He spent some quality time with them, and they managed to keep their phones off long enough to experience a slice of DeLeon County life. When he said he hoped they could return soon, they seemed receptive, and Emma even flashed a smile. Maybe something positive would emerge from all the upheaval he and Caroline had wrought on their lives.

Dancing at the wedding reminded Nate of a summer day he once spent with his father. They attended a church picnic in Vesely, a small community southeast of Hadlow. On the way back from Houston, he took a detour and revisited the church grounds.

Vesely was once a thriving town before the demise of cotton farming. It had a cotton gin, a cigar factory, two stores, a school, a dance hall, a blacksmith shop, and a Catholic church. Now only the church remained, a white wooden structure of traditional design sitting along a bend in the farm-to-market road.

Nate parked in the church parking lot, near the cemetery, and walked over to a cluster of buildings sitting in a grove of post oaks. The place looked very much like he remembered it. The buildings were white like the church, and they had large flaps with hinges that could be raised to make open-sided stands for selling food and drink. At both ends of the grounds sat pavilions with metal roofs and concrete floors.

The picnic had been on an afternoon in June or July, one of those days so hot the leaves droop listlessly on the trees, craving a breeze, and the shade offers little relief. They arrived about mid-afternoon, long after the noon meal had been served, and Nate soon ran into Darrell and his brother Michael. His father handed him a few dollars, telling him not to spend it on beer, and he ran off with his cousins. Games were set up under the trees, and Nate quickly spent all of his money on the ring toss and beanbag throw. Darrell won a small plastic football, and they played catch until they were hot and sweaty.

Needing more money, they walked around with cardboard boxes collecting empty cans, which they turned in at the drink stand for a few cents. Nate eventually earned enough to buy a snow cone.

While eating his snow cone, he searched for his father. Close to the drink stand was a dunking booth, and the parish priest was taking his turn on the seat. Nate wandered by the bingo stand and listened as the numbers were called, and the players, some with ten or more cards, scrambled to cover their squares. On one of the pavilions, the auction was in full swing. The auctioneer rattled away, taking bids from the crowd as he stood on a flatbed trailer surrounded by donated items of all kinds—farm and garden equipment, housewares, quilts, potted plants, furniture, cakes.

Not seeing his father at the auction, Nate walked by the beer stand, and then over to the dance pavilion. A band was set up at one end, playing polkas and waltzes, all sung in Czech, with a few country and western standards mixed in. Couples twirled around the concrete floor, which had been sprinkled with cornmeal. Onlookers surrounded the dance floor, seated at tables in metal folding chairs. Nate spotted his father at a table in the corner, sitting with Jerome, Ruthie, and Leroy.

Ruthie found him a chair, and he sat and watched the dancers as they frantically tried to keep step with a fast polka. Clarissa was among them, slender and lithe, wearing cutoff shorts, a red tank top, and a straw cowboy hat, her long dark hair tossing wildly as she danced. She made quite a scene.

The man she was dancing with whispered something in her ear, and she threw her head back and laughed in that carefree way of hers. She seemed so totally and fully alive, so completely into the moment, as if only the present had any significance.

When the song ended, Clarissa gave the man a hug and walked back to their table. She was out of breath, fanning herself with her hand.

"Hey there, Nate. You're bigger every time I see you."

She adjusted one of the straps on her tank top and took a drink from a can of beer. Then she sat down between Ruthie and

Jerome, across from Nate. Sweat ran down her neck, pooling in the hollow above her collarbone. She exhaled rapidly through pursed lips, struggling to catch her breath. Jerome sat a bit away from her, leaning back in his chair with a leg crossed, coolly sipping his beer, looking as if he would rather be elsewhere.

Later in the afternoon, Nate stood by his father between the beer stand and dance pavilion. His father was talking to another man. When the band struck up "Waltz Across Texas," Clarissa came up from behind and tapped his father on the shoulder.

"Can I have this dance, cowboy?" she said sweetly, with an affected twang.

He shook his head and politely said no, but she tilted her head and smiled, the kind of smile that plunges into the heart like a dagger. She grabbed his hand and pulled him toward the dance floor, and he allowed her to, but reluctantly. He stopped long enough to turn and hand his beer to his friend, and to look at his son.

Nate tried to remember what was in that look. Was it shame? Regret? Or was it sad and weary resignation, the look of one who has fought with courage and determination but is facing an adversary who is far too strong.

Twenty-Two

After returning to the house that afternoon, Nate decided to visit the Alois Holub farm. He first tried calling the number Ruthie had given him. She said Alois probably wouldn't answer the phone, and when her prediction proved correct, he drove straight out.

Thick ruby clusters of phlox and yellow squaw-weed encircled Alois's mailbox. Nate crossed the cattle guard, followed the short drive, and stopped in front of the house. Dappled sunlight flickered across the stone steps, but the house was otherwise in deep shade. Two tall shutterless windows flanked the door, eyes staring at him, the edge of the sagging porch a mouth, curled into a sneer.

Nate slowly got out of the car, then walked up the steps onto the porch. The windows were open, and a light breeze stirred wispy white curtains. A calico cat got up and stretched before moving off the doormat. Nate knocked on the screen door. When that brought no response, he called out to Alois and waited, listening to the song of a treetop dove.

After a few minutes, he walked back to his car and leaned against the hood. To the right of the house stood an old bladeless windmill and crumbling wooden water tank, and beyond that a barn and cattle pens, mostly hidden by trees.

He walked toward the pens across a stretch of shady ground, sidestepping pieces of old farm equipment. The boards of the nearest pen looked weathered and mossy, rugged and brittle to the touch. As he peered between them, memories flashed like fireflies in the night sky—the bustle and lowing of cattle, tails swishing, horns clacking on the sides of the alleyway, the odor of manure, sweat, and dust mixed together, hanging in the hot air like a shroud. The cattle close, looming above him, hooves pounding, the ground shaking, dust choking him. He was on the ground, trying to crawl away. Then a strong arm was around his waist, pulling him up, lifting him high in the air and setting him down in the cool shade. Then a voice, calm and reassuring.

Nate circled the barn and pens and walked back to the house. A picket fence adorned with morning glory vines came off the corner of the house at an angle. When he reached the fence, he saw the back doorstep and a flagstone patio. A stone path led from the patio toward an arbor covered in climbing roses and crossvine, their yellow and crimson blooms mingling gloriously in bright sunshine.

Nate waited. Then, throwing caution to the wind, he opened the creaking gate and walked across the patio. He stepped onto the path and followed it through the arbor. What he saw on the other side made him stop and catch his breath.

The terrain descended sharply toward a pond surrounded by towering sycamores. Stone pathways stepped down the hillside and crisscrossed between planting beds thick with roses of all colors, shapes, and sizes and other beds dense with blooms—lantana, winecups, daffodils, spiderwort, daisies. The blooms cascaded over low walls of white limestone. A cluster of Mexican plum trees, their limbs bursting with small white flowers, stood beside a dilapidated tool shed with a green door and a single broken window.

Nate slowly walked the stone pathways. Between the planting beds stood masses of rusted metal, and after closer inspection, he realized they were sculptures made from parts of old farm implements, tools, and other machinery, all welded, wired, and fitted together in intricate and creative ways. Some were recognizable as animals, while others were more abstract. There was a grasshopper with body segments made from balls of tightly wound wire and tractor gear shift levers for antennae. Another was a dinosaur-like creature with rows of teeth made from the cutting bars of an old combine. A life-sized horse or mule, composed of gears, springs, shovel blades, brackets, hinges, and pieces of chain for mane and tail, trudged with its head down, pulling a plow with a bent sword for a plowshare.

Sculptures of stone were also scattered about, some appearing unfinished. One was a great horned owl perched on a tree limb, wings slightly opened, looking like it might suddenly take flight. Another was a deer fawn, curled up in a bed of daisies. The artistry of the work was stunning.

Nate sat down on a rock wall near a dense thicket of rose bushes. Nearby stood a sculpture composed of jumbled barbed wire, pitchfork tines, and the spidery wheels of a hay rake. In the middle of that chaotic snarl of metal, seemingly suspended in midair and rocking precariously in the wind, hung a blue glass ball with splotches of green and brown paint. As Nate watched the ball spin, he realized the painted areas had the rough outlines of the continents.

From where he was sitting, Nate could see the pond framed between rose bushes and the wild green jungle of the creek bottom beyond. The air in the garden was so fragrant, the setting so inviting, that he forgot he was trespassing on the property of a virtual stranger.

He had been on many farms since moving to DeLeon County, but he had never seen anything remotely like this place. Ruthie hadn't mentioned anything about a garden. Did she even know about it? Did anyone know?

Nate eventually got up and continued exploring. In the far corner, close to the pond, he descended stone steps to a small patio of tightly packed gravel shaded by a single rusty blackhaw. At the base of the tree stood a bench of rough-hewn cedar posts. The bench faced a large flowerbed that seemed more carefully maintained than the other beds in the garden. In its center, surrounded by a lush growth of white irises, was a stone sculpture of a girl. She lay on her side with her head resting comfortably on her folded arms, her long hair flowing over her shoulder. Her eyes were closed, a look of perfect contentment on her face.

Nate sat down on the bench. He listened to the birdsong as he watched the ghostly reflections of the sycamores shimmering in the pond's dark water. He watched bees flitting tirelessly from bloom to bloom, then followed a line of geese across the sky as they headed northward, their calls growing fainter and fainter. The garden wrapped him in its embrace, making him feel strangely at ease.

Nate's reverie was interrupted by a shadow on the ground in front of him. Startled, he looked to his left to see the gaunt figure of Alois Holub standing on the patio, pointing a bolt-action deer rifle at him. He wore dirty gray pants, an untucked red flannel shirt, and a battered brown fedora topped with a white feather.

"Who the hell are you?" he said, his voice gravelly.

Nate swallowed hard. "I'm sorry. I'm just admiring your garden here. I'm Nate…Nate Holub…your great-nephew."

Alois moved a couple of steps closer. "Say it again."

"Nate. Dennis's son."

Alois grunted. "You'd be the new vet then."

"That's right."

Alois walked over slowly and sat down on the opposite side of the bench, laying the gun in his lap. He had amber eyes and a wizened hollow face with a heavy growth of whiskers. He smelled faintly of mothballs and wood smoke, and a toothpick jutted from the corner of his mouth. Nate saw how much he resembled the pictures he had seen of his grandfather. Both had the same chiseled features, the same ponderous brow. He also saw more than a trace of his father in that face.

"Sorry to surprise you like this," Nate said. "I knocked on the door first. I thought maybe I'd find you back here."

Alois squinted at him but said nothing.

"I've been wanting to meet you since moving here." Nate looked around. "I didn't know you were a gardener."

Alois studied him, then looked away. "This is my wife's garden. We worked on it together."

"It's beautiful."

"My Miriam loved green things. She was from West Texas, out around Sonora. That's nice country out there, empty and quiet, but nothing much grows." He surveyed the garden, scratching his chin. Then his face twisted into a scowl. "With everything going to hell like it is, this place will be that dry someday." He brought his hand up and flung the toothpick to the ground with sudden anger. "Damn them all, the lying greedy sons of bitches."

They sat silently as Alois brooded.

Nate leaned over and ran his hand over a wall of cool rough limestone at the base of the tree. "Is that where all of this rock came from? West Texas, I mean?"

"Some of it. Miriam's daddy ran cattle on four sections. Had more rocks than grass. We'd haul some back every time we drove out there. Didn't make a dent."

Nate looked up the hillside. How had Alois found time for building all of this while working, running a farm, and raising a family? It had clearly taken a lifetime of work. "Grandma mentioned you worked for the CCC during the Depression. Is that where you learned the stonework?"

Alois glanced at him. "That's right."

"The metal sculptures are impressive too."

"Just something to piddle with. Can't do it anymore. Don't have the strength."

"They're very imaginative."

"I used to drive all over the county looking for old equipment. People said I was crazy." He caressed the stock of his rifle, then ran his finger along the trigger guard. "Maybe I am."

Their eyes met and Nate smiled, but Alois just stared.

Nate fidgeted, scanning the garden. Where was Tilly? Was she in the house? The woods? Somewhere in the garden, watching them? He wanted to ask about her, but he wasn't sure how to bring her up.

"And you made this?" Nate said, pointing at the sleeping girl.

Alois shook his head. "No, that's Miriam's work. She learned it in Albuquerque. Worked for a sculptor there."

"She should have been a professional."

"She sold a few pieces…here and there. Mostly she just made them for the garden."

Nate marveled at how such beauty and creativity could go unnoticed. Alois and Miriam had constructed a sanctuary for themselves and their children, a refuge from the madness.

"I can't remember my dad ever mentioning this garden. Did he ever work here on your farm?"

"He helped me a few times, before he moved away. He and Jerome both."

"Working cattle?"

"A little. They baled and hauled hay mostly. Built me some fence a time or two."

"Did he ever work cattle for you *after* moving to Houston?"

Alois shrugged. "Could be. I got rid of my cattle a long time ago. Got tired of messing with them." He reached up and scratched his ear. "I liked Dennis well enough. Had a weakness for the ladies, but no matter."

A mockingbird swooped down to the patio and caught an insect, then flew up to the top of the blackhaw.

After a lengthy silence, Nate said, "This garden must take a lot of work."

Alois nodded.

"Does Tilly help you with it?"

Alois sat still for a moment. Then he frowned, took off his hat and set it on the bench between them, and rubbed his bald freckled head with a calloused hand. He leaned over, close enough that Nate could see the tiny vessels in his bloodshot eyes. "Who the hell told you to come here?"

Nate shook his head. "Nobody."

"Ruthie?"

"No, I just wanted to meet you."

Alois shoved his hat back on, his ears turning red. He gripped his rifle tightly with both hands. "I don't know what you've been told about my daughter, but you listen to me. She's of a right mind when she's here on this farm. If you take her away, she can't handle it. We tried more than once."

"I wasn't—"

"I know what you're up to. Ruthie, Viola, somebody put you up to this. They've been telling you about my daughter. They don't understand her. Nobody does…but me."

Before Nate could explain himself, Alois pushed himself to his feet.

"I got things to do. You can stay as long as you want." He started walking in the direction of the house. Then he stopped, turned, and waved the rifle barrel in Nate's direction. "But don't ever come back."

It was late afternoon when Nate left Alois's place. Before heading back to the house, he stopped at the farm. Viola didn't answer his knock, so he opened the screen door and found her napping in her living room recliner.

In the hallway, Nate glanced at the stairs. He hadn't seen the upstairs bedroom since he was a kid. Curious, he walked slowly to the top.

The room looked smaller than he remembered. It was long and narrow with a window on each end and a vaulted ceiling with exposed rafters. This was the room his father used after returning from Korea.

He pulled a string to turn on the single bare light bulb. A double bed stood in one corner, opposite a small add-on closet. The other side of the room had a tall dresser and a table stacked with boxes. More boxes were piled along the walls, almost completely hiding one window. A coat of dust covered everything.

Nate browsed the boxes. Some held old clothes, one had Christmas ornaments, and another had old issues of *The Texas Farmer-Stockman* magazine. On a shelf in the closet, he found a Hadlow school yearbook from 1951. He sat on the bed and thumbed through it, finding his father's picture among the junior class, right there between Martin Havelka and Anita Hrncir, his young face brimming with vigor and hope.

After putting the yearbook back, Nate pulled a framed photo from behind an old fan. It showed Sammy in cap and gown on graduation night, standing with Viola, stadium lights in the background. He had keen blue eyes and a tranquil smile. He clutched his diploma in his left hand, and his right arm was wrapped around Viola's shoulder. She wore a blue dress, and her brown hair had only a few hints of gray. She gazed not at the camera but up at her son, her face aglow, her eyes shining. Nate stared at the photo for a long time before putting it back and returning downstairs.

Finding Viola still asleep, he walked back to the kitchen. A thin layer of noodle dough lay on the table, spread out to dry, and another was draped over a chair. He remembered Viola making noodles when he was a boy—cutting the rolled-up dough with a knife and unraveling the long strips. The thought of her chicken noodle soup suddenly made him hungry. He left her a note and went out the back door.

The bermudagrass was almost knee-high in the bottom hayfield as Nate walked down to the creek. Dewberries bloomed along the fence lines, a few tiny green berries just starting to form. He went to his usual spot on the creek bank and leaned back against the cottonwood, his thoughts returning to his talk with Alois.

What would eventually happen to Tilly? There was the sister, Isabel. How involved was she in looking after her father? Maybe she and her husband would move back when Alois was gone, if not sooner.

Nate imagined Alois's life, filling in the gaps as best he could. He bounced around CCC camps throughout the Southwest in the 1930s, working on roads and bridges, trails and picnic areas. His body, already tough and wiry from farm life, became even more so, his skin as bronzed as the bigtooth maples lining the canyons and arroyos in which he worked. He loved the dry air of the Southwest—cool at night, redolent of juniper and sage in the afternoon heat—and the stone masonry work appealed to his creative nature. He dreamed of settling down and living the rest of his life somewhere in that vast desiccated land, building his own home out of native rock and filling it with a brood of dusky barefooted children. Then the war came along and shattered his daydreams.

And that wasn't all it shattered.

The creek bottom felt damp and cool, but Nate was warmed by a column of sunlight descending through the canopy above. The late night from the wedding and the drive to Houston that morning had left him more tired than usual. He closed his eyes, listening to the wind whispering in the treetops, and drifted off to sleep.

He dreamed he was fishing with his father, just as he had as a boy. He watched the bobber floating on the water's placid surface. The sky was overcast, looking like it might rain, and the water was an inky black rather than its usual sepia. Nate turned to his father and saw him staring down at the water. When he turned back around, the bobber had disappeared. He stood and started reeling, thinking he had a fish hooked, but no matter how much he reeled, the fish wouldn't surface. He finally dropped the fishing rod and grabbed the line, leaning back and pulling as hard as he could. Something finally emerged from the dark water, and he was shocked to see it was a human body, clothed in jeans and a white t-shirt. He reached down, grabbed an arm, and pulled. The body rolled over and bobbed up and down in the water, the face hidden by long dark hair. He pulled the hair away, and Clarissa's ghostly white face appeared, her eyes open and glassy.

The creek bed suddenly lit up with bright sunlight, and the water resumed its usual tone. Nate was sitting on the ground. He turned to his father but saw a woman sitting on the cottonwood trunk instead. She was petite with a freckled face, green eyes, and long hair like corn silk. She wore faded jeans rolled up below her knees, a paint-splotched tan shirt, and a straw sun hat with a chinstrap. She looked away quickly when Nate turned toward her.

He stared at her, finally realizing he had been dreaming and was no longer asleep. He leaned forward slowly. "Tilly?"

Her short legs didn't reach the ground, and she kicked her sandy bare feet back and forth, her arms straight down at her sides.

"I'm Tilly Holub. You're Dennis's boy, aren't you?"

"That's right. I'm Nate." He got to his feet cautiously, worried he might spook her back into the woods. He sat down on the trunk, but not too close. "I saw your garden earlier. It's beautiful."

She scooted away from him a few inches, put her feet on the trunk, and curled her arms around her legs. "Mama taught me before she died. She got cancer." She started rocking back and forth gently. "That's a red-bellied woodpecker."

"What?"

"A red-bellied woodpecker." Her eyes were closed now, her rocking more pronounced. "Don't you hear it?"

Nate listened carefully.

"It's up in that walnut." She pointed across the creek, her eyes still closed. Then she turned her head and pointed behind her. "They have a nest in a hollow up here in this elm. Every year they nest in that same spot."

Her voice had a childlike, singsong quality, and there was a youthful delicacy about her movements. She so resembled the young girl of his imagination.

Nate said, "The other bird singing right now, do you know what it is?"

The sun went behind a cloud, putting the creek bottom into deep shadow. Tilly stopped rocking, held very still for a moment, then started rocking again.

When she didn't answer, Nate thought he had her stumped. "Is it a cardinal?"

Tilly shook her head. "It's not just one bird singing. There's a Carolina wren and a tufted titmouse over there." She pointed across the creek. "And a mockingbird up here in this willow."

Nate looked at her in wonder. It was the mockingbird he had asked about. He hadn't even noticed the other birds.

"See these possum tracks?" Tilly pointed at the mud below them, her eyes still closed. "I saw a mama with babies on her back the other day. Might be the same one that left these tracks, but maybe not. Lots of possums around here."

She stopped rocking, folded her legs beneath her, and rested her elbows on her knees.

"Do you spend a lot of time down here?"

Tilly opened her eyes, looking in his direction but not making eye contact. "Every day, unless it's raining…or cold. Daddy doesn't like me going to the creek when it's raining. Or when it's cold."

"You don't worry about snakes? I mean…with your bare feet?"

She shook her head. "I saw a rattlesnake yesterday. A big one. Over by the bridge. Daddy kills snakes. Gets a hoe and chops their head off. But I don't tell him about the ones I see."

The sun emerged from behind the cloud, and the sunlight gave Tilly's hair a pearlescent glow. They sat quietly, listening to the sounds of the woods. Sitting with Tilly, silence didn't seem awkward. Nate wondered if his father had encountered her on his many excursions to the creek bottom.

"Tilly, did you know my dad very well?"

"Dennis died a long time ago…Clarissa too."

"That's right." Nate shifted to face her, lifting his knee up on the cottonwood. "Did you ever talk to him?"

"Sometimes."

Tilly raised her legs again, wrapped her arms around them, and laid her head on top of her knees, looking away from him. She resumed her rocking.

Nate waited. Why had his father never mentioned Tilly? Maybe he had, and he just didn't remember. Or maybe he purposely hadn't, thinking it was too complicated to explain.

"Tilly, did you know Clarissa?"

She continued rocking and began humming to herself softly.

Given her secluded life, it seemed unlikely Tilly would have met Clarissa. But perhaps Clarissa had come to Alois's place when his father and Jerome were working there. Maybe she brought them lemonade like she had that day in the hayfield. Nate pictured her parking her white convertible in front of the house, walking down into the garden, finding Tilly kneeling by a flowerbed.

He asked the question again, but she didn't respond. A shadow swept over as the sun went behind another cloud. The only sound was a rustling of leaves in the wind. Even the birds had stopped talking.

Nate finally rose. "Well Tilly, I better go. It's been nice talking to you. I hope I'll see you again."

He waited, then started walking away.

"Goodbye," she said, so softly he almost didn't hear.

He stopped and looked back. Tilly was still turned away from him, rocking gently and humming, ensconced in a world that only she knew.

Twenty-Three

Over the next few weeks, Nate was consumed by work as calving season continued unabated. The intricacies of bovine obstetrics slowly became less intimidating, and even C-sections began to seem routine. On one particularly busy day in mid-April, he did three C-sections, all in the field, and delivered four other calves.

When Nate arrived at the office early one Saturday morning, he was relieved that a line of trailers wasn't already waiting. He nudged Chewy off his chair and sat down to enjoy a moment of quiet before the morning rush.

Everett was at his desk, holding Ana and a steaming cup of coffee. She had her head on his chest, her arms around his neck. "Morning, Dr. Holub," he said.

"Good morning," Nate said. "Somebody is sure up early for a Saturday."

"Yep, this one is always up at the crack of dawn. She's usually awake before we are and climbs into bed with us."

"So how did it go yesterday?" Nate had been out on the road with Russell much of the afternoon, getting back well after five. They dewormed some goats, delivered a calf, and repaired a cervical prolapse.

"Not too bad. Dogs and cats mostly." Everett's face suddenly lit up. "Oh, I almost forgot. You'll enjoy this. Late in the afternoon, Harold Lubojasky came in. I was talking to Roy Heath underneath the oak out there, over by the barn, and Harold came storming up, interrupted our conversation, and just let me have it about being overcharged seventeen dollars on his last bill. It was trivial and could've easily been handled with a phone call to Jennie, but he just had to make a scene."

Everett took a sip of coffee.

"While standing there, I happened to look up, and believe it or not, stretched out on the tree limb just above Harold, probably no more than three feet away from his head, was Daisy. That crazy reptile survived the winter somehow. So in a low, very concerned voice, I said, 'Harold, listen to me carefully. This morning, a dangerous lizard escaped from the clinic, and I just now spotted it. Stay very still, and do not look up. It's right above your head. These lizards can spit venom into your eyes, so *do not* look at it.'"

Ana raised her head. "Daddy, what's venom?"

"Poison, honey. I was joking. Daisy's not poisonous. So anyway, Harold thought I was full of it, and of course he looked up, and I just wish I'd had a video camera. He bolted out of there like a scalded dog, cussing a blue streak. Roy and I were laughing so hard we were almost rolling on the ground. Harold got back in his truck, slammed the door, and drove off."

Everett chuckled. "Hopefully, that's the last we see of him, but I doubt we're that lucky. I managed to catch Daisy with a net, and this little one's happy to get him back. Isn't that right?"

Ana smiled, nodded emphatically, and laid her head back on his chest.

Russell was off that morning, and his absence slowed everything down. Audrey helped in the office, as she occasionally did when they were shorthanded. It was a typical busy Saturday morning. After the last client—Helen Meissner, owner of Sparky the coughing Chihuahua—walked out at one o'clock, Nate collapsed into his chair with a sigh of relief.

Irene walked in and handed him a note with a name and phone number. "Do you know Nina Bradshaw?"

Nate studied the note and shook his head.

Everett came into the room with a heaping sandwich, a bag of chips, and a glass of iced tea. He motioned toward the kitchen. "We've got smoked turkey, fresh from Chaloupka's. Y'all help yourselves." He sat down at his desk. "Did I hear you say Nina Bradshaw?"

Irene nodded.

"Was it Poochie Bartosh that called?"

"*Rodney* Bartosh."

"That's him. Don't tell me—there's a calf that can't nurse, and Poochie wants us to come out."

"You got it."

Everett smiled. "Nina and two of her friends from Houston

own a place near Almyra. They have tea parties out there and look at the wildflowers, I guess. They've got a dozen old cows that should've been sold a long time ago. Most have big bottle teats, so when a calf's born, it can't suck. Poochie takes care of their cattle, but he's too lazy and usually too drunk to do anything but call us. If I know Poochie, the cow's not in the pen."

"You're right," Irene said.

"I'll go on out there," Nate said. "Where is it?"

"You've been to Hugo Schulte's place, right?" Everett said.

Nate nodded.

"Hugo is right there on the corner where Klecka Road meets FM 2644. If you keep going down 2644 past Hugo, Nina's place will be on your right. You'll see an old farmhouse with a red barn and a big cedar tree. There's an entryway that says Sunflower Acres, or some such shit. You can't miss it."

"Okay, thanks."

"You could use some help getting her penned. I doubt Poochie will be around. Too bad Russell's off today. I'd go with you, but Olivia has a piano recital."

Nate looked at Irene. Something in her expression boosted his confidence. "Hey, you want to come along?"

She looked at Everett, then down at her feet.

Nate stood up. "Dumb question. You have to get back home to Zach. I'll manage."

Everett said, "They've got a decent alleyway out there, so no need to take the portable chute. I always block the cow up tight and have enough room to work between the boards. Make sure you tie her leg back though. Don't get your arm broke."

"Thanks for the advice."

Nate started walking toward the exam room, and Irene touched him on the shoulder. "I can go. Zach's on a camping trip this weekend with the Cub Scouts. I'll call Mom and tell her I'll be a little late."

Nate shrugged. "Okay, good. We can eat a quick sandwich and head that way."

The day was warm and sunny. As they drove away from the clinic, Nate glanced at Irene. She was wearing her hair loose and had a t-shirt on, having shed her flannel shirt. He liked the way she looked in the t-shirt, the way the sleeves hugged her freckled arms.

"How's your mom doing?" he said.

Irene frowned. "Not so good. She's having an okay week, but she's up and down. Her doctor thinks her kidneys are failing. She'll probably have to start dialysis soon."

"I'm sorry to hear that."

They drove on in silence, Irene staring out the window, the mood a shade or two darker than it was before.

Nate went by his house before heading to the Bradshaw place. Early that morning, one of Bruno's cows appeared to be very close to calving, and he wanted to check on her. They found her on top of the hill, near the old house, well away from the rest of the herd.

Nate circled her in the truck, looking carefully. "Nothing showing yet, but she's getting close."

They drove on into town. After climbing the bluff and going south on 34, they took a right on FM 2644, which followed the river for several miles. Before leaving the river and turning southwest, they passed a large stone entryway on the right with a W engraved in the arch. A long lane led up a hill to a sprawling ranch-style home shaded by big trees. It was the Duke Woller place—some two thousand acres of manicured hills and fertile bottomland—only a fraction of the Woller land holdings in the area.

What went through Wink's mind when he drove by here?

Three miles later, they pulled up to the gate at the Bradshaw place. Irene got out and opened it, using the combination Poochie had given her, then hopped back into the truck. "He told me the cow was an 'old tiger-stripe with tipped horns,' if that helps."

They soon spotted a cow fitting that description standing along a fence line, and as they got closer, a calf's head rose out of a clump of tall grass. The cow's udder was distended with milk, all four teats much larger than normal. The calf got to her feet as Nate pulled to a stop.

"This is the one we're looking for," he said. "Let's see…the pen is up there by the barn. How about you drive the truck and I walk? If we're lucky, maybe we'll get them in the pen."

"Okay."

Irene slid into the driver's seat after he got out.

Nate waved the cow forward, and she started walking toward the barn, the calf at her heels. The pasture was treeless, and the only obstacle in their path was a large stock pond. When they reached the pond, Nate wanted the cow to go right, below the pond's tall earthen dam. He shouted to Irene to drive on top of the dam, but the cow got there before she did. Deciding to push the cow along the dam, he motioned to Irene to drive around and meet him on the other side.

After Nate walked onto the dam, the calf suddenly darted to the left, and he watched in disbelief as she plunged into the water and started swimming, heading toward the center of the pond. Thinking she would surely drown, he frantically pulled off his boots and waded into the murky water, which was soon up to his waist, and then his shoulders, so cold it took his breath away. He swam out to the calf, grabbed her around the chest, and began paddling back to the shore. The calf kicked and wriggled out of his grasp, but he managed to get her back to shallow water.

The cow charged into the water, snorting in rage. Nate released the calf and lay with his arms over his head, feeling the cow's breath on the back of his neck, thinking his luck had finally run out. But with the calf safely ashore, the cow retreated.

Nate crawled out of the pond and sat on the bank as Irene came running up.

"Are you okay?"

He gulped for air. "Yeah…but it's a little early in the season for a swim."

After he caught his breath, Nate retrieved his boots. "Excuse me while I get out of these wet clothes." Standing on the other side of the truck, he changed into a pair of coveralls, wrung out his socks, put his boots back on, and washed the mud off his arms and face.

The cow and calf stood at the far end of the pond. When Nate and Irene continued driving them toward the pen, the cow slipped between them and ran below the dam. Unable to keep up, the calf lost her footing and fell. The cow stopped and looked back, but the calf was too exhausted to rise.

Nate ran over to the calf, picked her up, and carried her to the truck. While he struggled to lift the wet slippery calf into the bed, the cow came running back, bellowing loudly. With his heart pounding, Nate tried one last heave, but he lost his grip and the calf slid halfway to the ground. Carrying the calf, he quickly ducked around the rear of the truck just as the cow arrived. She caught the heel of his right boot with one of her horns, nearly tripping him.

He yelled to Irene, "Open the door!"

She leaned over and pushed the door open, and he scrambled into the cab with the calf in tow, slamming the door behind him.

Irene's eyes were wide. "What are you doing?"

"Go ahead." He nodded toward the pen. "She'll follow us now."

Nate held the kicking calf across his lap as Irene drove to the pen. The cow trailed them closely, still bellowing. Once they were inside, Nate got out and shut the gate. Then he had Irene drive into a corner so he could get the calf out of the truck.

After a few minutes with the calf, the cow settled down. Nate ran her into the alleyway and blocked her off, tied her right rear limb to a post, milked all four quarters until the teats were smaller, and then held the calf up and let her nurse. Afterward, as he let the cow back into the pen, a mud-splattered white truck pulled up.

"Impeccable timing," Nate said, just before Poochie Bartosh lumbered out and shuffled over with a bow-legged waddle. He had bushy black hair, a ruddy oversized nose, and a watermelon gut. His eyes were small and bat-like, well suited for his natural habitat—the shadowy beer joints of DeLeon County.

"Well hell, it looks like y'all got her done already," Poochie said, extending his hand. "I'm Rodney Bartosh."

"Nate Holub. And this is Irene."

"Pleasure to meet you." He took his cap off and scratched behind his ear. "You know, I didn't think we'd have a problem with this cow. She had a calf last year, and it sucked good."

"I'd keep them in the pen here so you can watch them. The calf will hopefully keep it sucked down now, at least one or two quarters." Nate figured Poochie knew the drill.

Poochie put his cap back on. "That sounds good, Doc. I really appreciate it. If you would, send the bill to Ms. Bradshaw. That's Ms. Nina Bradshaw, 1493 Willow Trace in Houston, Texas, 72192." He enunciated the name and address clearly, making sure no mistake was made in the billing, and just to be certain, he started to repeat it. "Miss Nina Bradshaw, 1493 Willow—"

"I believe we've got the address on file. Thanks."

While Nate and Irene were walking back to the truck, Poochie said, "You didn't have any trouble getting 'em in the pen, did ya Doc?"

Still walking, Nate turned his head. "No, not at all." He glanced at Irene and gave her a wink just before getting into the truck. He started the engine, put the truck in gear, and started driving down the lane.

"What are we getting for aquatic rescues these days, anyway?" he said as he turned left onto the farm-to-market road.

When Nate turned to Irene, he saw something totally unexpected…something wondrous…something that made him momentarily forget about his fears, his failures, the nagging sense of impending disaster that constantly permeated his thinking. Somehow, despite it all, everything might just work out.

Irene was smiling.

Twenty-Four

Irene's smile so invigorated Nate that he did a surprising thing, something completely out of character. On impulse, he decided to take a different route back to town, one he hadn't mapped out in advance and wasn't sure would work. He took a right on Klecka Road, thinking it might eventually come out on Highway 34.

The road was narrow and winding. After half a mile, they approached an unpainted wooden building sitting close to the road. A rusty Dr. Pepper sign adorned one side, and two antique Texaco gas pumps stood out front. Several vehicles were parked nearby in the shade of a mossy live oak.

"Are you thirsty?" Nate said. "This old place looks kind of interesting."

"This is a store? Way out here?"

"I think so. Let's check it out."

Nate parked beside a 1960s-era blue truck with hay bales in the bed. They got out and approached the screen door, hearing laughter inside and the click of dominoes on a hardwood table. Nate grabbed the faded Rainbo Bread door handle, opened the door, and they cautiously stepped inside.

The place smelled of dust and tobacco, and it took a few seconds for their eyes to adjust to the dim lighting. On the right stood a few grocery shelves partially stocked with a handful of basic items—sugar, flour, bread, coffee, breakfast cereal, canned goods. On the left was a long counter with an old cash register, and behind it were shelves extending to the ceiling, cluttered with empty bottles and jars, stacks of magazines, cardboard boxes, tools, framed photographs, signs, old clocks, and more than one sleeping cat. "Blue Eyes Crying in the Rain" emanated from a small portable radio on the end of the counter.

Several people huddled around a table in the back, all staring at Nate and Irene as if they had just landed an alien spacecraft on the county road. Nate looked for a friendly face, but he didn't see anyone he recognized. A rotund, iron-jawed, gray-haired woman got up from the table, irritably wiped her hands on her apron, and walked behind the counter.

"What can I do for y'all?" she said in a loud raspy voice.

"Uh…can we get a couple of drinks?" Nate said.

"Whatcha want?"

"I'll have a Sprite, and…" Nate looked at Irene.

"Diet Coke, please."

The woman walked over to an old upright drink cooler and shooed off a large gray cat. She slid the door open and reached down, then turned and plopped two cans on the counter—a 7-Up and a Pepsi.

"That'll be a dollar fifty."

Nate pulled out his wallet. "What's the name of this place, if you don't mind me asking?"

The woman put her hands on her hips and squinted at him. "Where you folks from?"

Nate realized he probably looked odd in his coveralls, and he likely still smelled of tank water and cow pen. "From Hadlow. I'm kind of new to the area though. I'm Nate Holub, and this is Irene…Irene Winfield."

"Holub, you say?"

Nate nodded.

"You're that new vet?"

"That's right."

"I'll be damned."

She glanced at the others, who looked back with blank stares. Then she took her apron off, threw it down, and came around the end of the counter with a clear sense of purpose. Nate took half a step back as she approached, not sure what to expect. When she stood in front of him, she threw her arms open wide.

"We're kin!"

She grabbed him around the chest and gave him a bear hug, nearly lifting him off the floor. "I'm Bernie Orsak, but I was a Skrivanek. My daddy and your grandma were brother and sister. I remember you when you were just a little boy. I've been meaning to bring Toby in for his rabies shot and say hello."

"It's great to see you," Nate said, trying to catch his breath.

Bernie shook Irene's hand, then led them to the back and introduced them to the others.

"You play forty-two?" Bernie's husband Gerald said as Bernie pulled up chairs for them.

"I played a bit in college, but that was a long time ago," Nate said.

"Good enough. And you?"

"I can play," Irene said.

"Y'all got time for a game?" Bernie said.

Nate and Irene exchanged glances, and then Nate shrugged. "Sure. Maybe one quick game." He sat down across from Irene, and they played as partners against Bernie and Gerald.

The game of forty-two is similar to the card game spades, involving bidding, trumps, and tricks, and it came back to Nate quickly, but he made several early blunders, and Bernie and Gerald capitalized. Irene was a good player though, and she helped them keep it close.

While shuffling the dominoes between hands, Bernie said, "You know, I haven't talked to Viola in quite a while. How's she been doing?"

"Okay, I guess," Nate said. "But I'm not sure how much longer she'll be able to stay on the farm."

Bernie nodded as she picked up her seven dominoes. "My daddy died in the war when I was just a baby, so I never knew him. But Mama used to tell me some of the stories he told her, stories about growing up on the farm. You know Viola was like another mother to him." Bernie scowled at her dominoes. "Lordy, lordy, who shook this mess?"

Gerald chuckled. "You did, honeydew."

"So I did. You know, Nate, one story Mama told has always stayed with me. Daddy and Viola were about as poor as you could get growing up. Mamma said Daddy liked to talk about his first trip to town. I guess he must've been no more than seven or eight, and Viola couldn't have been much more than a kid herself. Viola used to haul their cotton to the gin in a wagon, and one time she took him along. I think he was always her favorite. They usually sold at the gin in Almyra, but one year it burned down, and they had to haul it all the way to Hadlow. It took the whole day to get there, I guess. They slept on top of the cotton that night outside the gin. The next day they sold it and then went shopping on the square. She bought him some candy and took him to see a movie. Boy, I bet his eyes got wide when that movie screen lit up."

"I imagine so," Nate said.

"One time I asked Viola about that trip, and then I wished I hadn't."

Nate waited for her to continue, but she only stared at her dominoes, her jaw set, her eyes moist.

After finishing the game, they were persuaded to stay for a second, and then a third. Bernie talked about the family gatherings at the Holub farm, which she had attended with her mother and Gerald. Nate had only the vaguest memories of them being there.

"Bernie, do you know Alois, my great-uncle?" Nate said.

Bernie looked up from her dominoes, blinked at him, and shook her head. "Don't know the man. I used to see him carrying the mail, years ago, but I've never talked to him." She looked at Gerald.

"Same here," he said.

"Grandma doesn't like to talk about him for some reason," Nate said. "There seems to be some history there."

Bernie nodded. "The way it was told to me, Cap and Alois didn't get along too good. Their daddy Emil favored Cap. Alois was always more interested in reading books and roaming the woods than farming. And then when Viola moved in, Alois finally had enough and left home. I'm sure she was pretty headstrong, even back in those days. You know Cap and Alois's mama died young. I've always imagined Viola moving in and taking over the household. Alois probably didn't like getting told what to do by some teenage girl about the same age as him."

"What happened when he came back from the war?"

"Well, Emil died during the war. Had a stroke, if I remember right. He left most of the farm to Cap, but he left Alois the fifty acres across the creek. Most of it was just woods. They say Alois never could hold a job or nothing. He became kind of a bum around town."

"The war changed him."

Bernie nodded. "They have a name for it now, but back then nobody knew what to make of him. Then one day he up and disappeared."

"Disappeared?"

"They say he was gone for months before anyone knew where he was. One day your daddy ran across him in the creek bottom. Alois was camping out down there, living off the land. He was filthy, his hair all long and shaggy. Dennis didn't even recognize him at first. Cap tried to talk him into coming back home, but he just moved deeper into the woods. He'd walk to town every now and then to get supplies, looking like some kind of wild animal."

Nate envisioned Alois, bearded and hollow-eyed, wandering the woods, hounded by nightmares and grappling with fear and remorse, having fled a world he could no longer comprehend or negotiate.

"Did he get some help?"

"He lived like that for a long time, several years I believe, and then one day, out of nowhere, Miriam showed up. He met her before the war. I guess he must have written to her, but maybe not. She helped him get straightened out. They got married and rented a house in town. Then he got the job with the post office. Later, they built the house where he lives now."

Nate finally thanked Bernie and said they needed to get back. Bernie and Gerald won all three games, but Irene's play kept it from being a total rout.

"Drop by again sometime," Bernie said.

After getting back into the truck, Nate said, "That was kind of unexpected. Sorry to keep you. You're probably wanting to get back and check on your mom."

"No, that was fun. I haven't played dominoes in a long time."

"I'm just glad we weren't playing for money." He started the engine and backed the truck. "So where did you learn how to play forty-two so well?"

"At home. My dad loved to play. Whenever there were three other people around, he had a game going. All of us kids played."

Nate knew so little about Irene. He had avoided asking her personal questions, not wanting to seem presumptuous or to bring up Clint. "How many brothers and sisters do you have?"

"There are five of us all together, three older than me and one younger."

"Where are they now?"

"Scattered all over. I'm the only one in Texas. We moved around a lot when I was growing up. My dad was in the army. But he grew up here. So did my mom. I think playing forty-two reminded him of home. He planned to move back when he retired." She paused, staring out the window. "Dad got sick. He died when I was in high school."

"I'm sorry. I lost my dad when I was young too."

They drove through a leafy creek bottom and crossed a low bridge. The road then gradually climbed to the summit of a high hill. As they came around a curve, a sweeping vista opened up. Nate slowed down to take in the view, then pulled over and stopped.

"Look at this."

He turned off the engine, stepped out, and walked over to a barbed wire fence.

The land descended to a shallow draw containing a towering pecan tree, its branches bursting with tender new leaves, then rose again, rolling toward the horizon in every direction. The late afternoon sun bathed the landscape in soft golden light, rich as honey, and a steady breeze sent cascading ripples through the hillside grasses and made the spidery shadow of the pecan tree dance. The pasture nearest the road was awash in color—Indian paintbrush, evening primrose, dandelions, prairie nymphs—all achingly beautiful in the sun's glow.

"It's wonderful," Irene said.

Nate turned and saw her standing by his side. He smiled and turned his gaze back to the landscape. Wonderful indeed, but wonderful didn't begin to describe it. He felt so thoroughly alive at that moment, as if just roused from a very long sleep. All of his senses were heightened. The caress of the wind on his skin, the twittering of a pair of scissortail flycatchers pirouetting in the sky above, the fresh grassy smell of spring—all of it was suddenly discernible, and the intensity of it was overwhelming. He took a deep breath, held its sweetness in his lungs, and slowly exhaled.

When Nate turned back to Irene, the sun was behind her, and she looked radiant, strands of her hair glowing like embers as they tossed in the wind. He searched her eyes, wanting desperately to hold her—for her to be part of the joy he felt, for her to share in that joy—but the space between them was a chasm too danger-ous to cross. He toed the precipice, wanting to step forward, but his feet wouldn't move. His heart pounded, feeling like it might explode. Unable to bear the anguish any longer, he turned and leaned on a fence post.

To the west, Nate could faintly see the water tower for the town of Wiley, and the steeple of St. Anthony's was visible far to the east. "This must be the highest point in the area. I wouldn't mind having a house right here."

A pair of crows flew up from the pecan tree, cawing loudly, and circled around before disappearing back into the foliage.

"Wouldn't you worry about lightning?" Irene said.

He looked at her and smiled. "Maybe." Then he told her about his close call at the dairy, realizing she was the first person he had told.

"That's pretty scary." She twirled a strand of hair around her finger. "You know I'm surprised more *animals* don't get struck by lightning. I mean, you always see them standing under trees during thunderstorms." She leaned on the fence post next to him. "Who knows? Maybe more get struck than we think, and it just doesn't kill them."

Nate remembered Ruthie's story about Viola's heifers. Then he thought about the time Darrell lied to him about an electric fence being off when they were kids, and he had naively touched the hot wire. He avoided electric fences after that at all costs.

"Wait a minute," he said. "It doesn't kill them?"

"What?"

"You just said something about animals getting struck by lightning without it killing them."

Irene nodded.

Nate turned and walked away from her. He started pacing back and forth along the fence line. He stopped in front of her and almost spoke, then started pacing again.

"Are you okay?" she said.

"That's it. That *has* to be it."

He ran back to her and grasped her elbows with both hands, squeezing them. "Thank you." He turned quickly to go back to the truck but tripped over a clump of tall grass and almost fell.

She lunged forward and grabbed his arm to steady him. "Thank you for what?"

He held her arms again, his eyes wide. "I think I just figured it out."

"Figured what out?"

Nate had already turned and was walking swiftly back to the truck. He got in the cab and started the engine, then looked back at Irene, who was still in the same spot. When he motioned for her to come, she sighed, shook her head, and hurried after him.

Nate continued driving down Klecka Road. Following his instincts, he took a left, then a right, and then another left to come out on Highway 34. He told Irene about the problem on the Kollatschny dairy and explained his theory about what was causing it. He tried calling Ruthie, but nobody answered, and he remembered she and Leroy usually went to church on Saturday and then out to eat.

As soon as he put his phone back in the breast pocket of his coveralls, it rang. He answered quickly, thinking it might be Ruthie, but it was an emergency call. A woman had a dog with a fishhook stuck in its mouth. He told her to bring the dog in.

When they pulled to a stop at the clinic, Nate slapped the steering wheel. "Damn it. I completely forgot about Bruno's cow." He looked at Irene and shook his head. "Oh, well. This dog shouldn't take too long."

They got out of the truck. "Thanks for coming along," he said as he reached for his wet clothes in the back.

"Glad I could help. Now I know what it's like when you're out on the road."

"We don't always stop for dominoes. Sometimes it's a game of pool and a few beers."

Irene smiled, again that wonderful smile. "Do you need any help with the dog?"

"No, it should be easy enough. Thanks though."

"I need to get home and see about Mom."

As they parted, their eyes met and lingered there, ever so briefly.

While Irene was driving away, a green SUV pulled up. A woman and three kids got out, one leading a chocolate Labrador retriever on a leash. A chubby girl with blond hair said, "We were fishing, and Mocha jumped in after the bait. Our dad said that instead of a catfish, we caught a dogfish. Isn't that funny?"

The family lived in San Antonio and was spending the weekend with the grandparents. The dog wouldn't hold still long enough to be examined, so Nate sedated her and then had no trouble removing the hook. He pushed it all the way through the lip, cut the barbed end off with a pair of wire cutters, and pulled it out.

"She'll sleep off the sedative this evening and be back in the water tomorrow," he said.

By the time Nate got back home, it was just past seven o'clock. He stopped at the house only long enough to pick up Roscoe, then drove into the back pasture to look for the cow. He found her still on the hilltop, not far from where she had been earlier. She got to her feet as he drove up, and he was relieved to see a calf on the ground nearby. The calf got up and walked over to her on unsteady legs. He nuzzled her flank, found a teat, and started sucking, bumping her udder vigorously with his head.

"Well Roscoe, it looks like both mom and baby are okay. There was no need to worry after all."

Nate drove over to the old house, sitting stark and lonely in a clump of post oaks. The front door was missing, weeds poked up through gaping holes in the wraparound porch, and most of the windowpanes were lost or broken. It had gingerbread along the gables and ornate porch balusters—much nicer than the average farmhouse of its day. Nate found forgotten old places like this compelling somehow. He had been meaning to ask Bruno about it.

He got out of the truck and walked up to the house. Peering into a window, he saw a wood stove in the corner, the rusty frame of a bed, a few scattered bottles lying on the dusty floor. He walked around the corner of the house, past a pile of decaying lumber and an old well pump set into a cracked concrete block. He tried to work the pump handle, but it was frozen in position. He descended the hill toward the back corner of the home site, where he came upon the rusting body of a car, circa the 1930s, almost completely hidden by brush and vines. The car's doors were gone, and the front seat was missing, leaving only the springs.

Nate leaned on the car's fender and looked back up the hill. He saw the old house silhouetted on the horizon, sunlight casting an eerie glow through a broken window. Who had lived there? What were their dreams and passions? This place was once the center of someone's world, but they were long gone and only the house remained, sitting mute and desolate, forever keeping its secrets.

Would the Holub farmhouse have a similar fate? The image sent a chill through him.

It was almost twilight when Nate drove back to the house. As he approached, he saw a car parked under the hackberries and someone standing beside it. When he was closer, he was surprised to see it was Irene. He looked at his phone, making sure he hadn't missed a call.

She began walking slowly in his direction.

He parked and got out. "Hey, what brings you out here?"

Irene didn't answer. It was the first time he had seen her without her glasses.

"Is everything okay?"

Irene looked down, shifting her weight from one foot to the other. "I thought you might need some help with the cow."

"I just checked on her. She had the calf. They're both fine."

Irene glanced at him and then down again. "That's good."

"Is your mom all right?"

"She was asleep. I didn't want to wake her." When Irene looked up, he saw tears running down her cheeks.

He took a step closer. "What's wrong?"

She wiped the corner of one eye, sniffling, trying to smile. A gust of wind blew hair in her face.

Nate reached up and pulled the hair back. Some strands were matted to her cheek from the tears. He picked up the wet hairs delicately and pulled them away, a few at a time.

Irene grasped his wrist.

Nate started to pull his hand away, but she held on to it.

He leaned forward slowly. His fingers moved under her chin, and he softly pulled her face up toward his. He looked into her eyes and held his breath, feeling his heartbeat, and when their lips met, the sensation pulsated through him, all of his fatigue instantly melting away. They wrapped their arms around each other and held on tightly, cheek to cheek—a deep, warm, desperate embrace. He buried his face in her soft hair, smelling of lavender, and ran his hands up and down her back. He feverishly kissed her neck, feeling her rapid pulse, and then all over her face, wet with tears.

They stumbled toward the house, arm in arm, stopping at the yard gate and again on the porch to embrace and kiss.

While Nate made love to Irene that spring evening, the dying sun cast a golden glow high on the bedroom wall, framing the gently quaking shadow of a tree branch. Long suppressed desire was released like a dam breached, the wave crashing over him, washing away the accumulated loneliness and despair. For one glorious moment, their wounded souls coalesced into one jubilant whole.

Afterward, Nate held Irene's trembling body close and gently caressed the smooth supple skin of her shoulder. She wiped a drop of sweat from his upper lip and tasted it on her fingertip, and then she put her head down on his chest. They lay in each other arms quietly for a long time, watching the patch of sunlight on the wall dwindle slowly, eventually leaving them in darkness.

While stroking her hair, he whispered, "I want you to be happy."

Irene propped her head up with her elbow and looked at him. A single tear ran down her face and landed audibly on the sheet. She cupped his chin gently with her hand, and he placed his hand over hers. She smiled and laid her head back on his chest, sighing deeply, her breath warm as an April wind on his bare skin.

Twenty-Five

Early the next morning, Nate searched online for a journal article he remembered seeing years earlier. After reading it, he called Ruthie and told her he was coming over, not saying why.

When he pulled into the lane at the dairy, he saw Leroy sitting on the porch with a cup of coffee, petting a black and white cat on the chair next to him. He stood up abruptly when he saw Nate coming. Ruthie came out and joined him as Nate parked the truck.

"What's the matter, Nathan?" she said. "Something wrong?"

"Hey Ruthie. Nothing's wrong. I just want to run something by you. I have an idea…about your cattle problem."

Leroy arched his brows.

"Let's walk out back and look around," Nate said.

Nate examined the milking parlor thoroughly. While Leroy and Ruthie stood by, giving each other puzzled looks, he shined a flashlight into every dimly lit corner and carefully checked each milking machine and food trough. He walked around the outside of the building, then came back and repeated his inspection of the interior.

Leroy finally couldn't take the suspense. "What is it, Nate? What're you looking for?"

Nate walked over. "I'm not certain about it, but I think it might be stray voltage."

"Stray what?" Ruthie said.

"Stray voltage. It can happen when there's faulty wiring or electrical equipment. It's a documented problem on dairies." Nate frowned and shook his head. "I should've thought about it sooner."

Leroy scratched his chin. "But…but how would that cause what we're seeing in the cows?"

"It gives them a mild shock when they touch the feed trough or water trough. They get nervous at milking time and don't eat or drink as much as they should. Milk production goes down, and the poor nutrition and stress lead to other problems—more mastitis than usual, other infections, just overall poor health. I think it could explain everything."

Leroy leaned down and touched one of the water troughs. "I don't feel anything."

"I'm not sure you would. It might be a very mild shock. And it might only happen at certain times. I'd get an electrician out here as soon as possible and have them look the place over, check the wiring, test the whole system. I may be completely wrong, but it's worth a try."

Leroy pushed up his sagging glasses. "You know, Nate, you might be onto something. All the wiring we've got is pretty old. I'll call up Freddy Emler tomorrow and have him come out and take a look."

They walked back to the front yard. The wiring looked pretty crude to Nate's uneducated eye. He hoped the electrician would find something obvious.

Before he left, Ruthie said, "Nathan, if you're right about this, I'm making you the best dewberry cobbler you ever ate."

Nate drove into town, stopping at Kubena's for some apple strudel, then he headed south up the river bluff, on his way out to the farm. As he passed the bluff's final curve, he slowed and looked toward the edge, as he always did.

The cold dread he once felt there had never returned, but in its place was a hollowness, a dull aching deep inside, a void he knew would never be filled. He couldn't pass that curve without seeing Clarissa's white convertible, her dark flowing hair reflecting the moonlight, the look in his father's eyes when he realized it was too late, the flames leaping into the night sky.

When Nate pulled up and parked outside Viola's picket fence, he saw her walking toward the house from the direction of the barns, carrying a basket. He got out and met her at the back gate.

"Good morning. You out doing chores already?"

"Just getting the eggs is all."

Nate followed her as she trudged slowly to the back door. "Feels like it's gonna be a hot one today," he said. "I guess summer will be here before we know it."

He held the door open and watched as she eased herself up the steps. He was relieved to see an emergency alert device around her neck.

They sat down at the kitchen table. Nate told her about his visit with Ruthie and Leroy that morning, but she only nodded distractedly. She was having one of those days, the kind where she shrinks into her inner darkness, unwilling to let in the light. The strudel sat untouched.

Nate wasn't in a talkative mood himself. He couldn't keep his mind off Irene. It had been only twelve hours since they parted, and he already yearned to hold her again. He wanted to talk to her, but he wasn't sure if he should call so soon. He knew he loved her, but that was the only thing he knew for sure.

Realizing conversation was futile, he excused himself and went outside. He walked to the garden and did some weeding around the beans and tomatoes. After finishing that, he went down to the creek.

The morning was warm and muggy, and the grass in the hayfield glistened with dew. The leaves of the big pecan drooped languidly in the still air, a few tiny pecans beginning to form among the stringy green blooms.

Nate went to his usual spot along the bend in the creek, sitting down with his back against the cottonwood. This place had become more familiar to him than the living room of his house. He had watched it change through the fall, winter, and spring and knew its many moods. By now, the starkness of winter had been replaced by the exuberance of late spring, and every limb on every bush and tree had erupted with verdant new life. The creek flowed full from recent rain, and he watched pieces of drift float by in the muddy water.

Nate scanned the foliage across the creek, looking for Tilly. Since their meeting, he had been back on three Sunday mornings, each time hoping to see her again, but each time leaving disappointed. He worried their meeting had been only a chance occurrence, that she was no more likely to reemerge from the woods than the bobcat he saw that cold winter morning.

Feeling restless, he got up and walked upstream, looking for tracks in the mud, stopping as he rounded each bend to scan the banks. It was still cool along the creek, and a light fog hovered over the water. Along one stretch unfamiliar to him, he saw a smaller creek joining from the opposite side, a narrow shadowy channel with high banks, green and mossy, so tortuous he couldn't see past the first curve.

Nate took off his boots and socks, rolled up his pant legs, and waded across, the water coming up to his knees. He entered the channel of the smaller creek and cautiously followed its twisting murky course, walking in the water because of the steep banks. The bottom was sandy, the water only an inch or two deep and clear. After several bends, the way forward was obstructed by a fallen tree, but the bank on the right was lower, so he climbed up and out of the creek channel.

He put his boots back on and entered a shady grove of bois d'arc trees, the ground between them carpeted with ferns. Grapevines rose out of the leafy green bed and extended up into the tree branches, some hanging down in swing-like arches. It was an enticing spot, and he lingered for a moment, but then he pushed on, threading his way through an impossible bramble of yaupons, vines, and briers, having to crawl through some places on his hands and knees. When he finally emerged from the thicket, he stood at the base of a steep rise of earth, the sky hidden by the interlocking branches of sycamores... Alois's pond.

Nate climbed to the top of the dam and peeked out from behind the trunk of a sycamore, scanning the garden for any sign of Alois or Tilly. The morning was calm, and the garden looked as still as a painting. From this vantage point, it was even more beautiful than he remembered, the colors cascading down the hillside to the pond's reedy edge.

He walked along the bank, ducking from tree to tree. At one end of the pond, he passed the remnants of an old dock. Nearby, a decaying rowboat lay upside down, grass growing up through a hole in its stern. He found a trail and followed it up into the garden, and then he carefully walked the winding garden paths, pausing every few steps to watch and listen. He slowly worked his way up to the arbor at the top of the hill and cautiously poked his head through. Nothing stirring around the house.

Retracing his steps, Nate went back into the garden and found the small patio he discovered on his previous visit. He sat down on the cedar bench and leaned back, the fragrance of roses hanging in the air. The pond looked perfectly still, like molten metal poured into an earthen cast to cool. The silence was near complete, the birds seemingly hesitant to begin their day. Nate stared at the sculpture of the girl, still asleep in her bed of irises. Something about her spoke to him, but he couldn't decipher the words.

Nate imagined Alois laboring away in the garden for years. He had loved Miriam dearly, and following the war, she helped him slowly heal his fractured psyche. He focused all of his energy on the needs of his wife and young daughters, the entire light of his being funneled into one glowing spot, intense and purifying. When Isabel left home and he later lost Miriam, he shifted all of that energy to Tilly, and caring for her became the most important thing in his life. During the months of despair following Miriam's death, it may have been the only thing that saved him.

Nate sat for a long time, watching the sky change from smoky gray to silver, the feathery outlines of individual clouds slowly taking shape. The garden stirred something deep inside him. Like at his creekside retreat, he somehow felt closer to his father here.

Had his father known this place? Had he too been under its spell? Had he come here looking for solace? For absolution?

Nate heard a slight rustle behind him. He turned to see Tilly standing on the edge of the patio, leaning over a pink rose, pulling the stem toward her. She wore jeans and a faded purple blouse. Her straw sun hat hung down on her shoulder, held by its strap. She had a bemused expression, as though she had just spotted a rare butterfly flittering among the blooms.

"Hi, Tilly."

She broke the rose off by the stem and carried it to the low stone wall in front of the bed of irises. She sat down and brought the rose up to her face, inhaling deeply and smiling, her eyes closed.

Nate walked over to the wall and sat down near her. "It's good to see you. How've you been?"

She opened her eyes and gently caressed the flower's petals, wholly absorbed in it, her head tilted.

"That's a beautiful rose. What kind is it?"

Tilly turned her attention to the stem, tracing its smooth glossy length with thumb and forefinger, testing the sharpness of its thorns, one by one.

"I heard a woodpecker a few minutes ago. Like the one we heard last time. Remember?"

She raised her bare feet and folded them beneath her, then laid the rose on her lap. The knees of her jeans were dirty, the neckline of her blouse damp with sweat.

"Have you been working in the garden?"

Tilly blinked a few times, then turned her head slightly in his direction. "Weeds, weeds. I've been pulling weeds every day. Bermudagrass mostly. Daddy says there's no way to get rid of it, short of maybe dynamite."

Nate smiled. "It's a wonderful garden. You're doing a great job with it."

"Mama taught me. She got cancer. Mama loved green things. She loved roses most of all."

"I can tell."

Tilly cocked her head suddenly. "Hear that? It's gonna rain."

Nate listened. A hollow staccato bird call echoed through the creek bottom—a long series of rapid notes slowing down and changing character at the end, becoming plaintive and haunting.

"What is it?"

"Rain crow. That's what Daddy calls them. Mama said they're yellow-billed cuckoos. They like to hide. When you hear one, it means it's gonna rain. That's what Daddy says."

Nate looked at the sky. "Maybe he's right."

A loud creaking sound echoed down the hill and across the pond—a door opening. The tool shed? Nate looked around, planning an escape route.

Tilly picked the rose up and turned her back on him, resting her feet on the wall with her knees up. She wrapped her arms around her shins and laid her head on her knees.

"Tilly, when we talked last time, I asked if you knew my father very well, and you mentioned his accident."

Tilly started rocking slowly.

"Do you remember talking about that? And then I asked if you knew Clarissa?"

"Clarissa drove a white car. She liked to drive fast."

"That's right. So you knew her?"

"She gave me a ride in her car one time. Daddy doesn't know about that."

Nate scanned the path descending to the patio, then looked back at Tilly. "Did you ever see the two of them together? My dad and Clarissa, I mean?"

Tilly stopped rocking and laid the rose at her feet. "Daddy asked me that too."

"He did? When?"

"Right after they died. He knew I sat out on the front porch every night to watch the lightning bugs. I never saw them together though."

Nate leaned forward. "So you were on the porch *that* night? The night of their accident?"

Tilly raised her head and nodded. "I was eating peach pie. And Dennis came by, driving Clarissa's white car."

"He did? Are you sure?"

The loud creaking returned, followed by the slam of a door.

Tilly put her head back down and resumed her rocking. "He drove by the house at ten thirty. I was eating peach pie and watching the lightning bugs. I never see them anymore. Daddy says pesticides killed them all."

"Ten thirty? Are you sure?" The accident report stated that the sheriff's office received the call at ten forty-four.

She rocked faster. "I know because Mama always told me to come inside at ten thirty when the news was over. Daddy never watches the news. He says it's just the same old thing, over and over. He's in bed by nine most nights."

Nate heard the rattle of metal on metal, and then the slow squeaking of wheels—a wheelbarrow. He looked up at the path, feeling short of breath. He moved a few inches closer.

"Tilly, you're sure it was him?"

Tilly nodded. "He was driving Clarissa's white car. It's all grown up now, but you could see the road back then. He drove by, going toward town."

The sound of the wheelbarrow got louder, rattling as it bounced down the steps of the path.

"But didn't you say earlier that you never saw my dad and Clarissa together?"

"That's right."

"But...I don't understand. They had to be together at ten thirty that night."

Tilly suddenly stopped rocking, turned, and put her feet on the ground. For the first time since they had met, she looked directly at him, just for an instant, just long enough to get a glimpse into the emerald depths of her eyes.

"No. He was by himself."

Twenty-Six

Nate drove to the Hadlow Cemetery one day after work that week. He looked for some time before he found his father's grave in the shade of a weather-beaten old cedar, a couple of rows over from Cap and Viola's plot with its common headstone. He regretted not visiting the grave sooner. He had almost done so on several occasions, but like St. Anthony's, the place held memories he preferred not to revisit.

The stone was generic enough—a slab of gray granite with only his name and dates and nothing else to distinguish it from any other. Casual observers would note that this was the grave of Dennis Holub, who lived for forty-one years during the mid-twentieth century. They wouldn't know that he could repair a hay baler, tell a good joke, or lay down a perfect drag bunt. They wouldn't know his laugh, or the sparkle in his eye, or what kind of a father he was to his children. He was just a name on a headstone, cold and sterile, adrift in a sea of other names, other poor souls whose memory had died, or would die, with those who had known them.

Since his talk with Tilly, Nate had slept little, and the pace at work was still intense. He kneeled on his left knee and leaned on his right, feeling light-headed. He brushed some cedar leaves from the base of the stone, then ran his hand across it, contrasting the coarseness of its edges with its burnished front. His fingers followed the indentations of the letters, their sharpness already dulling with age. He wanted to say something to his father, but words escaped him. The long years had put too much distance between them.

Nate sat down with his back against the cedar. He listened to the whistling of the wind through the headstones, the shrill call of a blue jay echoing across the cemetery. Two squirrels chased each other through the branches of a nearby oak. At his feet, a tiny black beetle scurried through the leaf litter.

So much life amid all this death. Life surges forward in its inexorable rhythm, not hesitating for those who are mired in the past and cannot appreciate the present. His father had known this, and if he were standing there today, he would grasp his son with his firm grip and implore him to live, to live for the both of them.

Dennis Holub survived only four days after that fateful April night, and Nate's last memory of him was his most vivid. His mother brought him and Sarah to the hospital. His father lay in the bed, covered with tubes and wires, looking more machine than man, his normally ruddy skin a sickly gray under the dim fluorescent lighting. A bandage covered his forehead, and another was over his left eye. The only sounds were the beeping of his heart monitor and his gentle faltering breaths into the oxygen mask. Nate touched his hand, and the skin felt cool and dry, like grass after a killing frost, the life slowly ebbing from him.

As his father clung to life by a thread in that cold foreign place, Nate felt numb, unable to comprehend the pale ghost of a man lying before him. He couldn't remember seeing his father sick, not even for a day, and certainly never bedridden. Most of his memories of him were outdoors, working on the farm or in the garden at home. He seemed to come indoors only to eat and sleep, and when he had to be inside, his nervous energy kept him bouncing off the walls like a moth in a jar.

His mother stood between him and his sister, and she put her arms around their shoulders and held them close. She must have been reluctant to bring them there, fearing the sight of him in that state would be too traumatic.

Sarah, barely eight, looked up at her mother. "Mama, is Daddy going to die?"

His mother kneeled, held Sarah's face in both hands, and then gave her a long tearful hug, unable to find the words to comfort her.

Nate didn't cry that day. He had arrived at a new place, and the abruptness of the journey left him disoriented, not yet certain of what had been left behind. The tears came later, a trickle when he was first told of his father's death the following morning, and then a torrent when he came to the full realization of what those words meant—that he was gone…forever.

The finality of it was shocking, and no promises of a reunion in the afterlife offered any solace. Never again would he see that familiar wink and grin, reassuring him everything would be all right. Never again would he feel that strong hand on his shoulder, holding him upright in the maelstrom.

After so many years, the pain was still there, and it was becoming more difficult to reconcile as it drifted farther out of reach, into the haziness of the past. Nate knew his only hope of finding peace lay with one who had known his father better than he had...one for whom the past was a constant living companion...one whose suffering far exceeded his own.

Twenty-Seven

Nate found Viola on the front porch when he drove up on Saturday afternoon. She sat with her hands clasped in front of her, her extended index fingers resting on her chin, the translucent skin of her hands scarcely hiding the bones beneath. When he greeted her, she stared straight ahead, her eyes watery and bloodshot. He pulled up a chair and sat down beside her.

As he gazed westward toward the creek, his thoughts took him on a serpentine course through the bottom's tangled depths, then along the muddy banks, shady and drift-choked. He longed to be in that lonely place, hidden away from it all, watching the shifting shadows, the swaying branches, the dappled sunlight on dark water. Life was pure there, uncluttered and unrepentant, the past inconsequential.

"I found something interesting down at the creek last weekend," he said finally, "a little side creek I hadn't seen before, on Alois's side. I waded across and explored it a bit. It has high banks, very narrow, moss growing along the sides. Do you know the place?"

Viola turned to him and blinked, as though she had just noticed him.

"I wonder how far it goes," Nate said.

After a long pause, Viola cleared her throat. "Not far. There's a spring back in there." She took off her glasses and rubbed the corners of her eyes. "It's always run, even during the worst droughts. That's what Cap used to say."

"Is the spring on Alois's place?"

She nodded.

"Have you ever been there?"

Viola put her glasses back on, then looked at him wearily. "Where?"

"The spring…or…Alois's place at all. I mean…I know Alois keeps to himself, but have you ever been over there?"

Viola looked away.

"He has a garden behind his house. Have you seen it?"

She drew her lips together, a thin hard line.

"It's not a vegetable garden, but more of a flower garden—beds and pathways, all built with rock. And there are these sculptures, some made out of old farm equipment and others out of stone. It's really amazing. He could charge admission." Nate looked at her hopefully. "Surely you've seen it, or maybe heard someone talk about it?"

Viola shifted in her chair, crossing her legs. "What Alois does is no concern of mine."

Nate stared at the floorboards below. He watched an ant follow a wandering path over the rugged surface, stopping and redirecting when the way became impassable, finally disappearing into the rotting base of a porch pillar.

"I think I was over there when I was a kid. Daddy and Jerome were working cattle. I must've been pretty young."

Viola started rocking gently, the heel of her shoe barely rising off the floor.

Nate leaned forward, elbows on his knees, arms folded. "I talked to Alois a few weeks ago. He told me my dad and Jerome used to work over there—hauling hay, building fence, that type of thing."

Her eyes were closed. She gripped the arms of the chair tightly as she rocked, her knuckles sunspotted and knobby.

"We never went by there when I got older. Alois said he sold his cattle. I guess there wasn't any more work to do."

Nate looked toward the creek again. The shadow of a cloud drifted slowly across the bottom hayfield. The rocking chair's rhythm marked the time, the floorboards whining softly in protest.

"I've been wondering what it's like for them…for Alois and Tilly, I mean…living the way they do. I've had a hard time imagining it." Nate pivoted toward her. "But after being there, in the garden, it makes more sense to me."

Place is everything—Alois in his garden, Viola here, on this crumbling farm. One cannot be understood without the other. Nate tried to envision the farm as Viola knew it—the endless tiring days folding one on top of the other, the bustle and laughter of children, the smell of wood smoke and bacon grease on a cold morning, the feel of good soil between the fingers, cool grass between the toes. For her, the farm was alive with spirits—some comforting, others terrifying. He longed to visit that place, if just briefly, but he feared what awaited him there.

"I talked to Tilly the other day," he said finally, rubbing the back of his neck. "It was the same day I followed that little creek."

Viola's rocking slowed. She folded her hands in her lap.

Nate leaned back, his eyes closed. "While we were talking, Tilly said something very odd." He took a deep breath, opened his eyes, and looked at Viola. "She said she was sitting on the front porch the night of Daddy's accident…and she saw him drive by in Clarissa's car."

Viola looked straight ahead, still rocking.

"The odd part is that he was alone. He was driving toward town, apparently from here, and it was only minutes before the accident."

Viola stopped rocking. She unfolded her leg and smoothed a wrinkle in her pants.

"I know that was a long time ago, and her memory may not be reliable, but she seemed certain about it."

Nate waited. The sound of crows echoed on the wind, distant and raucous.

Viola slowly pushed herself to her feet. "I'm going in now. I'm not feeling too good." She took a step forward, and Nate reached out and grasped her arm.

She stopped and looked down at him.

"Grandma…please…is there anything you can tell me?"

Her face was rigid. "Don't pay attention to nothing Tilly says. She don't know if she's coming or going."

He suddenly felt like a child again, withering under her flinty gaze. He released her arm.

She walked to the screen door.

When she put her hand on the door handle, Nate said, "Grandma?"

She stopped, but didn't look back.

"I know it didn't happen the way everybody thinks."

She stood with her hand on the door handle, tottering slightly.

"I think you know the truth."

She turned her head and looked at him. He waited for her to say something, but she only stared.

Nate rose and walked toward her. He gently grasped her elbow. "Please."

She focused on a point somewhere beyond him, her pupils small in the harsh afternoon light. She held the door handle, seemingly suspended there. She looked at the door…then at him…and then the door again. She finally closed her eyes and lowered her head, a look of intense pain washing over her face.

Nate led her slowly back to her chair.

She sank into it, making it groan as it rocked back.

He sat and leaned toward her, feeling his pulse, his mouth dry.

She sat very still.

"It's okay," he said. "You can tell me."

She stared straight ahead with an intensity that startled him. "I was gonna take it to the grave."

Nate fidgeted, looking down at his feet.

She swallowed hard, then took a slow deep breath. "*She* was here that night." The word had an edge to it, sharp enough to draw blood.

Nate waited.

Her eyes narrowed. "I curse the day I met her…the first day she stepped foot on this farm." She shook her head slowly. "I hated her. Hated her with all my heart."

Nate had never seen her like this—her lip curled, her face rife with loathing.

"That night she came looking for Dennis. She had him, just like she had Jerome. She had to have 'em all." She leaned forward in the rocker, looking down at the porch, her breaths getting shorter and faster.

Nate put his hand on her shoulder and felt her trembling.

"She came into the kitchen like she owned the place. She always looked down on me like I was trash. I told her to leave Dennis alone and to get the hell out of my house. And she just laughed… *laughed*…after what all she'd done. With Sammy and all."

Viola rubbed her hands together, still staring at the porch, her eyes on fire.

"I cursed her and told her to leave. She gave me a look I'll never forget, and said some things I won't repeat, and then she laughed again. I grabbed her arms and shook her. I had to make her stop laughing. And then she slapped me."

Viola raised her shaky right hand and leaned her forehead against her palm. "She turned around and started walking to the door, and that's when I…"

Nate sat on the edge of his seat, breathless. He took her left hand in both of his. "What happened?"

She looked at him. "I…I picked up the fire poker that was leaning against the stove, and…" A single tear, large and glistening, hesitated at the corner of her eye before plunging down her cheek. "Nathan…I hit her with it."

She pulled away from him and took her glasses off, burying her face in her hands.

Nate pulled his chair closer.

"She grabbed the back of a chair and stood still. I thought she was gonna turn around, but she started breathing hard. She leaned over, then she fell on the floor. I heard Dennis drive up. By the time he got into the house—"

Viola's glasses fell on the porch with a clatter, the sound echoing in the warm afternoon air.

"By the time he got there…she was gone."

Nate stared at the floorboards at Viola's feet, feeling dizzy. The porch was moving. He was floating away. He grabbed his left leg with both hands and tried to hold himself in place. Then he realized she was still talking.

"…and he started pacing around the house, yelling at me. He'd been drinking. I picked up the phone to call the sheriff, but he stopped me. He said he didn't want me charged with murder. R.J. Woller never did like me. We was in school together. He thought his daughter should've done better for herself than get mixed up with the likes of us."

Viola lowered her hands to her lap, shaking her head slowly. "So Dennis come up with this idea. He'd drive her over to the bluff and push her car off. Make it look like an accident. He said he'd walk back here. Said it wouldn't take him long to go down the river and then up the creek."

Nate stared at her.

"We argued about it. I told him he was crazy. I didn't want him blamed for what I'd done."

She closed her eyes and put her hands over her face again, leaning back in her chair. "I should've tried harder to stop him. Goddamn it. I should have tried harder."

Nate stood up. He walked shakily to the edge of the porch, and then back. "So, how did he…"

"I don't know what happened. He must have slipped and fell.

I've thought about it every day since, but I just don't know."

She started sobbing softly.

Nate walked to the corner of the porch. He put both hands on the corner pillar and leaned against it, trying to steady himself. A mockingbird sang serenely from a branch of the live oak. The treetops in the creek bottom tossed gently in the wind, their leaves shimmering in the bright sunshine. Feathery puffs of cloud floated slowly northward as a turkey vulture soared below them, making long sweeping arcs through the blue. Nate took note of each of these things, things he knew to be real, points to anchor himself in a world turned upside down.

Viola slumped in the rocker, her arms limp. "I don't regret that she died, God help me. But I'll curse myself to the grave for what happened to Dennis."

Nate walked back over and sat down. "Sammy...you mentioned Sammy. What did you mean?"

Viola opened her eyes, her face streaked with tears. "She and Sammy was close to the same age. They dated for a little while. He thought she loved him, but she just used him, like all the others. It wasn't just a crush for him. When she left him, he took it hard...too hard. He was always like that. I couldn't talk no sense to him. He quit school and joined the army before we even knew what happened."

Nate sat for a long time in stunned silence while Viola wept.

Eventually, he leaned over and wrapped his arm around her shoulders and cupped her head with his hand, pulling it to his cheek. The only sounds were her gentle sobs and the distant lowing of a cow, faint and doleful.

She felt so frail, reduced to a withered husk. Her wounds were much deeper than he had ever imagined, festering slowly, incapable of healing. Sorrow and guilt had eaten away at her over the years, and her hardened exterior had been necessary to keep the whole intact. He tried to console her, wanting her to put her demons to rest, to find the peace that had eluded her for so long. But he knew nothing could reverse the damage she had already done to herself.

They sat quietly, the dead limbs of the live oak swaying gently, casting quivering shadows at their feet. Shadows...memories... both ephemeral, perpetually changing before vanishing altogether.

Nate's memory of Viola would forever be rooted to that lonely hilltop. Her essence would pervade it. Whenever he came there, it would be her voice he would hear, disconsolate and haunting, whispering softly on the breeze.

Twenty-Eight

Viola Holub was buried on a somber gray morning in the middle of May. The air felt crisp from a weak front that had arrived the day before—the last hint of cool air DeLeon County would experience until October. It was almost a year to the day after Jerome had been lowered into the same sandy loam.

Two weeks after Nate's visit to the farm, on a sultry Saturday afternoon, Ruthie had found her lying in the garden, alive but unresponsive. By the time the ambulance arrived, it was too late. The official cause of death was heatstroke. She had been chopping weeds and was still gripping the hoe when Ruthie found her. Her emergency alert device was later found in a kitchen drawer.

A thick blanket of low clouds enveloped the cemetery that morning, allowing only a flat dismal light to filter through. Tree leaves fluttered gently in the feeble north wind. The ground was soaked from rain, and the headstones sagged under their weight, sinking slowly back into the earth.

Nate was consumed by grief and remorse. He regretted not visiting her again during those last two weeks. There was more he wanted to say. He wanted her to know that he didn't hold her responsible. He went over everything said that day again and again, hoping to remember something he may have forgotten, some little nuance, gesture, or word of hers that might have indicated understanding.

As he sat under the graveside canopy with pensive Emma and tearful Marianne on either side, the flower-draped casket in front of them, Nate realized it was impossible to fully comprehend Viola, to truly appreciate her grim reality. She had been a riddle to him for all of his life, and just when she started coming into better focus, the image was already fading.

The priest completed the rite of committal, "May her soul and the souls of all the faithful departed, through the mercy of God, rest in peace." Nate, Leroy, Darrell, and the other pallbearers removed their boutonnieres—pink carnations—and placed them on the casket.

Nate stared down at the casket, thinking about Viola's last words to him that Saturday afternoon. When he stood to leave, she had reached up, grasped his hand, and searched his eyes imploringly. "Get on your knees every day…and pray you don't outlive those two girls of yours."

He knew he would remember those words for the rest of his life. He wrapped his arms around Emma and Marianne and pulled them close. The thought of losing either one of them was more than he could bear.

Before leaving the cemetery, Nate walked the girls over to his father's grave. Someone had placed a bouquet of flowers on it, the petals starting to wilt and fade. He knew it must have been Ruthie.

As they stood over the grave, he said, "Girls, this is your grandfather. I wish you could have known him."

Marianne sniffled and wiped her nose. "What was he like?"

Nate turned to her and put his arm on her shoulder. He realized it had been years since he told the girls anything about his father. Looking back at the headstone, he searched for the right words. "That's a difficult question, and I don't have a good answer. He was complicated, I guess. I never got to know him as well as I would've liked."

Nate hoped he could tell them more about him in the future, that they would stay close enough to talk about such things, and that they would care enough to ask.

During the reception and luncheon at the parish hall, Ruthie gave Nate an update on Wink's condition. He had been diagnosed with a rare form of cardiomyopathy and was hospitalized in Houston awaiting a heart transplant. Nate hadn't talked to him since learning of his diagnosis, but he planned to visit him at the hospital after dropping the girls off that afternoon.

On the drive back to Houston, the sky cleared. The roadsides north of Hadlow blazed with color, thick stands of Mexican hat and Indian blankets shimmering in the afternoon sun.

Nate's thoughts turned to his mother. He spent the previous night at her house, wanting to pick the girls up early in the morning. She had been moody, and he wondered what effect Viola's death had on her. He didn't tell her Viola's story. He hadn't told anyone, and he wasn't sure he ever would.

Nate looked in the rearview mirror at Emma, who was sullenly chewing on a thumbnail. He extended his hand back to her. "You okay?"

She took his hand and squeezed it. Their eyes met in the mirror, and she gave him a faint but reassuring smile.

"She's probably thinking about *Henry,*" Marianne said from her usual position in the front seat, as she busily texted a friend.

"I am not."

"Henry?" Nate said. "That's a nice old-fashioned name."

"He's just a boy in my art class."

Nate had more reason to worry about the girls than usual. That morning, on the drive to Hadlow, Marianne told him Caroline and Vicente had been arguing a lot. Vicente traveled frequently and was gone for long periods, and the implication was that he wasn't being faithful. For the girls' sake, Nate hoped the relationship worked out. They needed some stability in their lives.

Marianne turned and looked at Emma. "Dad, you'll be glad to know that Emma wants to be a country vet. You've like…inspired her or something." Having performed her role as spokesperson, she turned her attention back to her phone.

Nate glanced back at Emma, who was scowling at her sister, but her face softened when she looked at him. "Is that true?"

She nodded. "I think so. I really like science, and I think what you do is pretty cool…I mean, riding around in the country… and working with animals and stuff."

Nate smiled at her. "That's interesting. We'll talk about it."

He never imagined one of his daughters might want this life he had chosen, a life that until recently he wasn't even sure he wanted himself. He had experienced a lot over the past nine months—stress, long hours, physical punishment. His parental instincts told him to caution her against it, but at that moment he couldn't help feeling a surge of pride, and maybe even a sense of validation for the choices he had made.

In the weeks following the funeral, life gradually returned to normal. The summer heat, permeating and oppressive, had all of DeLeon County firmly in its grip by early June.

One Saturday morning at work, Nate got a call from Ruthie. She said they needed to talk and that she would come by his house that evening. Nate hadn't seen much of Ruthie or Leroy since the funeral. Leroy had called him once to report that milk production was back up after an improperly grounded connection had been repaired in the milking parlor.

After leaving the clinic, Nate grabbed a quick lunch at Rita's. Then he had a couple of farm calls—a colicky horse and a feverish show lamb—before heading back to the house. The rest of the afternoon was quiet.

By the time Ruthie arrived, it was almost seven thirty. She carried a covered dish. "Here's that cobbler I promised you. Hope you like it."

Nate hugged her. "You're a saint, Ruthie."

"It's the least I could do, considering what you did for us."

He took the cobbler inside and brought back two glasses of iced tea. They sat down in lawn chairs in the front yard shade. The cold tea and a light but steady southerly breeze made the heat bearable.

Ruthie's face looked haggard, her cheeks missing their usual blush. The last few weeks had been hard on her. The shock of finding Viola, her death and its aftermath, Wink's health—it had all taken its toll. Wink had received a new heart only days after the funeral, and Ruthie had been keeping the kids while Wink's wife Valerie stayed in Houston.

"How's Wink?" Nate said.

"He's doing good, thank God. Coming home this week. His doctor says his body ain't rejecting the heart, so he's got a good chance." She sighed. "You know it's funny. He's like a new person. You'd never know it was Wink. I've known that boy his whole life, and all of a sudden, he's different. I guess something like that changes you."

They sat silently, a tractor engine humming in the distance.

Ruthie took a sip of tea. "Nathan, Mama left the farm to me. I don't know what we'll do with it. Lease it out, I guess. Maybe use the hay patch. The only thing I know for sure is that we won't sell it. Mama wanted it to stay in the family, and that's what I'm gonna do. But that farm is yours too, you know. You go out there whenever you want. I'm gonna tell Wink the same."

"I appreciate that, Ruthie."

The farm meant a lot to him, he now realized. It was a tangible connection to his father…to his past. His family had always worked the land, going back many generations, all the way back to the dim prehistory of the old country. Each generation had nurtured their patch of ground, always with the assumption that it would be there for their children, as fertile and life-giving as it had been for them and made even more so by their loving stewardship. Nate imagined Viola stubbornly holding on to that assumption until the end.

"Leroy thought maybe we could move out there and let Darrell have our house, now that he's pretty much running the dairy. But the place needs a lot of work, and I don't know if I really want to live there. It might make me think about Mama too much."

Ruthie leaned toward him, put her hand on top of his, and looked him in the eye. "Mama told me her story, Nathan. Probably only a couple of days after she told you."

Nate shifted in his seat. He waited for Ruthie to continue, his hand suddenly numb from holding the cold glass of tea.

"You know I never knew about Sammy and Clarissa," Ruthie said. "Mama never told me. I'm not sure if anyone but her really knew why he ran off and joined the service like he did. I don't think Dennis knew, or Jerome either. Sammy was always kind of high-strung, so I guess we didn't think too much of it." Ruthie shook her head. "I always knew Mama hated Clarissa, so much she couldn't even bring herself to say her name, but I never understood how bad it was. I just wish she'd talked to me about it."

"Clarissa wasn't around much when I was growing up," Nate said. "It all makes sense now."

Ruthie nodded. "There's one more thing you should know about Clarissa, Nathan. Mama didn't tell you because she didn't know herself."

Nate moved to the edge of his seat and leaned forward.

Ruthie studied his face. "Clarissa had the same disease as Wink."

She paused to let it sink in.

"I never knew. Nobody did, except Jerome. She had probably only a year or two to live once the doctors told her what she had. There wasn't no treatment back then. Jerome told Wink about it once he was older. Wink told me just yesterday."

Nate stared at the ground. Then he looked at Ruthie, his eyes wide. "With a condition like that, she could've died any minute. Do you think—"

"Yeah, I do. It was probably her heart that killed her. We'll never know for sure, but that's what I think happened."

"And Grandma never knew."

Ruthie shook her head sadly. "If only she and Dennis had known, things might have turned out different."

Nate sat still for a long time, trying to make sense of it all.

Finally, he poured out the rest of his tea, set his empty glass on the ground, and leaned back. The hackberry leaves above, green and delicate, tossed in the wind, each seemingly tethered by the most tenuous of holds. The sweet odor of freshly baled hay drifted in from the neighboring farm. He looked north, across the distant pastures, fields, and woodlands, a mosaic stretching to the horizon, flushed with the deepening colors of early evening. A low bank of lavender clouds gave the illusion of a distant mountain range, enticing yet unattainable.

Life is inscrutable, he decided, but oddly beautiful, made even more so by its absurdities…and by its very fragility. Each day is an exquisite gift, not to be squandered.

He suddenly rose. "Thanks for coming over, Ruthie. I appreciate it. And I appreciate you." He leaned down, gave her a hug, then planted a big kiss on her cheek, causing her to look up in surprise.

"Irene's coming over later. I want to get some work in while there's still daylight. I've been wanting to start a garden, and now's as good a time as any." He smiled at her and took off briskly toward the tool shed.

He was halfway there before Ruthie collected her thoughts. "It's too late to be getting a garden in, you know!"

Nate did not respond or even look back. His mind was made up, and the soil, dark and rich, was beckoning.

About the Author

Brian Porter lives in College Station, Texas, where he works as a veterinary pathologist. He previously worked in private veterinary practice and once taught high school chemistry. *Dreams of Arcadia* is his first novel.

Acknowledgments

Many thanks to those who helped make this book possible. I am indebted to my family, especially my parents, my wife Karen, my son Benjamin, and my sisters Donna and Glenda. Jodie Toohey brought the novel to life, and I greatly appreciate her commitment and patience. Peter Gelfan's astute early edit pointed a wandering ship in the right direction, and Ann Kellett, Charles Salzberg, Kathryn Mattingly, Ralph Storts, Sylvia Dickey Smith, and Evelyn Byrne-Kusch offered encouragement and advice. Three literary journals, *The Boiler, Visitant,* and *Origami,* published adapted excerpts, which kept a novice writer hopeful. Thomas and Barbara Lenarduzzi, Kirk Remmers, Karen Ashley, Sean McDonough, Anthony Allen, and Steve Wikse provided inspiration and/or stories. Margarita Dimova helped with the front cover art, and Iana Videk created the back cover art. Books that proved useful include *From Can See to Can't: Texas Cotton Farmers on the Southern Prairies* by Thad Sitton and Dan K. Utley, *We're Czechs* by Robert L. Skrabanek, *Krasna Amerika: A Study of the Texas Czechs, 1851-1939* by Clinton Machann and James W. Mendl, and *Tales of Old-Time Texas* by J. Frank Dobie. I also thank David Carriere for his unwavering support.